C000147468

The Sleepwalkers' Ball

The Sleepwalkers' Ball

Alan
Bilton

To Kate and Ben

Hope you enjoy

Alan Bilton

ALCEMI

First impression: 2009
© Alan Bilton, 2009
This book is subject to copyright
and may not be reproduced by any means
except for review purposes
without the prior written consent of the publishers
Alcemi is represented in the UK excluding Wales by Inpress Ltd — www.inpressbooks.
co.uk. In Wales it is represented by www.gwales.com

Editor: Gwen Davies

ISBN: 9780955527265
Printed on acid-free and partly-recycled paper.
Published by Alcemi and printed and bound in Wales by
Y Lolfa Cyf., Talybont, Ceredigion SY24 5AP
e-mail ylolfa@ylolfa.com
website www.alcemi.eu
tel 01970 832 304
fax 832 782

For Pamela

Letter from Gilbert Roland to Clara Bow, 1953

Hello Clarita Girl,

I am truly sad that you don't feel well. Sometimes when I go to church and I think of you I say a prayer. It will be heard. God hears everything.

I hope someday they show 'The Plastic Age'. It would be wonderful to see that dancing scene, you and I. It would be pleasant seeing how I looked when I was your beau, and you were my dream-girl. It would be pleasant seeing that. And then it might be very beautiful and suddenly it might be very sad.

It seems you are in my thoughts.

It's good I feel that way.

It's good I have never forgotten you.

God bless you,

Gilbert

PART ONE

Our Grand Tour

Right this way, ladies and gentlemen, watch your step! The way down from the castle is awful steep, and there's broken glass and dog mess everywhere. Sorry Madam, no refunds! It's a wee squeeze in places, so keep one eye on your valuables and the other on the road ahead. That's it, sir, mind how you go: the steps are treacherous and the handrail is kind of loose. What's that sir, something on my breath? Merely the slightest nip against the cold, nothing to be concerned about — the engine won't start without juice! Quick as you can now please: our time is short and the sky is threatening rain.

Look — the cutting is coming to an end and the old town is opening up before us, concertina-like between the blackened cannons and the lone kebab shop. There now, can you see? Granted, it's not much of a view and the town is kind of grey, but... Miss? Miss, if you please? To the east you can see the chimneys of the breweries, followed by a line of long cooling towers and the beginnings of the industrial park; to the west, a crooked line of hills and the inky squiggle of the river-bank, the railway running alongside, as straight as a ruler. And just ahead? A jumble of huddled grey houses, darker tenement blocks and little old yards which belong to the time of the castle itself. What a sight, eh? Like the coals of a fire which has just gone out. And hidden amongst the dour municipal housing is a gloomy wee yard, held together by row after row of stiff-drying laundry, a little shoebox theatre wrapped up in washing. Ah, do you see? A line of socks and smalls flip-flap in the wind and two doddery old pigeons footer about amongst the aerials and the dishes. And all the way at the bottom some kid is kicking his ball between two piles of bin bags, his innocent mug without a care in the world. There, Madam, just below that big striped sheet; he's dribbling it up and down the yard, a tiny little kid, just a speck really... He runs up, gives a little hop, and boots the ball clear over the line of washing. No sir, don't run and get it! The kid's scuttling off to fetch it, happiness written all over his mucky little face.

Funny little kid, eh? Just messing around, a little kid and his ball. Wee Hans boots his ball up and down the yard, while above him the TV aerials creak in the wind and the sky gets darker and darker... Ah, my friends, do you remember a time when you were happy doing nothing, messing around for hours, every day stretched out as if hung up on a washing line? Mm, weren't we happier then, in our own little world, killing time… What's that sir? No, just leave him, he's fine, just a funny little kid. Let him be, eh? We'll go on in a minute…

See, the lad fires between two big piles of bin bags and then a window opens up above him, some woman poking her head out and yelling to the kid. Quite a gal, eh? Her face as round as a birthday cake, with two black raisins for eyes. Well, it seems that she wants Hans to go to the shops before his dad comes home, to get a few things, you know, for their tea. The gal throws her purse out, a shower of cake-crumbs following it down, the lad waiting at the bottom with wide-open arms. Down, down, down it goes, no more than a little black spot; when the kid catches it he jumps up and down and waves, no more than a little black spot himself.

But what's he doing now? He's chasing a little cloud of sparrows and hopping in and out of the drains. Hey kid, kid! But it's no use; he's over by one of the smelly black grates, poking around in it with a long stick. What about the shops, you little squirt? But the boy's not listening. No, he's playing hide and seek between the rows of washing, painting stripes on the sheets with his long slimy stick. Blimey, he's going to get it when his dad comes home! Kid, kid, look up! The light's fading and it's going to bucket down any minute! I mean, just look at that sky — like a cup of black coffee about to spill over. What's wrong with the boy anyway? Now he's painting funny figures on the walls with his manky stick, his tongue sticking out and his hands completely filthy.

Listen kid, I know what I said earlier, but you can't just muck around all day. I mean, look at those windows, those doorways, the big black eye of the sky; ah, kid do you think you can't be seen? Look, some old biddy is already hobbling into view, hurrying over to where the boy dabs at the bedding with his long sticky pole. Blimey, she's ancient; like the shadow of a shadow and crooked as a hairpin bend.

Well, the kid's in for it now. I mean, just look at the way she's holding her stick: she probably gave Adam what for when he was a little lad. But hold on, what's going on? The old bat's smiling and rooting around in her cardy and doesn't seem to have noticed the kid's scribbles at all. Nope, she's heard that the boy's popping out to the shops and wonders if he could pick up a little wet fish and maybe some tinned fruit, you know, something to tide her over till her daughter comes round in the morning. The old girl pulls a stub-end of sweets from one sleeve and the boy pops one in his mouth.

"That's a good boy," the wifey says and hands over her purse. It's as round and wizened as she is.

Granny, granny, are you sure? You might as well give your purse to a monkey...

"You're a good boy," the old woman says again and the little kid beams. A gust of wind suddenly sweeps across the yard and the two of them wobble on their pins. Yessir, the wind is really getting up now! No place for kids or grannies!

"Off you go then," says the old woman, pointing the way to the shops. Her pale eyes are kind and watery. Then she pats him twice on the head as if he were a little dog.

Ho, what a daft old bat! Imagine trusting that tiny little kid with your cash! I mean, look at the size of him; no more than a smudge on a page. That granny must be as dotty as they come to lend her purse to a kiddie like him. But what can you do? There she goes, shuffling back over to the stair-well, bent over her stick like a little letter 'm'. And whilst she's climbing back up that stairwell, painfully picking her way amongst the rubbish and the loose steps, what d'you think the kid's doing with her purse? Why, he's tossing it up in the air and using a pair of boxer shorts as a basketball hoop. What a monkey! What a brat! Does he think that old gal's made of money? The purse is sailing through the air and little Hans is chucking it higher and higher, laughing and clapping as it slides down the pants, until the purse gets caught in some fold or other and won't come down again. Oh kid! It's hanging high above him and the boy looks up at it with wide-open eyes, his grubby paws outstretched. The wind blows, the sky darkens, the laundry starts to flap, but the purse isn't going anywhere. What a twerp, what a clot... And what's he doing now? Chucking his ma's purse in to try and dislodge it! No sonny, don't do it! Look at that black sky, d'you think it augurs well? Anyway, we all know where this is going — yes, now there's two purses hanging high above his head and the boy's still marooned in the yard. Ah kid, couldn't you have seen what was going to happen? What a pup, what a brat! Little Hans, little Hans! What will save us from the perpetual stupidity of youth?

Meanwhile the clouds are closing in and the sky is growing darker and darker. Best look for shelter, ladies and gentlemen! An awful gale is blowing in from the East, an ill wind indeed... See how it makes the laundry twist and spin, the trousers running on the spot, a line of black tights jogging along next to them. Yes, the sky is heavy and angry: atop the flats, telephone wires zip and twang and a chimney pot wobbles and blows loose. Ah, my friends, hold onto something solid and try to stay together! Mm, what's that, miss? The kid? He's over by a big pile of cement, a tiny little midge blown this way and that in the wind.

Kid, kid, over here! I mean, doesn't he care about all the trouble he's caused? A scrap of paper blows off down the yard and the brat follows it, flapping his arms like he's about to take off. Weeeeeee, he shouts. Then two of the bin-bags topple over, and a welter of rubbish chases after him, a great wave of litter and sweepings. But what about the old woman's fish? And something for his dad's supper? Mm, does he think that no one will notice?

The boy jumps over the rubbish-pit and crosses over into another, smaller yard. There he comes out by the row of buckets and rusted tools which dot the outside of the caretaker's run-down shed and suddenly grinds to a halt. It's a little more sheltered here, and you can find interesting things hidden amongst the rotting railway sleepers: old paintbrushes, the skeleton of a stepladder, a nest of rusted lawn-mower parts.

The kid hugs the wall and tiptoes toward the caretaker's bothy, a ramshackle hut which looks like a railway carriage inexplicably abandoned in the middle of the yard. In the doorway, the caretaker, a squat, hairy man, sits by a three-bar fire. He wipes his mouth and peers at the boy with two bleary eyes, a telly on behind him, some type of quiz show, laughter. As the child draws near, the fella gestures toward him, his gut struggling to get out of the chair.

"Kid, hey kid!"

The caretaker's round and meaty and covered with a heavy pelt. He scratches his shaggy head and rises up as if wakening from some great and terrible sleep.

"Hey, kid, kid — you doing anything, eh? You got a minute?"

The boy examines the fellow closely. His big bushy brows look like felt-tip marks and his stubbly face seems badly shaded, as if somebody has scribbled over all the lines.

"Take my dog for a wee trot, will ya? Just up the castle-walk and back."

Wee Hans looks back at him blankly as the caretaker fumbles in his pockets.

"G'wan, be a pal, eh? There's a pound in it for you."

Ah, kid, don't fall for it! D'you think the fella's asking you for no good reason? Why, look at that sky: like a great black balloon just waiting to burst! And we've all heard tales of the caretaker's ferocious hound...

But the fella shuffles back into the bothy and pulls a big metal chain down from a nail on the wall.

"Good boy, you're a good boy. He's tied up by the garages, okay?"

Ah, kid...

"Off you go, then. There's a pal."

Hans takes the lead and holds it in both hands. Blimey, it's big! Like a loo chain with the end sawn off. Nevertheless the kid inches away and the fella settles back down in his chair. The shed smells of calor gas and methylated spirits and there are bits of old newspaper everywhere.

"G'boy. You're a good boy."

With that the fella settles back in his chair while the boy scampers away, trailing the lead over by the railway sleepers. Well, we'd best go after him; I mean, who's to say what might happen? But it's pretty grim here — engine parts, old sacks, piles of discarded rubbish. Ah, watch your feet, Miss! Something's taken a dump all over the ground, great mounds of crap. Where are we now? There's a horrible, piss-stained wall, a number of half-collapsed sheds and, further on, a line of firmly secured lock-ups and a skip. All sorts of weeds are growing in the middle of the tarmac, and a puddle of thick, black oil oozes out from one of the garages. What a place! The shapes seem obscure, indefinite, the light heavy and mottled. And the turds are really piling up here, big dumps everywhere. I mean, I don't know what that fella is feeding his dog on, but....

What's that, Madam? No, the kid's still going, even though he looks smaller than ever now, no more than a little black dot really. After you, sir: the yard is dismal and louring, a collection of shapes without origin or purpose. One side of the alley is made up of solid blocks of darkness, and the other is even worse, as if we're wading through thick black ink. Still, there are a few recognisable things: a drainpipe, bin-bags, plastic sheeting ...and amidst all this nothing, something is breathing. Yes, the thing's right there, slumped in the darkness, a denser patch of shadow amongst the gloom. Best not get too close, Madam; its tum is going up and down and a terrible smell emanates from its rear-end. And yet the boy is inching toward it, his silhouette no more than a pencil-stroke. He gingerly puts out one hand and ... What's that he's doing? Untying the thing? A sudden gust rattles the garages and the shutters bang and creak. Stay together at the back! The kid is right by its mouth now, unhooking the chain that's looped around its ruff. But it's terribly dark in there and the beast is awful hard to see. All I can make out is a long pink tongue and now the kid's right on top of it, his little head just above the creature's maw. Don't push, Madam! The boy is practically tickling its whiskers, his face obscured by the gloom...

And then suddenly the kid freezes. Kid, kid, what are you doing? He stops and lets go of the lead, the dog giving a low growl as the chain plops on his paw. Foolish boy! The beast is untethered and you're standing there like a loon! I mean, just look at that thing — like a rolled-up carpet but with teeth. Oh miss, I wouldn't do that if I was you! I'd leave that thing well alone. Aye, let's go! The kid's scampering away and we'd be best advised to follow him. The boy's hopping between the oil and broken glass, his little black shape disappearing in the gloom. And the dog? It's shaking its great head, a row of teeth in space. Yes, the beast is dark and shapeless, more of a smell than a form, a crude daub of darkness licking its chops. Let's go, let's go...

Miss? Miss? If you please? Back along the alley-way... that's it, dodging the wire and the dog muck, over the wooden boxes, past the bothy and the sleepers ... Mm, we're back in the main courtyard now, the yard a little darker but otherwise undisturbed. A few lights are coming on now, and if you look up at the tenement windows, you can see the old woman laying out her knife and fork on the kitchen table, the boy's mum staring into her oven, an enormous room lit by a naked bulb. The yard's brighter here, but colder too. Best button up your coat, sir! That wind's blowing straight from the east. I mean, just look above you ladies and gentlemen; the clouds form a long black line, like a dam waiting to spill over.

What's that, Madam, something panting in the yard? Just the coming gale, my dear, no need to worry. The hound? No, no, nowhere to be seen. Now everyone over to the bike-shed, the rain will be coming soon. Sir, sir? No shoving at the back!

And the kid? Still footering about by the rubbish-tip, his grubby little mug as guileless as ever. Look, there's the kiddie over by the rubbish heap, staring off into space, watching the laundry twist and turn. If only he knew, eh? Up on that line hangs the whole sad livery of our lives, nightie, pinny, and thermal breeks; and at the end some dark things all plastic and rubbery, reeking of disinfectant and old folk's pish. Ach, such sorrow! The little boy's shape looks smaller than ever there, his daddy's overalls and ma's pants flapping in the gale.

Kid, kid, when will your dad be home? Purse lost, bike uncleaned, dog loose in the yard. Oh my lad, what do you think you're doing?

Well, what happens next is no surprise. A screech of brakes, the swish of tyres, the slight clatter of a loose mudguard; yes, his dad is home, his bike just starting to free wheel into the yard. Fast as a monkey the boy leaps into one of the great white sheets and hauls himself in (aye, with his mucky shoes on too!), his little legs swallowed up beneath him. From the bedding the lad can see his dad locking up his bike and slowly taking a plastic lunch box from out of his saddlebag, his orange vest the only colour in the yard. Then the fella — stooped, round shouldered, and with a big bristly moustache — checks his lock, takes off his bicycle-clips, and walks over to his son's bike, lying upturned by one of the smelly drains. Yes, it's as he thought — nothing has been done. The fella shakes his head and sighs through his 'tache. Ah Madam, have you ever seen such a sorrowful face? Sad eyes, sad chops – even his moustache seems weighed down by the sorrows of the world. But then he straightens up, looks up at the black cauldron of the sky and thinks to himself, well at least I beat the rain. Grit blows crazily across the yard and the fella props the kid's bike up, scoops up the lad's ball, and walks stiffly across to the stairwell. Dad, dad! But the boy doesn't dare cry out in case he gets into trouble. No, he just lies there wrapped up in wet bedclothes, one more rag hanging on the line. There's the fella's orange safety jacket and there's his big heavy boots and now he's away up the stairwell and the kid is all on his own.

Kid, hey, kid!

But he isn't coming down.

No, the lad's just hanging there, swaying gently above the concrete and rubbish. Mm, is he ever going to climb down? Or is he going to stay there forever, his little dot just another lump in the lining, one more bump or form... I mean, the boy feels kinda safe in his hammock, like he's been swallowed by an enormous cloud, a cloud which smells of bath time and soapsuds... Yes the wind bellows and the dog growls but the lad's all tucked up in his little white nest, his body a wee round ball, curled up against the cold.

What's that? Doesn't he miss his mummy and daddy? Why, of course he does, Missy, his little heart is breaking! But, in his heart of hearts, he knows he can never go home again. His purse is lost, the dog is loose, the little old wifey will never get to eat her fish — and in the meantime the sling rocks to and fro, the boy one more scrap swinging on the line.

So did he ever come down? Well, you have to remember that all this happened a very long time ago. It's true, sir; even that block of flats isn't there anymore. Ah, ladies and gentlemen, there's no use complaining, time marches on, even in a little grey town like this. And the kid? Well, of course eventually he had to climb out of the sheet and face the music; I mean, after a while he got hungry and lonely and the sheet was all damp and cold. And were his mum and dad mad? Sure, I mean, you saw what the little brat got up to! But what do you say we leave him there a little while longer? That's right sir; let him lie there a little bit more, suspended softly above the life that's yet to come. After all, he's only a little kid and doesn't know what's what; let him swing there for a little while more... Yes, the kid's in his hammock and just starting to drop off... Let him be, sir, let him sleep...

Hm, what's that? The first drop of rain! Well, we'd best be going, ladies and gents; our tour is only just starting and we've a long way yet to go. What's that? No, no, let the boy be. He'll be fine. Take a swig from the bottle and off we go; the pavement's terribly uneven and the rain is coming down in buckets. Miss, miss? The kid's still there, though the heavens are opening and the little line of laundry is blowing this way and that. Miss? It's time to go. Right this way ladies and gentlemen, keep together and follow me. You too, Missy, after me...

II

The poky little pub was squeezed in between two big concrete blocks, one of those spit and sawdust joints frequented by students, piss-artists, glue sniffers and the like. Tonight though was something different: tonight some kind of coach-party and their guide were crammed into the wee snug, the fella necking pint after pint while the rain poured down and the heavens bellowed and bayed. Tubfuls of rain exploded out on the dingy street and the drains gurgled and belched, like a plughole about to overflow. What a hole! The snug swirled and lurched, the tour-guide got hammered, and the coach-party huddled together, looking kind of nervous.

Over by the pool table a bunch of young guys were lounging about, knocking some balls together in a desultory fashion. One of them was supposed to be finishing an essay and another had to prepare for some class or other, but instead they ate crisps and flicked beer-mats across the pool table. Work-shy skivers! Every once in a while one of them would poke his nose out of doors, check that it was still raining, and then buy another pint; the glasses were lining up now 'cause the barmaid couldn't be bothered to pick them up, and a lackadaisical air hung over the establishment, two old bods talking about football, and the barmaid reading a magazine. Some of the walking-party grumbled and muttered but nobody wanted to go back outside and no wonder. Outside, the wind shrieked and threw itself at the door, the windowpanes rattling in their frames. Better to stay indoors, even if the place was kinda dumpy, its tartan decor all mottled and stained.

Well, it was just about then that the doors flew open and this scrap of a girl blew in, drenched from head to foot. She looked around, blinked twice, and then shook herself down like a dog.

"Okay," she said. "Who wants to buy me a drink?"

She wandered over to the clump of students and struck a provocative pose. The gal was little and skinny but had a big round face, like a silent movie star. By her side was a scuffed wee case.

"What do you say?"

Nobody made much of a move.

"C'mon fellas, I'm drowned!"

She was quite pretty actually, but had a whopping great bruise on one cheek. Her eyes were two dark caves, her eyebrows two little fish.

Reluctantly, Hans put down his cue.

"I've only got a pound…"

"That's okay, just something fizzy! The bubbles go straight to my head."

Hans walked over to the bar, the girl shivering and clapping her hands.

"I'm freezing!" she announced, jumping on the spot. "My pully's soaked through…"

He didn't know what to say. The barmaid was finishing her word-search and barely looked up.

"Are you from the Uni?" she asked, bobbing up and down.

"Um, yeah."

"What'cha doing?"

"The History of Art."

"Really?"

"Mm."

He eyed up her tiny wee skirt and tried to guess her age. What a crazy dame, he thought.

"Coke alright?"

"Mm, great."

"Diet?"

"That sounds lovely."

The gale was picking up strength outside. It sounded like the roof was about to fly off and the pub creaked and groaned.

"Art, eh?"

"Mm."

"So would you like to paint me?" She assumed a dramatic pose and Hans thought she's got ants in her pants this one; can't she just stand still?

"No, I don't paint. I just write about them."

"Oh. Hey, I'm really hungry, you know."

"I…"

"How about some chips?"

Hans looked out the window. Big chunks of debris were blowing down the street and you could hear funny clanks and bangs.

"My pully's just drying out…" the girl said.

Instead, he bought her some crisps ("Hey, you've got more than a pound" she muttered) and watched as she devoured them. Her mouth was tiny, like a little black bud, but she managed to pack 'em in.

"Art, eh? Mmm."

Clara was a packer in a biscuit factory, which was all right, though there was a guy there who wouldn't leave her alone. He'd corner her in the stockroom and try and grab her bum or else he'd squeeze past her in the corridor and try to look down her top.

"It's true!" she said. "Every time he saw me he'd start to act up. Once he tried to get me to go up to the roof with him 'cause he said he'd seen a squirrel but I knew what he wanted."

She took a big swig of Coke.

"You see guys are always after me! Like when I was a cashier in a petrol station and this bloke who delivered the confectionery there said that he was in love with me. Well, I said to him 'are you serious?' and he said 'sure I am' and I said 'well prove it', 'prove it how?' says the fella, and I say 'any way you like' and the fella laughs and says 'look, I'll streak through the car-wash' and I say 'well let's see you do it' and the fella runs outside in just his boxers and gets hit by the rollers and when we got him to the hospital he needed seventeen stitches. But guys have always been crazy about me!"

"Ah."

The girl's eyes flashed defiantly.

"They can't help it! I mean, there was this one bloke when I was a hairdresser…"

"You were a hairdresser?"

"And what's so weird about that? One day this old bloke comes in with, like, hardly a hair on his head, and asks for a quick wash and go and well, I do him quick, 'cause there's not much to be getting on with, and at the end he puts twenty quid in my hand and says, awful polite, 'That was lovely Miss, but could you do it again and this time a little hotter.' Anyway, you know, he's the customer so I do what he tells me, but when I'm done he produces another note and whispers, 'I don't suppose you could let the shampoo run down into my eyes

19

could you?' so I do and he shouts 'Hotter! Hotter!' and 'Give my head a good scrub!' and 'Fetch me a rough towel!' and afterwards he sighed and said 'Just once more, if you'd be so kind' and I was just about to do it when he sticks his hand up my skirt and so I have to squirt perming solution in his eyes and clout him one with the clippers. 'Oh, Miss, oh, Miss,' he says, 'will you marry me or no?' Now what do you say to that?"

Hans looked at her kinda suspiciously. "You did all those jobs? You look kind of young to me."

"I'm not that young, you know," Clara said, batting her eyelids. "Anyway, how about another Coke?"

He counted his pennies and went off and got one. When he got back, the girl was perched on the pool table, chatting to his mates.

"Hi there! Martin's given me a pound for the juke-box."

"Great. Here's your Coke."

"Mm! Are you sure you don't want to paint me?"

"I wouldn't know how."

She yawned and there was a crash from outside like a bin was rolling down the road. Rain bounced against the windowpanes like bullets.

"Which bit would you do first?"

"I…"

"My legs? My knees? My eyes?"

Her eyes were two dark cherries framed by long black stalks.

"Really, I can't paint to save my life…"

She wrinkled her nose up and skipped over to the jukebox. A few seconds later a pop song came on at top volume but nobody shifted; the two bods continued to argue, the barmaid nibbled the top of her pen, and the studenty-types looked down at the table. Outside the heavens roiled and spun. The tour-group was still there.

"This song reminds me of a guy I once knew," the girl yelled. "He worked in a record shop and would get me whatever I liked. He was great! He did this song for me but I accidentally taped over it and we broke up."

"You know a lot of guys."

"Yeah." Her eyebrows were two black commas on a crisp white page. "It's like I can't help it! Now, what about those chips?"

The students looked at one another sleepily. The two old blokes had grown tired of their argument and were now quietly supping. The barmaid yawned.

"Well?"

It was as if the pub were the only point of dry land in a vast and terrible ocean. It bobbed to and fro whilst everything else was torn apart and pulverised by the gale.

"Okay, okay. Let me put my jacket on," Hans muttered. "I'll see you guys later, okay?"

The snug seemed to be the last dry place on earth. Outside, the void roared and leapt. The rain came down in one long deluge, and within seconds the two little stick figures were drenched.

"Can you hear my stomach rumbling?" yelled the girl and the squall cracked open the sky, tearing the clouds to rags. The rain came down in stair-rods and cascaded down the flooded little street.

"When I was little they couldn't keep me out of water," she said. "I was always falling into rivers, paddling pools, ditches, hoping some fella would fish me out."

Her big, wet face was lit up by the streetlight and she pulled a long black hair from her mouth. She still had her case by her side.

"Lucky, I don't mind getting wet."

"Mm."

They took the short cut by the churchyard, the steps a little waterfall, the flailing trees clawing savagely at the sky.

"Look at that," she said, and they watched a flock of black tiles cut through the air and smash into the warehouse opposite.

If I don't hold onto her then she'll blow away, Hans thought, though he didn't know whether or not to bother. Ah, when was the last bus back to Uni? Meanwhile, Clara was off on her own skipping through the puddles.

"Do you want to hear about my last boyfriend?" she asked. "He washed dishes at this fancy restaurant and he used to say that my face was a big round plate and when he kissed me he could see his own face smiling back." Hans didn't answer. More debris went flying off into space and the wind blew rainwater in his ears. "We split up 'cause he was sick of all the guys chasing after me — but what can I do?"

Her hair blew in front of her round, white face, and it was like a lunar eclipse, the girl's eyes and nose and mouth disappearing in the darkness. All he could see was the bruise.

What a gal, thought Hans. But what was she doing with a suitcase in the middle of the night anyway?

The chip shop was on the main road to the bridge out of town and a weary yellow glow emanated from its dreary interior. The spotty guy behind the fryers looked just bored out of his brains and the only customer was some little old dear waiting quietly for her fish.

"Double chips please!" said the girl. Water was streaming from her clothes and sizzled on the hot counter. The pair of them were soaked to the bone.

But where should they go with them? Hans wasn't even hungry. They sheltered in a tenement stoop near the bridge. Outside, cars splashed along the main road and the rain lashed down in barrels. When he poked his head out, it was like a bucket of water in the face.

The girl was shivering. "These chips are lovely," she said.

When he kissed her she tasted of vinegar. He couldn't see very well and water kept trickling in his eyes. Close-up the girl looked even prettier, her bruise an ugly crater on the moon.

And Hans thought: If I could paint her then I'd put her head on upside down, make her eyes as big as saucers, and her mouth a tiny hole in the canvas. Then I'd draw her body like one skinny line with this big white balloon on the top, a light bulb on inside.

Clara's lips were warm but her teeth chattered.

The gale battered the low stone bridge, picked up water from the river, threw it at the town. It wailed and hollered. Heavy black clouds came down and obliterated the skyline, flooding the rooftops, the steeples, the grey granite hills.

"There was this one guy who was mad keen on me," said the girl between kisses. "I mean, he was really crazy. One day when I didn't show up he burst into tears, took off all his clothes, and jumped out of his tenement window. It's true! But it all went wrong 'cause, like, he fell really awkwardly and got himself caught up in all the washing-lines which were strung across, and he ended up sort of tangled, one leg slipped into a stiff pair of shorts and one arm stuck in an apron, and there he was, hanging there above the yard, all dressed up. Anyhow, after a while a crowd came to watch him and eventually someone called the fire brigade. They came in a big red lorry, with smart black uniforms and shiny helmets, and everyone clapped and cheered."

And Hans thought: look, her pullover's like a dish-rag. She's shaking.

She was the shape of a lollypop — skinny with a big round head. And where had she got that bruise from? Hans felt awful tired and wet but the girl was stuck to him like a plaster.

Had somebody really thrown themself out of a window for her? Raindrops sparkled in her hair and her eyes were dark and saucy. But I don't know, Hans thought to himself; his neck was sore and he had these cramps in his legs. I don't know. Tch, he blinked his eyes and looked down at her case. What was in there anyway?

After a while they stopped kissing. "I'm still a bitty hungry," she said. "There's a Spar just round the corner. Could you get me some chocolate?"

He mentally counted up his change and said, "Okay." When he looked back her face was this big round headlamp in the darkness.

Clouds exploded and great grenades of water bounced off the road. The wind blew the water into great swells, which coursed down toward the overflow. Hans crossed the channel and ran over to the shop.

Just look at him, though: he's tired and he's wet-through, with his hair stuck flat to the top of his head. Bugger this, he thinks to himself. There's a leak in one of his trainers and his essay is due in tomorrow.

Outside the Spar is a bus stop and he stops and thinks about the cash in his pocket. Ah, he thinks, isn't it easier to just go? A great weariness seems to descend upon him and all he wants to do is to lie down and sleep. But then he thinks about the girl shivering and waiting for her chocolate and starts to feels bad. How old was she anyway? The rain pours down in a never-ending stream, splashing from the guttering, spilling out from the overflows. He pictures her face, a big round balloon with a smile crayoned-on, and then he pictures her case, all battered and scuffed, sitting next to her like an obedient dog. What a crazy girl! The wind is trying to grab his glasses, his trainers two grey puddles beneath his trouser-slops.

But amazingly, the headlights of a bus are approaching. Is it the right one? Yes it is.

Ah, me, he thinks. It's awful late.

So what's he doing now? He's climbing on the bus and giving the man his money. No, really!

The fella is on the bus and he's fishing in his pocket for his loose-change. Kid, hey kid! Ah, it's as if he can't be bothered; he stumbles down the aisle already half-asleep, swaying from side to side and falling over half the seats. Lucky the bus is empty; he makes it to the back seat and throws himself down, his clothes one big wet bundle. Ah, what's he thinking about d'you think? The girl? Her case? The gales? No, nothing. The kid is thinking about nothing. A mysterious lethargy seems to overwhelm him and he slowly closes his eyes. Look – the bus is starting to pull away and the fella is starting to disappear...

Lethargy! Lassitude! Indolence! O, the listlessness of man! The bus is disappearing and back on the stoop the girl seems to vanish too. Yes, there's a sudden flicker and her little headlamp goes out, swallowed up by the darkness. But the kid's asleep and doesn't even notice. Listlessness, torpidity, indifference; what will save us from these?

III

Outside on the pavement, our little group of tourists clustered together for warmth. Ah, what a night! Above us the clouds were being wrung out like dish cloths, huge spouts of water pouring down from the sky. Rain surged along the guttering, cascaded from the overflows, and gurgled in the drains. How cold it was and how heavy! But what could we do? We watched the little bus pull away and felt the sky rumble and flush, terrifying water-bombs exploding above our heads. Even the darkness felt wet.

"On we go," yelled our guide. He was four sheets to the wind by now and his eyes rolled erratically in his sockets. "We're leaving the old town behind. Ahead lies bleak industrial parks, housing estates, closed down shops. But don't worry! The silhouette of the castle will stay with us, and the shadow of those grey-black hills."

But, oh, where were we going? Outside the supermarket, a flock of trolleys ranged freely across the car-park, whilst over by the off-licence a ragged mass of bin-bags looked like a great black cloud fallen down to earth. We were so wet! The pedestrian walkway was more like a paddling pool, the dark underpass flooded and impassable.

Our boss-eyed guide glared at us impatiently.

"If you please, ladies and gentlemen... no time to lose!"

One hand held a now-empty bottle, the other the black stalk of an umbrella.

"Right this way!"

Tell me, what could we do? We were cold, wet, bedraggled. We hung onto each other in fear, soggy wee ticket stubs crumpled up in our paws, water dripping down our forlorn little faces. And so on we went. We clambered over some railings and stumbled across a patch of muddy waste-ground, every step heavy, every patch of earth a puddle.

"This way, this way," cried our guide. "Watch out for any sink-holes or sudden drops! There's no time to go back for your shoe now, sir: you can scrape that off when you get back. Miss, stop crying, please! Hold on tight and the storm may spare you."

Suddenly he came to a halt, the stalk of his umbrella pointing up toward heaven. What was going through his head? His eyes looked wild and maddened, his long grey face as flat as a spade.

"Shhh", he said, pointing to a battered 'No Trespassing' sign. His umbrella was a little black hole cut out of the sky. "Not a sound, do you hear me? Not a sound!" And with that he ushered us forward, over a high wall and across some wire, his umbrella shaking from side to side.

The cluster of blocky buildings were piled up in a dull, grey compound, bereft of life. Only one block was illuminated, a low concrete shed with a row of fat chimneys and a thick tangle of pipes running along the outside. Well, maybe we'll find shelter here, we thought, our sad little huddle shivering in the darkness. We crept toward it, a few steps behind our guide, and then we were in the compound itself, staring through the window of a grey out-building, water trickling down our faces and pricking our eyes.

The place was some kind of launderette, but not the ordinary kind, open to the general public: no, it was one of those huge industrial jobs, with enormous machines, massive drums and vast dryers. It was just as noisy inside as out. The drums span, the tubs gurgled, water surged and rolled, blasted in terrible jets. And in the middle of this turmoil, this little bloke lay dozing over his newspaper, his head cradled in the sports pages.

Our guide put one finger to his lips.

"Quiet as you can," he whispered. He shuffled over to a little side-window and jemmied it open with his brolly.

Then we crept in a little closer to see the skiver close-up.

Was that wee Hans? Aye, weak chin, watery eyes, a mug like a cake that won't rise. "And look at the length of those finger-nails," whispered our sozzled guide. "He's never done a day's work in his life."

We were well inside the launderette by now. All around us, washers chugged, boilers droned, machines whirred and hummed; everything whizzed and spun but the whey-faced lump just sat there, dozing.

"Pfff," said the guide, shaking his brolly dismissively. His ragged umbrella looked like one of the torn black clouds fallen from the sky.

But just then one of the machines finished its cycle and the fella had to get to his feet and haul out all the washing. Blimey, he looked bored, limp as a sock. Hans fished out the laundry and dumped in the next load with a kind of stubborn slowness. Work-shy layabout! He could scarcely be bothered to check the setting for the next boil-wash and just left the dials where they were.

I don't know — Hans looked down at his paper and sighed. He drew funny beards on the film stars, comedy scars on the models, poked daggers through politicians. Then he ringed the telly programmes he was missing, checked his answers to the Kwik-Quiz, filled in all the o's in the money section. What a lump! His face looked as washed-out as the laundry.

Meanwhile our guide was telling us how the launderette dealt with big orders from local firms, overalls, uniforms, tabards, aprons and the like. Caterers' apparel came in smeared with sauces, sweat, stains, factory workers' coveralls smelling of chemicals and oil, a feint tang of machine-parts. But by far the worst were the big orders from the old folks home, bibs and pinafores painted yellow, red, brown, encrusted with who knows what. Mm, what a job! The windows rattled, the door shook, and inside the tubs the garments reeled and slew.

Hans watched the machines for a while and then went back to his newspaper. But after a while his eyes started to wander, his pulse slowed down, and even his breathing seemed to grow heavier and more pronounced. One eye drooped and then the other. His face seemed to sag and crumple. And then he started to mutter something in his sleep, cradling his sagging noggin in the crook of his arm.

Inside his head, he'd taken off his socks and shoes and was paddling at the edge of a foamy tide. Hi ho, he thought. The waves smelt of detergent and conditioner, spumes of soap flakes breaking over his hairy toes. He rolled up his trews and waded in a little deeper. The water was hot and lathery and breakers of froth rolled over him. What's this, he said to himself, it's lovely and bubbly in here. Suds swirled around his head and his feet scarcely seemed to reach the bottom.

But at the same time he couldn't help noticing that something wasn't quite right. The crash of waves on the shore sounded strangely like a knocking or a banging, and the further he bobbed out to sea, the louder the knocking seemed to be. Hans looked down at the bubbles and blew some more of his own. Where was the banging coming from? Something in the tub? Glug, glug, glug, said the fella, screwing up his eyes.

But the drumming wasn't coming from the tub at all – no, somebody was hammering on the front door of the launderette, heavy, insistent blows like thunder-claps, and as the sound echoed across the linoleum, Hans made himself get up and go over and have a look.

If anything the thuds were getting louder. The tide receded and the fella stumbled over to the door.

'Blimey,' thought wee Hans, 'who is this?' Rubbing his eyes he unlocked the security grill and stared out into the gloom, where he saw a dark shape standing beneath a bottomless sky, a sort of scribble squatting there in the doorway, curled up against the rain. No, really! 'Twas more of a bundle than a man, a sopping heap of mismatched clothes all bundled up in a pile.

"Are you open?" yelled the heap, the wind howling round him. He was holding a big plastic carrier bag with both hands, the bag starting to tear at the seams.

"No, listen," Hans tried to say, "we're a private…" but his words were blown off across the yard.

"What's that?" cried the stranger, his hair blown crazily in the gale.

"Not open to the public," cried Hans, yelling as loud as he could.

"What?"

The gale bawled and wailed, a great disturbance in the heavens.

" … not that sort of launderette," Hans shouted, but his voice was carried away over the rooftops, off past the garage, and down by the charity-shops. Besides, the fella wasn't listening anyway. He pushed his way past, seated himself on the mannie's chair and stuffed the soggy bag between his knees.

"Ah, thanks," he said. "Poor me!"

Hans scratched his crotch and lingered by the doorway.

"I…"

"Ah, dear, what a night!" The fella put two sodden feet on top of an enormous dryer. "You wouldn't believe the things I've seen; it's

28

like the whole world is disappearing down the plug-hole. Ah, but will you look at my bag."

Hans nodded and we took our chance and scuttled in, hiding behind a long row of grey plastic baskets.

"Look at the state of it. And look at the state of me! Not a bus to be seen, not a cab on the road. I don't know… I was glad when I saw that you still had a light on, let me tell you."

Hans scratched his head. "Well…" he said, rather uncertainly, whilst the stranger lolled back in his chair, dripping water all over the seat. The guy was short, round and had a kind of idiot grin plastered over the front of his face. It was hard to tell which clothes he was carrying and which ones he was wearing.

"I was just walking past the discount centre," said the funny-little guy, "when suddenly the awnings blew down and it was like a whole bath-tub had been dumped on top of me. And then, when I picked myself up, this van drove past and — splshhh — right in the face again."

"Really?" asked the attendant, watching what the mannie was doing on his chair.

"Yeah! And no sooner had I wiped the water out of my eyes when I noticed my bag was shooting off by the overflow, and I had to splash my way in to get it and my shoes got ruined and everything."

"Well, people should look where they're going."

"That's right…"

"I mean, you know, on a night like this…"

"'Specially on a night like this."

"That's right."

The funny little guy smiled at Hans, his mouth suspended between two round apple-cheeks. His eyes flashed mysteriously.

"You seem a sympathetic sort," he said to the skinny lad. "Will you join me in a bottle?" And so saying he produced a jar from inside his soggy jacket; the bottle had no label and the top seemed to be gummed shut.

"Um, well…"

"Ah, c'mon. Time for a quick one!"

"Well…"

"On a night like this? Don't be silly. C'mon, sit yourself down."

"You see I..."

"Sit yourself down! Nobody's checking up on you tonight."

"Well, I don't know," Hans said, but nevertheless he pulled up a chair and retrieved two manky old mugs from a sink.

Then he took a swig and felt his stomach lurch. The drink tasted of gin, aniseed and lighter fluid.

"Warms the cockles, eh?"

"Mm, yeah"

"Have another."

"Thanks."

Hans leaned back on his chair and looked at the little ball of a man with his little round cheeks and his idiot grin. "It's kinda late to be doing your laundry, eh?" he said, trying to figure out what the fella was doing here

"What? Ah, well..."

"'Cause you see, we're not open to the general..."

"Oh, don't you worry," said the little bloke. "I'm in no rush! Just glad to be out of the rain."

"Well, I guess," Hans said, watching the fella spinning round on his office-chair. He looked very much at home.

The roundy-man pulled off his socks and hung them out to dry over a big electric heater.

"Are you done with that paper?" he said, flicking through the attendant's things.

"Oh, yeah, sure."

"Much obliged."

The machines hummed, the dryers turned, and the drains frothed and gurgled. Hans started to explain that this place wasn't for public use but then realised he couldn't be bothered. Ah, it was late; might as well have another drink with the fella instead.

The launderette sounded like an enormous plane about to take off.

"It's a nice wee place you've got here," said the stranger, eying up the concrete washroom. "Warm, dry, awful cozy." He swung round on his seat again. "And this chair's a beauty!"

"Do you think?" asked Hans, sniffing the edge of his mug. "It's all shift-work you know — deliveries, loads, hauling stuff in and out."

"But... a place of your own, time to catch up on your reading," (and here he held up a picture of a model where the young fella had drawn a rope-ladder between her breasts) "nobody breathing down your neck... no, no, it's pretty good, considering."

"Well..."

The booze seemed to be having a strange effect upon our laddie, and Hans felt his tongue starting to go a little numb.

"I mean, look outside," said the strange wee fella, pointing to where the great black sky was tearing itself into pieces, a huge dark canvas coming apart at the seams. "No, you're better off in than out, sitting on your arse, putting out some washing once in a while."

"Well, thanks for saying so."

"Yes, nice little place," said the roundy-man, sagely, "a nice little place."

The two men drunk a little more and the stranger flicked through the paper. Various lights were flashing, and buzzers sounded, but Hans couldn't really be bothered. By now his tongue felt like the inside of a slipper.

"So what's in the bag, eh?" he slurred, nudging the carrier with one outstretched toe.

"Just a little washing, you know, this and that," said the squat wee fella.

"Oh yeah? Well who does their washing in the middle of the night? On a night like this?" And so saying Hans clinked his mug on the dryer.

"Bits and bobs," smiled the mannie, "bits and bobs. Here, your mug looks nearly empty."

Hans supped a bit more, but his throat felt furred, like the inside of an old kettle.

"This is lovely," he said.

"Look at the night outside, and think of what we've got right here. Best stay indoors, eh? Good company, something to drink, refuge from the storm... Who wants to venture outside on a night like this? Aye, the wind is sharpening its claws all right, and the rain feels more like grit. But we can turn up the radiator, have a game of cards, finish off the paper…"

"That's right."

"Let the storm blow itself inside out for all we care! Trust me, the night will keep."

Sloth! Lethargy! Laziness! No good will come of this, hissed our guide, shaking his brolly at the pair of them.

But who could be bothered… who could be bothered on a night like this, checking the panels, lugging out the contents, wheeling round the trolleys? I mean, overalls, uniforms, tabards, aprons… And outside the sky looked more and more like the sea, storm-tossed and roiling.

"Mind if I use the lav?" asked the wee fella and Hans said, "Why, sure," and pointed the way. To be honest, his legs felt kinda wobbly and his thoughts kept sticking to the inside of his head.

Hi-Ho, he thought. When he looked down he saw a little foamy wave breaking round his feet; it lapped around the bottom of the chair and smelt of chemicals and detergent.

I've got to wake myself up, Hans thought. What will the little guy think if he finds me sleeping on the job?

A few of the machines had started to bleat but Hans didn't get up; he couldn't remember what to do anyway.

When the stranger came back, he was dressed in some kind of bottle-green uniform, with a peaked-cap, a tunic-like jacket and stiff, formal trews.

"I found some dry clothes," he announced. "Is that okay?"

"Why sure," said Hans. "Don't want to catch a cold!"

"That's right!"

"Sure is."

"Have another drink."

So he did. Well, why not? Anything to break the monotony.

"Where did you get them?" Hans asked, gesturing toward the mannie's new outfit.

"Oh, round the back." The little fella ran his hand along one neatly creased trouser-leg. "Nice, eh?"

"Nice."

After that the night's spin-cycle drowned out the conversation for a while, the sky a great black pool pouring down on the grey little town. But then Hans spotted the fella's manky plastic bag and said, "Say, I forgot your washing…"

"Oh, don't you worry," said the mannie with the apple-shaped cheeks.

"No, but…"

"That's okay, I'll do it myself."

"Oh, no, I…"

"Don't worry! They're pretty badly stained and you look kinda tired. Let me…"

Hans stretched and leaned back on his seat. "That's very good of you. How about I see if I've got a couple of cans out back."

"You go ahead."

"Back in a second."

"Mm."

The fella smiled his big idiot smile but as soon as the attendant was out of the room, he scuttled over to one of the tubs and surreptitiously opened his bag. A terrible stench issued forth and the sack's lips drooped obscenely. What was in it? We couldn't see. But the fella was up to something; he checked the setting, opened the lid, and stuffed a whole bundle of things inside. Our guide shook his head, awful sadly. Then, when the young fella trooped back from the side-room, the roundy-man innocently closed the lid and wandered back to the table.

"Find 'em?"

"No, but I was sure…"

"Ach, well. Fancy a game of cards?"

"H'okay. I'll just…"

"Don't you worry! Sit yourself down. I'll fetch us a pencil and pad."

Hans parked himself on his chair and looked down at the floor of the unit. When he moved his feet up and down he seemed to be paddling.

"Hey!" he said, and then promptly forgot what he was saying. Meanwhile the fella set the dial to boil-wash and the machine began to hum.

"Rummy?" asked the mannie.

"Great!" Hans said and picked up his cards. We wanted to creep over to the machine but felt afraid; even our guide was silent for once, regarding the tubs with a mournful air.

Well, it was getting pretty late by now, but the little roundy-man seemed wider awake than ever. Beneath his peaked cap his eyes shone brightly, and the uniform seemed to make him look bigger somehow, almost a different person.

"Clubs!"

Hans looked knackered, barely able to look at his hands. His thoughts seemed sluggish and heavy, like wading through soup. The two blokes gabbed away for a while, but Hans kept nodding off, his chin tumbling down to his chest.

To be honest, he was finding it hard to remember what he was supposed to be doing here. He blinked at the fella in his bottle-green uniform and felt confused. Who was this guy? The jacket made his shoulders look wider and the shadow of the cap lent his features a rather fearsome aspect. Hans leant back on his chair and suddenly caught sight of the mannie's bag; it was empty but looked kinda sticky, squashed up into a strange shape. 'S'funny, he thought to himself, his head terribly heavy. Waves of soapsuds were lapping at his feet. Splish-splash. The water bubbled and frothed round his ankles and the tide seemed to curl lazily around him.

But meanwhile the guy in the uniform was watching him intently. As soon as he was sure he was asleep, the fella stole back over to the machine and eagerly checked the dial: hm, yes, nearly done. Illuminated by the flashing lights, his features seemed sinister, even diabolical. His apple-cheeks glowed and his idiot-smile beamed.

What was he washing? O, let us leave this place! This cannot end well. The fella placed both paws on the machine and rocked to and fro.

When it was done he leaned into the tub and began to rummage around in there, his large round face huffing and puffing. What was in there? We tried to creep closer, but our guide waved us back.

"No, no," he whispered, "'tis all too late…"

And just then a loud klaxon went off, water poured out of all the plugholes, and Hans suddenly jumped to his feet.

He looked groggy, dazed, his tongue lolling about in his mouth. Where was he? When he looked at the guy in the uniform and peaked-cap, he looked totally different, taller, wider, stern in countenance, with a fierce glint in his eyes.

"Okay pal, time to go," he growled, fingering the fella's collar.

Hans looked up at him like something waking from a long hibernation.

"What?" he mouthed, the words slow and heavy on his tongue.

"Yeah, yeah, time to go," said the fella in the uniform, frogmarching the other man to the door.

Something was wrong here; after all, wasn't he the attendant? Hans looked at the fella's uniform and grew confused. Wasn't this his job? If not, then what did he do?

Outside the door the heavens bayed and shrieked, the black sky a storm-tossed sea, savage and endless.

"Wait, wait," said Hans, staring out into the gale. But he couldn't think what else to say. He looked down at his clothes: jeans, T-shirt, and trainers. Then he looked over at the mannie's cap, tunic-like jacket, and formal trews. But why was he so confused? What was he doing here in the first place? Especially at this hour of the night, in this old grey town, when he should be tucked up in bed.

He looked around the bright, smelly launderette but couldn't recognise anything. Behind him the guy in the uniform, with the stern eyes and the podgy cheeks, seemed to grow even taller. "Don't give me any trouble, son," he said, and bundled a pile of laundry into his arms. Overalls, coveralls, tabards, aprons. "Out you go."

"I don't think…" said wee Hans, but the attendant shook his head.

"But, I…"

"Away with you…"

Confused, Hans looked back into his office as if from inside a washing machine; rain lashed down from all angles, was picked up by the wind, and then lashed down again. How cozy the little block looked! An electric-fire, a travel-kettle, two manky mugs. Ah, well. The rain stung his eyes. Hi ho, Hans thought.

His jeans, T-shirt, and zip-up top were soon soaked. He lingered by the window for a while, watching the fella and his uniform scuttling this way and that; the fella seemed to be busy with the control panels, pressing this one, turning another, checking each of the drums and throwing out the previous loads. But the young guy's face seemed oddly indifferent, impassive, sleepy. To be honest, he didn't seem to register what was going on. What was he thinking about? Home? His bed? Something good on the telly tonight? After a while, he walked away and didn't look back.

Join us friend! Our tour isn't over and there's always room for another! But our tour-guide shakes his head: no, no, such things are not to be. Friend, friend, where are you going? Wait for us! This is no night to be walking the streets alone! But our guide is signalling for us to move on. This is a haunted place, he says; nothing good can come from here. And inside, the idiot with the apple-cheeks removes something dark and stained from another plastic bag.

IV

To be honest, by now even the tour-guide didn't look so good. His shoulders slumped, his brolly drooped, one corner of his fake moustache had come unglued on his lip. But still he marched on, his bandy-legs capering this way and that in the darkness.

"This way, this way," he yelled. "No time to dawdle! No, no, ladies and gentlemen, we can't go back. Back to what? The very sky is coming unstuck and who knows what lies behind it?"

Delicately, he wiped the glass of his spectacles with one gloved finger.

"What a night, eh? Like the very rafters are coming apart. But let's keep going, Madam! There's bound to be something warm waiting for us at our journey's end..."

Crocodile-fashion, the tourists followed in a docile line behind him, heads bowed and feet aching, a line of ragged silhouettes cut out from an old piece of newspaper. The fella at the back walked with a limp.

"Sir, sir, if you please? Don't linger by the tree, sir; those branches will have you over in an instant! And try not to stray from the path, Madam; no, no, this way, over the little stone-wall, through the gate-way, across the wide, muddy field..."

Strung out in a line, the tourists flapped and shook. Only their feet seemed to keep them tethered to the ground, their hooves great clods of earth.

"Ah, ladies and gentlemen, we've left behind the town and the industrial park, the ring road and street-lights, all the trappings of modern life. Imagine; the world has slipped away and all we're left with are shadows, holes, black shapes moving through the darkness. What are we now? Just sticky blobs and dabs, black marks on a black canvas, a gaping void or some such thing...."

The tour-guide voice suddenly cracked and softened.

"Oh, my friends! Now we are approaching the very edge of the world, without light or colour or form. Mind how you go, sir; it's hard to know where the sky ends and the ground begins! All seems painted with the same black brush, the landscape as much as ourselves, less a great black brush than the very paint-pot itself..."

But there was something there. Across the field and over a rough fence, there was a petrol station, its forecourt illuminated by four large lights. Rain fell on its felt roof and petrol pumps, lit up by the lights like little strokes of a pen, while over by the carwash an old blue car stood parked, water bouncing off its top.

The tour-guide saw it but immediately turned his back, his eyes fixed on something thither. He scratched his chin and straightened the fingers of his gloves. The tourists however started to gesticulate wildly. One woman pulled on his sleeve whilst another started to hop up and down on the spot.

"Food, crisps, tea! Ah, food, sweets, soup!"

The tour-guide looked down at them condescendingly, his moustache just clinging to his upper lip.

"Ladies and gentlemen, please; we are so near the end of our tour, do you really want to tarry? No, no, let's go on. We have but one more stop to make, one last station of the cross before the end... I ask you, Madam, just look at that sky — the very heavens seem to tremble and the earth itself is starting to shake. Ladies and gentlemen, I beseech you! Remember our theme — listlessness, lethargy, sloth!"

But the huddle of tourists looked sullen and resentful. They shuffled their feet in the mud and gazed longingly at the little island of light, lit up like a kindly lamp in the darkness. Ah, there was nothing the tour-guide could do. Rain exploded over the spinning-signs, the row of pumps, the empty newspaper display.

"What a dispiriting place," grumbled the tour-guy, running his fingers along the top of a pump. "Lifeless, soulless, abandoned..."

And it was pretty quiet; no car raced past on the carriageway, no customers were wandering around over by the shop. The tourists were tired and hungry and they gathered outside the kiosk like the survivors from some great and terrible wreck.

Shhhh, said the doors.

Inside the light was bright enough to peel your eyeballs, and the wee clump seemed momentarily dazzled, a little lost amongst the food-displays and the magazine-racks. Loud music played out of the speakers and the tourists stumbled about, kinda shaky-looking, searching for familiar things, confectionery, vending machines. Outside, rain hammered on the windows, metal awnings, billboards.

"Ah, me," said the tour-guide. He strode over to the sealed-off kiosk area, where a young girl was sitting reading behind a sheet of shatterproof glass, her eyes seeming to slide along the surface of her book. Somehow, she seemed both bored and engrossed, and when she got to the end of a page her lips trembled and released the tiniest of sighs.

"Er, Miss? Miss?"

The girl didn't look up, but went on staring at her book. Her eyes were pale and her lips strangely faint, like somebody had drawn in her features but then rubbed them out in a hurry. Her hair was like straw, and seemed to poke out from atop her high forehead.

"Miss?" The tour-guide rattled his brolly on the glass grill, and the girl mouthed "Pump number" somnambulantly, though no sound penetrated the partition.

"I'm sorry?"

"Pumber," mouthed the girl, her lips the faintest of pencil-lines.

The tour-guide looked at the girl kinda craftily.

"No, no, we have no car," he intoned, with a theatrical flourish. "We've arrived on foot, wet, cold, buffeted by the gale... O, Miss, have you not looked outside at the night? The nails which held up the sky are giving way, and a great cauldron of water lies above us." He poked back one errant corner of his phoney moustache and rested his bony elbows on the desk by the grill. The girl's face was as vacant as the glass partition.

"Miss, Miss? Can you hear me? Ah Miss, look up from your book," whispered the tour-guide. "The sky is heavy and dangerous, as dark as the inside of one's head! Miss, Miss, what are you doing here? I mean, in a place like this, on a night like tonight? Marooned in the middle of nowhere, stuck in this plate-glass tomb..."

How pale the girls eyes were! The tour-guide couldn't tell whether they were open or shut.

"Ah, how did it come to this, eh? Dead-end job, lousy hours, sealed up in a glass box..."

The girl shifted in her seat and the tout-guide smacked his lips in disgust.

"What a dump this is! As empty as a plastic cup." He snorted but then shuffled over, closer to the mouthpiece of the grill. "But tell me, I'm looking for this place near here, a construction-site, do you know it?"

He looked down at his brolly and gave it a sharp little shake. A small pool of greyish water had formed beneath him.

"Just a few fields away, a big hole in the ground..."

The girl's lips moved soundlessly, and the fella's expression seemed to soften.

"Oh my dear, do you hear me at all?"

Her eyes, nose and mouth were no more than the faintest of furrows, and the tour-guide pressed his moustache up against the glass.

"You see, there was this fella I once knew, ach, a funny fella really, head in the clouds, a bit of a layabout if truth be told. And, well, maybe he even came in here. I mean, he worked on this building-site and, you know, I can imagine him coming in to get his junk-food, his tinnies, his microwavable snacks..."

Outside you could see the rain coming down in long, crooked lines, the wind tossing it against the glass with alarming force. From where the tour-guide was standing, it sounded like a machine-gun.

"Did you ever see him, Miss?" he asked the girl behind the grill. "Maybe he popped in in the middle of the night, this fella, a work-shy git in a pakamac, his hair too long and his mug unshaven, the laziest fella you could imagine..."

The girl's features seemed strangely indistinct, her features a kind of blur.

"And this fella, well, he came to a bad end, let me tell you. You see, he let himself slip away, drifted off and..."

But the girl wasn't listening. She put down her book, closed her eyes, and seemed to curl up in her own lap. How pale she was! Like a blank piece of paper. Rain exploded like shrapnel just outside but the girl rolled herself into a ball and went to sleep right where she was.

"Ah, well," said the tour-guide. "Ah, well."

He shook his head, grasped the handle of his soaking wet brolly, and walked back over to the other side of the shop where the tourists were gathering up whatever consumables they could find.

"It's alright, Madam; take whatever you like. The girl is asleep, and it's fair to say that our need is greater. No, sir, not the whole stand; just gather what you can carry, whatever you need before we make our final stop, the terminus which awaits us all…"

Outside the wind screamed and the rain bounced off the forecourt floor.

"This way, ladies and gentlemen. Quickly, before the sky tears loose entirely! Yes, I know, the wind is wild and the rain seeks every crevice, but we must brave the elements one final time, deliver ourselves up to the darkness…"

As soon as the tour left the oasis of the deserted little petrol-station, the little group seemed to vanish entirely. It's true! It was as if they had been swallowed whole by the storm, every last trace of them effaced from the world. Only the stentorian tones of the tour-guide could still be heard, his voice echoing strangely, as if he were yelling from the bottom of a well, or the centre of a terrifyingly black hole.

"Ladies and gentlemen, don't panic! No, hold on tight now, don't let go of one another's hands or try to run for cover. Ah, madam, though we be bereft of light or vision, though the very elements oppose our passage, we must not waiver or weaken, must not buckle under the weight of that terrible black sky… Sir, sir, are you there?"

"Sir, don't worry, the end of our tour is nigh. Look! This isn't a field but some kind of building site. We're not lost, just at the very outskirts of the town. It's true! There's a digger and a long row of pipes and some kind of portakabin, where one last light still glows. Follow me, ladies and gentlemen. Watch out for the trench and the markers…"

And so saying, the guide ushered them forward, his shape a crooked daub in the blackness. Whispering and muttering, the tourists made their way alongside the trench and climbed the few metal steps up to the prefab cabin.

"Say, can you smell gas?" breathed one of the tourists as they climbed inside.

The air in the portakabin was hot, fusty and malodorous, but they did not pause nor did they slacken….

V

Inside, the guide gently patted his moustache down and warmed his back by the fire. His voice was surprisingly soft and tender, his eyes dimmed to the colour of old coal.

"You see, the end, when it came, was like this. After a series of terrible jobs — waiter in a tea-shop, car-park attendant, handing out fliers in pubs — little Hans finally ended up doing casual security work on this building site out of town, ah, a call-centre, supermarket, or some such thing…" He glanced around the portakabin and propped his brolly up to dry. "But really all he did was lie around, kip by the fire, read a book. Honestly he was the slackest, laziest, most work-shy git you could imagine, I've never met such a dosser…"

The guide looked down at his feet and shook his head.

"And yet Miss, this fella, he meant no harm. No, he just looked around himself at this little grey town and thought, Ah, well, better the world of my dreams. Do you know what I mean, Miss? School, work, everyday life; it was as if he found fault with everything and rather longed for some other extraordinary thing. And this thing — well, it seemed to finish him."

The guide warmed himself by the fire and sighed. The tourists watched him warily, rain water drying on the back of their necks.

"He was a funny fella, you know, Miss. Slept all hours of the day, tufts of hair sticking up like a dog's curly tail. When he talked his head bobbed up and down and when he walked his long lanky legs slackened and bounced, like a spring."

The tour-guide shrugged.

"And yet," he went on, "it was as if he was only half there, as if the door between waking and sleeping were somehow propped open. And then, when he got his job on the building site, he settled into his portakabin and gave himself up to idleness entirely. Ah, sir! There's no other way of putting it. He rolled over, closed both eyes, and searched for this one miraculous thing, a thing which, as all sleepwalkers know, can only be found with one's eyes tightly shut.

"But then, sitting up in his cabin one night, Hans suddenly felt a shiver of doubt: did he really have a job after all? He stood up and looked around the portakabin, a shelter which somehow seemed unfamiliar and strange. O ladies and gentlemen, was he really the security-man? After all, he arrived at the building site after everyone had gone and left before the workers in the morning. Nobody asked about him, checked up on him, or seemed to take the blindest bit of notice. No, he slipped into his portakabin each night, rolled out his sleeping bag and was out like a light. Was he supposed to report to anyone? Was he still being paid? To be honest, he couldn't remember. He had a kind of jacket, and a security man's peaked cap, but couldn't remember where he'd got them. He didn't report to anyone, didn't have any badge or pass; if someone were to stop him and demand to see ID then he would be utterly lost. Luckily, however, he himself was the security guard, and so he let himself in every night, climbed inside his sleeping-bag and slept like a log.

"And when he was awake? Well, he footered around the cabin, tried to read a horror novel, stared out into the darkness… but he wasn't fussed. The walls were papered with naked girlies, but he rarely looked at them. Nor did he examine the building plans scattered across the table. What did it matter what they were building, call-centre, bus-depot, DIY store? He filled in no forms, filed no reports, kept no logbook. In the morning, he would cycle off and crash at a mate's house, but then it occurred to him that he hadn't seen his friend for a long time either. I'm drifting away, he thought to himself one day, drifting out to sea…

"Time went on. The fella grew a beard. He started to talk back to the radio. One night he was visited by this stray dog who'd wandered onto the site looking for scraps or handouts, a funny-looking mutt with grey fur and white paws. Hans fed him biscuits and crisps and patted him over and over, saying, 'You're a good boy aren't you? Yes you are…' The dog laid down by the fire and the guy said, Who's a good dog then? and rubbed his tum. He tickled the dog's ears and said 'Hello big dog. Hello big dog'. The pooch looked up at him, his tongue poking out like the filling of a ham sandwich. 'Hello big dog,' said the fella.

"After that, the dog came most every night. Hans would get a take-out from a nearby garage and then share it when he got to work, the pair of them curled up by the heater. The dog's fur was matted and smelly and crawling with beasties, but Hans didn't seem to mind; after all, he didn't look so clever either. Once in a while, when the weather wasn't too wet, they'd wander round the building-site together, picking their way through the mud and the darkness, four little paw prints and a pair of trainers. Hans would shine his torch over the pipes and trenches, saying, 'What do you think, boy?' or 'hey boy, what's that?' The place was full of holes, either being dug or filled in, and there were deep furrows everywhere. So much mud! The fella and his dog would wander about until the first birds started to sing or the sky started to change colour and then it was time to go.

"What's that, sir? Why, yes, I know. At times it still seemed like he was on the verge of this one miraculous thing, whilst at other times it seemed further away than ever. Strange thoughts pursued him. His head ached and his eyes ran. He started to make up different names for all the bits of furniture — Mr Table, Mr Chair, Mr Sleeping-bag. He was tired all the time and everything seemed to ache. Once, he heard some kids messing around by the main generator and when he went out in the morning his bike was gone. Another time, he looked out of his cabin window and saw a fox talking to his dog. 'Hello, big dog,' it said.

"Oh, Miss, he was slipping away! His thoughts seemed to have come untethered and bobbed crazily about the room. Worse still, winter was coming now, a winter of cold and sleet. The nights felt deeper and darker. 'Where am I?' whispered the fella, wrapped up in his sleeping-bag. To be honest, he was little more than a heap of bedding himself....

"But one morning Hans felt a little better, and managed to pull himself out of his sleeping-bag, stow his things, lock the cabin-door, and lope off along the carriageway, his hair askew and his clothes kinda fusty.

"And Hans, well, he walked past a soulless new industrial park, crossed an ugly grey housing-estate, and reached the old town bridge by the river. What a sight he looked! Like something his dog had dug up, his beard wild but his face as gentle as ever. But already disaster was coming, snapping at the idle fellow's heels...

"For, you see, Hans had forgotten where he was staying. His mate's house, his stuff, his telly — all gone. He shook his head but nothing came; it was as if he'd never been to this little grey town before in his life. Instead he strode up and down the twisty little lanes, past one row of shops and then another, but couldn't find the way to his friend's road, much less the flat where he stayed. 'Where am I?' he mumbled. 'And where am I going?' The town seemed flimsy and unfinished. Other people were abroad now, ordinary folk heading off to work, but Hans didn't dare approach them. He stared in the shops, wandered down by the station, and couldn't recognize a single thing. By ten o'clock it had started to rain, and Hans staggered back to his building-site. Blokes in hard-hats were milling around an enormous digger, and some kind of enormous pump was being delivered on the back of a lorry. Hans sauntered through the gates and casually wandered around, joining a gang of guys staring into a deep hole. Not knowing what else to do, he picked up a spare hat and stared in with them.

"What a dark and fearsome space, he thought. A space without any ending.

"But, he couldn't stay there forever though, no, not even on a building-site, not even in a dump like this. No, he had to hide behind the portaloos, shuffling this way and that, until finally it was clocking-off time and Hans could climb back inside his cabin, his feet aching and his trainers all a mess. How warm his portakabin seemed! His mug was there, and his peaked cap, and his bedding; but in the morning he would again be cast out, forced back into the mud and the rain, his feet sore and his hands freezing in his pockets. He tried not to think about it. The space outside his window seemed merely an extension of the huge hole the world was ceaselessly digging, a hole that would one day swallow him entirely. 'Why me?' he asked. Around midnight, his dog came back and looked at him, thoughtfully. 'Hello Big Dog,' said Hans, but the dog said nothing. Its eyes were as sad as the world.

"The second day seemed even longer. Every minute, every second, stuck like glue. After mooching around all day, the mannie was soaked to the skin and his trainers were two enormous clods of mud. On the third day, the rain turned to sleet. Hans didn't feel so good. Nothing on the building site seemed to be the right size and he had started to lose feeling in his hands and feet. On the fourth day, he tripped over a pile of piping and fell into a filthy trench; fortunately he ran away before anyone could grab him or ask what he was doing. However, when he went back to his cabin later, he couldn't find his key. A wave of icy panic suddenly swept over him. It was lost, lost! He scampered around the site but couldn't find it anywhere. It was dark now and dense black shadows filled up all the holes. He spluttered and coughed and pressed his face against the cabin window, a sense of utter desolation overwhelming him. Ah, that it should come to this! But, wait, what was that in his other pocket? The key! Not knowing what else to do, he immediately burst into tears. The wind was getting up again now and the rain came down in buckets.

"Well, that night, things came to some sort of an ending. The cabin rocked in the terrible gale and the fella felt hot and delirious. Crouched over his smelly fire, he turned to the animal at his feet and quietly related his woes.

"'Ah, doggy,' he said sorrowfully, 'things have come to a sorry state.'

"The dog rolled over to let him stroke his tum.

"'It's true! I've reached the end of something without finding my way through to anything else. Ah, old friend, I've nothing left, nothing to call my own. But listen, if we could somehow swap places, just for one night…'

"He furtively glanced toward the door, a strange expression on his face.

"'What do you say, doggy? One last chance to search for this missing thing, whatever it may be…'

"His eyes were large and glassy, his mug red and feverish.

"'Hey, boy, what do you say? The night is huge and empty, but I must leave this place, abandon these things…'

"He removed his jacket and cap and placed them on the hound. His teeth chattered and his body shook.

"'Cover for me, eh boy? Just for this one night?'

"He took off the rest of his clothes and patted his dog on the head. It looked at him suspiciously from underneath his cap.

"'I won't be long boy. Just one night, eh? Just one night.'

"And so saying he opened the door and ran out into the teeth of

46

the gale. The dog tried to stop him, but it was no use; the fella leapt through the air, let out a cry, and plunged into the full force of the storm.

"The cold, the cold! The wind immediately stung his eyes and the rain lashed his limbs, but at least it didn't reek of gas out there. No, the air was rich, wet, biting. He snuffled around for a time behind the bins, and then padded across to the main gate. There were new smells everywhere. He nuzzled open the latch, pushed his weight against the mesh and trotted outside. Now there was no need to stay by the roadside; the fields were boggy but smelt delicious. He stopped by a big old tree and had a wee. The sky above him was a big black hole but he was rooted in the mucky ground, his heart pounding and his lungs filling with air....

"And then he started to run, as fast as his legs would carry him. All around him, the elements raged and swore, great squally gusts pouring down from above, but the fella didn't care. The sky clattered and banged. The archaic machinery that drove the world seemed to scrape and to whirr, but the fella was running, his legs torn-up roots, his arms flailing branches. He bared his teeth and growled. All around him the nocturnal backdrop was tearing loose, the props starting to blow away...

"'Howl, howl!' Hans cried. He ran and he ran until the storm was left far behind, like a fever or a ferment or some such thing...

"Yes, ladies and gentlemen, that's exactly what happened! He ran and he ran until the storm was left far behind. After a while, the rain seemed to slacken and the gales to desist. All of a sudden, the whole world felt different. In an instance, the rain turned to drizzle, the wind to a dirty breeze, the night a different shade of black. Here and there one could even see tiny stars twinkling, like little nails holding up the sky.

"The fella slowed down and breathed in. Ahead of him lay the lumpen silhouette of a farm, the smells pungent and animally. Hans stopped and sniffed the air; it was heavy, mordant, flatulent. He could smell the beasts penned up by the fold-yard, the manure reeking in the midden-heap, the acrid whiff of the garage. Shaking himself, he walked closer. The cobblestones were slippy, filthy, covered in bits of straw and dung. He snuffled round the outhouse and trotted toward the yard. Was that a kennel? Yes, a kennel, long and black and smelling of meat. He padded across the cobblestones, his breath a pale misty balloon. All of a sudden his exertions seemed to catch up with him. His legs felt heavy, and his chest seemed to burn.

"Yes, all of a sudden the fella felt weary. His feet ached, his head bobbed, and he was cold. He ambled toward the kennel feeling utterly exhausted. The kennel was dark and smelly, like a black hole or a gaping, toothless mouth. Then the fella got down on his hands and knees and crawled inside. Somewhere inside him, a strange thought struggled to come to the surface: long ago hadn't he released some kind of hound from a place like this? When he was a little kid, no more than a speck — hadn't he messed up his chores, left everything undone, got into all sorts of trouble? Yes, and he'd been sent straight to bed with no tea and all sorts of crying and commotion… Ah, but that was in a different life, in a different place. Now he was tired and ill and everything he had seemed to shake. What a clod! The kennel was damp and dark, like a grave. Sniffing the air, the fella made his way in…

"What a dark and fearsome space! There was nothing to be seen, absolutely nothing. The interior was as black as the black sky above. Nothing seemed to penetrate the darksome spot and the fellow could see no limit.

"Aye, that was just how he climbed in: helplessly, idiotically, like a clot.

"You see, of course, none of this really happened. It was just that this guy's fire was on the blink and he'd gassed himself in his sleep, the gas filling the little portakabin, starting to suffocate all within. I mean, what can I say? He was the most useless dosser you could ever hope to meet! Oh my friends, oh ladies and gentlemen, if only he'd kept an eye on that fire; but he was never one for practical things, for the things which run our world…"

The guide rubbed the ends of his moustache absent-mindedly.

"What's that, Miss? The dog? Why, it slipped out of the door and stood guard outside the cabin all night, pawing at the cabin and whimpering through the night. But the wind blew the door tight shut and left the dog abandoned in the rain.

"In the morning the foreman arrived, looking furious. The gate had been left open and all the copper piping and coils of wire had been nicked during the night. Workmen ran this way and that through the mud, their faces angry, livid, red.

"Outside the cabin, the dog looked down at his pale-grey jacket and tried to shake the cap from his head. 'Uh oh,' his eyes seemed to say. 'How do I get out of this? But there was no escape! No my friends, there was no escape at all!"

And at this the guide slowly shook his head.

"No, the fella was carried out from the cabin still in his sleeping-bag, his skin all pasty and white. And as they carted him to the ambulance the laddie seemed to be sleeping like a baby, his eyes tight shut, still scanning the horizon for that one extraordinary thing, the one inexpressible sight that would change everything....

"Have you ever felt that, Miss? This feeling, this world? That one extraordinary thing? Ah, Miss! No there's nothing more to see here. Oh my friends, why are you looking at me like that? What's done is done. And now ladies and gentlemen, it's time to go..."

VI

Yes, it was finally time. The tour-guide dusted down his hat, checked that his moustache was still beneath his nose, and then picked up his brolly.

His face was flat, impassive. Outside the cabin, he looked both smaller and thinner, his voice no longer seeming to carry in the pale light of day.

"Ladies and gentlemen, the night is over and our tour is at a close. Look! The storm has worn itself out and a familiar greyness spills out from the east. Look how ordinary everything seems! How dull! The drab houses are still there, and have been all the time. Likewise, the ugly, congested ring road, the monotonous industrial estate... The sky is overcast, the distant hills dull and leaden.

"Back to the castle we go, for all tours must end at the same point they begin. What's that sir? Our theme? Why, the indolence of man, sir, lethargy, laziness and sloth. But maybe the fella wasn't so bad as all that; after all, he passed through this world like a little cloud of nothingness, causing no real harm, or pain or misfortune...

"Oh, stop your moaning, Miss; our bottle's empty and we can sup no more. We have awoken to a dreary dawn and our hearts are drawn and tired. On your right is an amusement arcade and chemist, to your left the most depressing shopping mall you could ever imagine. And next to the chemist is a travel-agent, card-shop, the local offy; and then there's a row of dark tenement buildings full of tiny little flats, and in the tiniest of all these flats, right at the very top, an old man sits waiting for his soup, a tiny little fella, half the size of nothing, neither whit nor scrap nor jot....

"And while the old fella waits for his soup to bubble and boil and watches the wee blue flames lick the bottom of the pot, what is it do you think it is he's thinking? Tell me, Miss: is it an old man dreaming of being young or a young man dreaming of being old? From here it's hard to tell – the fella's as thin as a crack, skinny as a hair, with a heavy fall of snow atop his nut. But his eyes, his eyes are cornflower blue, the only dab of colour in the whole dreary picture..."

At this our guide smiled and waved to the fella in the window, though the mannie didn't wave back.

"And there the old man stirs his soup, absent-mindedly waggling his little roundy spoon, shuffling about in his pyjamas and bare feet. There sir, can you see? The spoon trembles, his cloudless eyes sparkle, his whole body seems to vibrate like a tuning fork. But what is it that makes him tremble so, that makes his spoon dance like a pen, or a paintbrush, or a stick? Ah, that sir, is what we cannot know; all we can see are his cornflower eyes, his mop of white hair, a beard cascading from his chops like a waterfall…"

At this our guide rubbed his fake moustache and rolled back on the balls of his feet. He looked awful tired.

"Yes, our tour has taken in all the sights of life, sir, from the mewling wee bairn to the doddery old fool, from nappies to breeks, a span which passes as swift as the night, as fast as a black train under a black sky. But tell me, sir, is this all there is? A mere train-ride, a shunt along the tracks? Or is it that alongside this track runs other lines – repetitions, variations, contradictions — echoes of all those lives we failed to live and the things we failed to do? What do you think, Madam? Perhaps sometimes we can sense those other lives, second or dream-lives, make out some kind of secret door or an opening… And maybe these doors or windows look out on things left undone, journeys untaken, what we desired or feared but failed to realise… What say you, sir? Perhaps one should fix one's eyes not on what is seen but on what is unseen, for what is seen is temporary, but what is unseen is eternal…"

The guide paused and re-attached his moustache.

"Aye, we have followed the path of idleness, traced the path of a work-shy soul, a life made up of less what happened than what did not. It's true my friend: some things are doomed to repeat themselves again and again. Tch, can you smell that gas, Miss? The fella's stove is on the blink and the stench is everywhere — in his sheets, his pyjamas, the pot-bellied wardrobe in the corner. I mean, what's the old fool doing boiling soup in the middle of the night anyway? What a clot, a clown… Mm, what's that madam? The smell is making you sick? Well, there's no time to worry about that now: the new day is here and we all must get going. Yes, there are tasks to perform, jobs to be done, and let's not forget, tomorrow is another working day…"

We looked around, and slowly, reluctantly, rubbed our eyes. It really was starting to get light by now, a thin grey light creeping in from the east. The guide looked down on us, the brolly above his head an exclamation mark on the page.

"Tch, what's that, sir? How did the fella get from there to here? How did his back get so bent, his mane so long and hoary? Aye sir, isn't that the real question, the question we ask in the wee small hours of the night? How did the train go by so quickly? How did I get to be so old?"

Behind him the shape of the old man was already starting to flicker and to dim, and in the blink of an eye there was neither hide nor hair of him — not the top of his head nor the tip of his spoon, nor the bulge of his belly, no, not even the word 'nothing'. Rather, it was like a film that disappears when the lights come up, a silent movie drowned out by the clamour of the working week.

"Well, let us go," said our guide, taking another swig from whatever he carried in his bottle. "For now our tour is over and we have arrived at a point beyond which we cannot pass. What's that, Miss? The other shore? That mysterious country beyond? " Our guide smiled, and his smile seemed to contain all the sadness of the world. "Ah, Miss! No, take my hand, the way is steep and the steps are treacherous, 'specially in this half-light…"

Well, there was nothing to do but humph our way back up to the castle, the guide skinny as a scarecrow, his top hat lying low over his brow. Tired-looking commuters watched us with irritable eyes, somnambulists stumbling sleepily to work, their heads bowed and thin lips clamped tight shut. How pale they looked, like a legion of the dead… And what did they make of our wee group, cold, mud-spattered, soaked to the skin? To be honest, they were too knackered to care… Make way! Make way! We'd lost footwear, raincoats and most of our party. We limped, sniffed, staggered to and fro; our joints ached, knees stiffened, heads throbbed. And in this state we ascended Castle Hill.

Nestled up against the castle-wall was this little stone kirk, now a tourist centre and gift-shop, selling postcards, guidebooks, pencil-cases; alongside. that a little strip of green, a tumbledown graveyard, shadowed by the branches of a wizened elm.

Our guide sat down on a wee mound of grass whilst we perched atop the plinths and memorials, resting our tired feet and backbones. How quiet it was! A few snowdrops pushed their way through the wet earth and the ivy on the memorials was fresh and green.

Our guide stretched out, and turned over onto his back. For some reason the drone of traffic and purl of the town suddenly seemed very far away.

"My soul has been a lawn besprinkled o'er with flowers," he whispered, lying flat out on the grass. It had been a long night and the fellow looked exhausted. "And yet it seems to me that I never picked a single one. Ah, but it matters little now. I am tired, friends, very tired. Even the birds are sleeping, and the worms and the insects too…"

To be honest, we were all kinda sleepy. Somebody had brought sandwiches and we munched on them gratefully, glad of the rest. The sky was pale and delicate, the colour of mushrooms. We stretched and yawned. Was this the end of our tour? One by one, we all gave in to our weariness; all of us, man, woman, granny and child, closed our eyes and let the cool earth carry us.

"Yes, that fellow may have been a wee skiver, the worst kind of layabout and dreamer, but I don't know, sir, I don't know… maybe his work-shy life passed close by something else, another story, so to speak. And maybe from time to time voices drifted across from this other tale, as if through an open window, the crack of a door or a portal. What do you say, ladies and gentlemen? Perhaps if we close our eyes will we be able to trace its shape, make out the dim shadows of a second life, a girl with a suit case and the silhouette of the castle, a night as silent as a dream…"

And so saying, our tour began once more…

PART TWO

The Grey Circus

I

Is there anything more strange to us, ladies and gentlemen, than the mysterious world of the subjunctive, that country of endless possibilities, the shadowy world of *what if*? A realm where what we fear or imagine or dream holds as much sway as what truly takes place, a kingdom where that which might have been carries the same essential weight as the way things really are. What an idea, my friends, such an odd notion! And yet, that world is never far from us, its intangible border perhaps the finest line of all…

No, this other life exists, as it were, just across the water, its shoreline both a stone's throw away from our daily lives yet also a kind of smudge or blur on the horizon, a sort of shape half-glimpsed through the fog. And from time to time things are washed up from this other shore, the flotsam and jetsam of other lives — a suitcase, for example, or a pot bellied wardrobe, or a whole tangle of laundry — carried across the channel by sudden swells and high tides, the mysterious waves and echoes which lap across this world.

Ah sir, as we scan the vague, mist-covered horizon, its shadowy coastline seems somehow both familiar and strange to us, sometimes far away in the distance, sometimes so close that one can make out its landmarks and signs, hear the chatter of its inhabitants and the murmur of their dreams, aye feel as if one could somehow cross over, wade across that murky water, pass from one world to the next…

Do you feel that, Miss? This feeling, this world? Ah, Miss! Let's go, let's go…

II

You see, Miss, the yellow buds jumped down from the bus and paraded across the market-square, their figures blowing through the gloomy stalls like blossom. A few guys caught sight of them and started to call out, but the girls just waved back and pointed at one another merrily; they'd just arrived from the neighbouring paint factory, where work in the pigment department had dyed them the colour of sunflowers and caked their skin with powder and dust.

No sir, it's true — the girls were as yellow as canaries. Only the hairs on their heads, protected in the factory by cheap plastic hairnets, retained their original hue; everything else was painted the colour of the sun. Taking a swig from a bottle of cider they carried between them, the buds then marched unsteadily across the yard, stripping off their clothes to reveal patches of unvarnished skin. All the other folk out doing their shopping — old women with shopping-trolleys, wifeys in head-scarves, guys in donkey jackets, all of them dressed in greys and browns and blacks — got out the way pretty sharpish, parting before the girls like a dull-coloured sea. And who could blame them? Ah, the girls seemed luminous! They honked and squealed, swaying against one another and swearing loudly. Next to the blackened stalls they looked like flames licking the edge of long-dead coal.

But they weren't the only ones from the factory in the square. No, behind them, the evening shift was already queuing up alongside the factory minibus, an air of despondency hanging grimly above their heads. The line shuffled slowly along without speaking, their faces burnished deep hues from years spent working at the plant; these faces seemed less gaudy or florid, weathered and tinctured rather than freshly dipped. Once onboard, the factory workers stared blankly out at the square, their mugs as impassive as stained glass. One bloke flicked through a *Record* and another nibbled at a greasy pasty, the folds of his chops lined with ink. While all around seemed sketched from a muddy pallet of charcoal and ash, the men's moustaches were a blaze of tints and lacquers, the women daubed onto the bus with thick, heavy strokes. What a terrible shift! The workers stared out at the stallholders with blotchy eyes, their features smeared and smudged.

Eventually though the last of the last of the figures made their way to their seats and the doors wheezed shut. Tch, such a heap of junk, it was; like something out of the ark. The bus coughed, groaned and slowly pulled away from the square, taking its little painted cargo with it. In its wake the yard was dimly monochrome once more, the grey waters of the market rolling back in to cover up its dirty flagstones. Then the bus climbed the steep hill towards the plant and was gone.

In a café on the other side of the square, a sleepy young waiter — a waiter who looked kinda familiar to be honest, his drowsy features sort of recognisable — watched the bus disappear and sighed. The sulphurous factory girls had vanished into a titchy wee chemists round the corner and the young fellow felt sad and full of melancholy yearnings. Ah, why was beauty so elusive? Hans looked across at the clock above the menu-board but it refused to move. Outside in the market, nothing was happening. He ran a cloth across the counter and counted the change left for tips. Fifty-seven pence. A terrible emptiness seemed to fill his heart: there was nothing here, nothing! The guys on the market were packing up, the shops were switching their lights off, and inside the café there were still a few biddies drinking tea.

But when he looked over to the back of the room he suddenly saw a girl he'd not noticed before, puffing sullenly on a dangly cigarette in one of the place's gloomy corners. Where had she come from? He scratched the end of his nose and couldn't understand how he hadn't seen her come in. The girl seemed out of place among the other dumplings in the place, and he pegged her at seventeen, maybe eighteen, with pancake make-up, dark raisin eyes, and scrambled marmalade hair. He smoothed down his apron and went over. Once there, he noted down her big suitcase and sober, formal clothes as he took down her order ("Just a tea, thanks."), but she failed to look up even once and he went back to his counter again rather sulkily.

But who was she? From behind the counter he watched the girl glance round the place with a rather vinegary expression on her face, her skinny legs rubbing up against her case. Her pouty mug looked thoroughly miserable, but her knees seemed to have a life of their own, bobbing up and down as if on a seesaw. Hans rinsed out a cup, and regarded her thoughtfully. What was the gal doing here, looking so forlorn and so bereft? And why the big case? Tch, what would anyone be doing coming here? Taking refuge behind the girl's air of abstraction, he continued to stare across at her until some daft auld biddy leaned across to spoil his view, her hair-do completely blocking out the girlie and her case. Hans strained and stretched but it seemed that no matter which way he craned his neck, the drab wee wifey seemed always to be in his way. Cursing under his breath, he stared balefully at the old biddy's dull, graceless mug, her lip-sticked mouth and rouged, flabby cheeks; only the girl's lazy smoke could be seen behind her, curling upwards towards the stained yellow ceiling.

Ah, Hans thought to himself, well, let me think.

The girl's been sent to this little factory town by her mother, the two of 'em packed together in some little flat in a big city away to the south. There, the mother and daughter have been at each other's throats for years, both longing for some kind of respite from its four walls or each other or something. And then this letter arrives from the girl's uncle, hinting at a possible situation arising at a paint factory he's had some dealing with, a factory not too far way but quite far enough, if you catch my drift, in some grotbag little town the girl has never heard of. The plant, it seems, is recruiting at the moment and, accompanied by a suitable letter of introduction (the uncle works in the marketing department of one of the chemical firms supplying it) he sees no reason why his niece should find any difficulty in securing a suitable position should she present herself for interview on the 16th of the month.

Mm, thinks Hans, who can frame the strange patterns of fate? Straightaway her mother begins to make plans, and the girl, who'd been threatening to walk out of the gloomy flat for years, is completely taken aback by the speed with which her departure is arranged. Tickets are bought, her uncle's letter of recommendation arrives – and her mother seemed to draw breath only in order to pack her big, bulky case. But why does she need such a case? Ah, you see, the interview is on the 16th, and her uncle has arranged a tour round the site for the day before. But where's she going to stay? No worry, no worry, says her mum; there's this bloke at the plant, he'll put up. But why's her case so big if she was just staying the night? Because it's the only one we have. Yeah, well, why does she have to wear these clothes? And so on and so on.

III

Clara started to feel unwell as soon as she arrived at the station with her mother. Crossing the long tiled concourse her breath seemed to come in thin, ragged gasps, her case terribly heavy and cumbersome. Ho, what was in it? Her mum helped her to lug it past the shops and the ticket-office but their progress seemed terribly slow and faltering, and they seemed to be wandering further and further from the right platform. Where were they going? They staggered through a dimly-lit underpass and past some boarded-up kiosks, the platforms increasingly deserted, the signs getting harder and harder to read. The station was vast, loud, confusing. Eventually they left all the other commuters behind and found themselves in a neglected area far from the central plaza, the girl deathly pale and limp, her ma scowling furiously at her watch. The station-announcer's voice could still be heard now, but only very faintly, as if awfully far away. The whole station seemed to be buzzing.

Her mum told Clara to stay put whilst she went to look for a guard, and the skinny gal laid herself down on a discarded trolley, feeling desperately queasy and in need of the lav. She tried concentrating on the timetable opposite, but the print made her head dizzy and her stomach lurch, so instead she closed her eyes and waited for the nausea to pass.

With her eyes closed it felt like she was bobbing out to sea. How strong the tide is, she thought. When she opened them again, she was being carried along the deserted platform by two uniformed porters, a third following with her case a few paces behind, struggling slightly under the weight. Too weary to protest, the girl allowed herself to be picked up and carried toward a dimly lit train, the carriage full of tired and scowling passengers jamming their belongings into any nook or cranny they could find.

And Clara thought to herself, Mum, Mum, where are you?

She felt pretty anxious, to be honest, what with her poorly insides and all, but let herself be carried by the two uniformed bods, who took her to the very last carriage in the line and then loaded her onboard.

The train was awful busy. Hoards of weary commuters kept pushing up against her and the girl had to squeeze herself flat against the loo door, her chest sore and her breathing kinda strained. The coach didn't seem big enough to take another soul but the passengers kept on coming; heigh ho, thought the girl, where is everybody going? She looked out of the window, trying to catch sight of her mum or a vending machine or the platform number, all sorts of crazy thoughts going through her head. Strangers pressed themselves against her and stood on her feet and she didn't even know if this was the right train.

What is this thing and where is it taking me? she thought.

Outside of the carriage there seemed to be an endless crush of people but Clara couldn't recognise a single soul; the porters kept on pushing and the people kept on coming. So many people, she thought, but after just a few minutes the doors silently closed and the grey canopy of the station was slowly, soundlessly, rolled away. What a sight! It was like the sky was being opened rather than vice versa.

"Mum, Mum!" she cried, but it was already too late. There was the girl, squashed flat by the loo door, staring out of a train window at a dull, dishwater sky, and there was the station, swiftly disappearing someplace back along the line. Ah, mum! Clara felt giddy and sick, and her hands were kinda clammy where she'd been gripping the handle of her case.

All the seats were occupied so she struggled with her case along the narrow aisle, earning bitter glances from the other passengers as she did so. Most looked like packers bound for the nearby industrial park but they all seemed to be carrying piles of luggage and it took her ages to clamber over everything and find a seat. When she finally squashed herself into a tight little space near an abandoned drinks-trolley, she found that she couldn't get her case up onto the dark rack above it. Why me? she thought, hauling up the great weight. She struggled and strained, but couldn't even lift the great lump, which by now seemed to have expanded to jam up the entire aisle behind her. Ach, what to do? People were starting to stare and point, and the poor girlie felt embarrassed by her mum's dog-eared case, its bottom all swollen and scuffed. No, it just wouldn't fit; she huffed and she puffed but the big thing wasn't going anywhere. Why had she been given the case anyway? Passengers were whispering, laughing, gesturing, and the case kept on getting bigger and bigger. Ah me, she thought; either this thing is going to burst or I am.

Her arms were tired, her hands were sore, and the rack seemed to tower over her. How helpless she felt! She couldn't even do this one stupid thing. But then the fella sitting opposite leant forward, took hold of the case by its handles, and seemed to effortlessly swing it up into the hole above.

"Oh, thanks," she said, "thanks."

Too embarrassed to even look over, Clara lowered herself into her seat and glanced up at where her case had been swallowed whole by the darkness. How dark the void seemed! Like a hole in space itself. People were still staring at her, but instead she gazed pointedly out of the window, watching the countryside roll past her in a monotonous procession of brown-grey fields. Thankfully her heart was slowing down now. She settled back in her seat and started to breathe more easily, the air no longer quite so painful in her chest. Slowly, her hands relaxed on the armrests and her thoughts seemed to come less crazily. Every once in a while she stole a glance up at the luggage rack, but all the other passengers seemed to be gawping at the very same spot, so she sheepishly turned away. The case was nowhere to be seen.

After she'd been sitting there a little while, the guy sitting opposite tried to strike up a conversation, his hands drumming on the tabletop. He was some kind of quality control clerk at a nearby refinery, and he kept midering her about how light her case was, how easy it had been to pick up, how strong his arms were...

Clara wasn't listening though. She kept her eyes on the dull, flat landscape and refused to even look at him. Where am I going? she thought. It's like being swallowed by a big grey sack. In the distance the rough flattened fields give way to a crooked caravan of hills, pockmarked by industrial buildings whose purposes were impossible to guess. The guy's voice seemed equally flat and monotone, like he was reading from a series of flip charts. "Boy, my arms are strong!" he said. "When I lifted up that case I couldn't feel a thing..." But by now a loud blether had started up a few rows down the way, and Clara's little pink ears immediately started flapping.

Down the way, a gaggle of wifeys, all dressed in brown tabards, were squeezed round a single table, guzzling tea. They were gassing about some new girl that had been moved to the produce department of the plant where they worked. The gal was tiny and round and forever disappearing to the lav (so they said), because the smell in the place made her sick and gave her the skitters something rotten.

Such a round little tub! As soon as she clocked on, her skin went all blotchy and her belly started up. Can you imagine? With every day that passed, the girl seemed redder and redder and her roundy wee tum sounded louder and louder, like she was turning into some kind of drum. The poor lassie! Rumours began to fly in the canteen and meaningful glances were exchanged by the cutting table. Then one day the girlie ran off to the ladies just before the mid-morning break and nobody saw her for ages; she'd just downed tools and taken to her heels, dashing for the loo as if her life depended on it.

The word went round quickly and after a while a small crowd gathered outside the lavvy. What was happening in there? Five, ten, fifteen minutes went by, but there was still no sign of the girlie. The crowd were restless but nobody wanted to go in: after all, who knew what was going on? "Shhh," somebody called out, "was that a flush?" By now, everyone was staring at the lavvy door. The supervisor held her breath. But still the girlie didn't surface! No, it was as if she'd made a run for it or burst. Time went on and eventually the old guy from security had to be called, you know, that codger in the cap. Kinda reluctantly, the old fella breathed in, kicked open the cubicle's manky door — and the girl, well, the girl was nowhere to be seen! It's true — it was as if she'd disappeared without a trace! The only clue was this long line of toilet paper strung out from the dispenser and disappearing down the pan; the girl had written on it using some kind of eyebrow pencil, but just as the words had vanished from the paper, the girlie had melted into thin air.

"What's that?" snapped one of the wifeys. "What rubbish! The gal was simply sent home."

But not all the women were quite so sure.

"Tch! Imagine that…"

"Such a thing…"

And all the time the fishwives were chattering, the girlie – our girlie that is, the one with the long pale face and the marmalade-orange hair — wriggled awkwardly in her seat. What a stupid story, she told herself. *As soon as I get to this dump I'll jump straight back on a train and come on home....*

How poorly she felt! Her own belly was bubbling away like a cauldron and her ankles felt tired and sore. But what could she do? The train juddered across the sketchy landscape, its passage unmarked like white ink on white paper.

Yes, the grey fields stretched out like glue, the sky above somehow faint and rubbed out, like somebody had changed their mind. Everything was terribly drab. Clara tried shutting her eyes but couldn't sleep; when she opened them again, the scenery looked just the same. There was a lot of flat land and then some more of it. But the view wasn't quite as empty as she first believed....

No, on the horizon, long black chimneys pumped variegated fumes up into a pale, watery sky, a vague blush forming over some nondescript little town. Pylon wires and rusted walkways stretched over the tracks as the train approached, the town's outskirts an unappealing sprawl of rubbish tips and goods yards. Tch, was this it? The cloud of a black, dour-looking castle floated uncertainly over the little grey town like a bad dream or cartoon cloud. Clara shook her head. What a dump!

With this the girl looked up at the luggage rack and felt a sudden twinge in her belly. Her case seemed awful far away; and anyway the guy sitting opposite was looking at her strangely, his eyes sliding up and down her chest. What a creep! Clara couldn't reach her case and the fella didn't want to budge. She tried jumping up and lunging for the handles but it was no use; the station was already taking on shape and substance all around her, forming itself out of the gloom, while her suit-case was stuck up there on the rack, hidden away in the darkness. The train slowed down and there were billboards, posters, a waiting room, yet no one would lift a finger to help....

"Ah, do you think you could..." she murmured, gesturing at the black space above their heads, but the guy kept on looking at her top.

"Um, my case, I can't reach..."

Oh, why wouldn't the guy pull it out? The train was coming into the station now.

"Ah, sir?"

What was he doing? Somewhere, somebody was blowing a whistle.

"Please…"

For a second she was dazzled by a blinding white light, but then the case abruptly plopped down onto her head, Clara staggered backwards, and somehow she managed to fall painfully from the train.

She was on the platform before she could work out how she'd got there. For a moment she thought she was going to cry. Was this even the right place? The station was scabby and discoloured, all bleached-out posters and broken cigarette machines. What a hole! Wobbling from side to side, Clara approached the ticket barrier with a surly pout on her lips, looking for all the world like some sulky little kid about to get told off. What is this place? she thought. It looked almost derelict, with no other passengers around at all. The old goat on the gate checked her ticket and then let her through, and there was a ticket-office and a newsagent and a foul-looking waiting room and that was about it. Behind her she could hear the train pulling away and could sense all the faces pressed up against the carriage-window, their mugs all red and sweaty: she refused to turn round though. Let them stare, she thought, what did it matter? Her arms ached from hauling her awkward luggage and her hands were clammy and sore. Where was she anyway? "They can all go to hell," she whispered, dragging her case along the ground…

IV

The area close to the station was an ugly mess of car parks and warehouses, but once across the main road, the town grew older and more distinct. Steep, narrow streets picked their way amongst the tall gloomy buildings, many of them shabby tenements squatting above dismal little shops, their windows covered by a thick metal mesh. Apart from the pretty hills spread out across the horizon, everything felt weathered and discoloured. On some streets the paint had cracked and blistered to leave whole rows of buildings pallid and faint, whilst elsewhere pigmented clouds from the nearby factory had dyed the brickwork lurid shades, a garish bus-stop outside an emblazoned bookies, multi-coloured lamp-posts spread out like lolly pops along the street. Only the castle, more of a shadow than a thing, seemed wholly black, stamped at the top of the picture like a shape cut out from the sky.

And there was the girl — she was lugging her suit-case across a dirty market-square but looked kinda poorly and out of breath and had to stop in a shop door-way to rest. Nobody else paid much attention. Women were loading up shopping baskets with pale fruit and vegetables, their plastic carriers bulging. Everyone seemed weighed down, heavy, lumbersome....

Next to the shoe-shop was a little alleyway; and at the end of that, a mucky yard where a delivery-van was parked outside a rusting lock-up. Clara tottered unsteadily down the way and swayed from side to side. Her feet felt swollen and sore and she sat herself down on her case and sullenly examined the sole of her shoe. How forlorn she looked! A pale figure under a white sky. She looked around the yard and glowered.

What was she doing here? She imagined her mum coming home from a long shift at the bakery, her face dusted in flour, her skin tanned red from the oven. Were those white strands in her hair maize-dust or old age? Oh, but she was young, young! She only looked old 'cause she was stooped from lugging the hods from oven to oven. Her hands looked burnt and sore, but her fingers smelt like warm rolls.

Mum, Mum, what's happened to you? she thought. You should be young!

Even though Clara's eyes were closed she felt another burst of white light spilling out over her, and when she opened them again two huffing figures were slowly emerging from the yard at the rear, a kind of four-legged animal humphing a crate of empties between them. One was a man and the other a woman but you could have moved a moustache from one to the other without anyone noticing.

It's true! In close-up, they looked like one person carrying a mirror. Red in the face and overweight, they staggered to and fro as if they'd drunk the contents of the crate themselves.

"Ahhh," said the fella.

Together they hauled the load into the back of the van and strapped it into place. "O-o-o," said the man, rubbing his back and trying to straighten up. The woman watched him indulgently, minding his fingers on the hinge of the van door.

"Ahhhh," said the bloke again, rubbing every inch of his spine.

Blimey, the mannie was bent over! If the road was downhill, you could've rolled him like a tyre.

"Ah, dear," said the mannie, "my back, my back."

The woman sighed and helped to rub his hump. The fella really was stooped, his spine bent over like an old bent branch.

"This job is killing me," he grumbled. "These bottles, these crates — my back can't take it anymore. Oh, my dear, what's to become of us? Just look at me: my shoulders are coming together to form one roundy hill."

The woman nodded and patted his bandy back. What a pair, they made; like the sign for a hump-backed bridge.

"Tch, this job, these loads. And heavier, heavier everyday..."

Needless to say, whilst the fella moaned, his wife got on with the job, straightening the load and checking the straps on the crates.

"Are you done?" she asked. She finished counting up the empties and filled in the sheet.

The guy nodded, sadly.

"Tch, my dear! The eye never has enough of seeing nor the ear its fill of hearing. But for what, for what?"

The woman started to reply but then both of them caught sight of a figure sitting crouched in the courtyard, a skinny young girl perched on her suitcase, her hair the colour of egg-yolk, but her face awful pale.

"Who's that?" asked the wifey and elbowed the fella in his side.

The guy blinked and scratched his head. "Ah…"

"You wait here."

"Mm."

The wifey went over and offered the girl a can of Coke whilst the fella shook his head.

"Only a fool's work wearies him," he said softly to himself. "The fool does not know the way to town…"

He couldn't hear what the two women were saying so instead he turned and scraped the thick layer of crap that had collected on the windscreen. Breathing the air here is like chewing cardboard, he reflected mournfully; even the rain smells of petrol. By the time he'd got both wipers to work, his wife had lugged the girl's suitcase into the back and helped her up into the cab.

"We're giving her a lift," said the wifey.

"Oh, right."

He smiled at the girlie. "All right there?"

"Mm, thanks," she mumbled.

Unfortunately there wasn't much room in the cab, and when the wifey got in, the girl practically had to sit on their knees.

She didn't look at all well. Where was she going? The nearby plant. Was she meeting someone there? Aye. Was she going to work there? She shrugged. What time did she have to be there? She shook her head and pursed her pouty little lips. The fella started the engine and backed out. The little old town was just as dull as before. Would she like some fruit? No, no. The old pair made a fuss. The girl shook her head. No, no, she said. In truth, Clara felt strangely disconnected from what was going on. The air in the cab was very close and the plastic seating seemed to stick to her bum.

"Can we open a window?" she asked but the two old crusties didn't seem to hear her and nattered away about the town, their van, who knows what.

"Sure you wouldn't like some fruit?"

"No, no, thanks."

"An apple?"

"No."

"Banana?"

Clara's complexion was the colour of sour milk.

"No, thank you."

What was she doing here? What she really ought to do was get back on a train and go home. But now the van was leaving the lacquered old town behind.

Ah, well, she thought, too late, too late.

V

They passed an unkept playing field, a line of depressing, run-down discount centres, a row of orange gas-towers. After a while only a few grim-looking buildings remained, surrounded by high-fences and barbed wire. Beyond these lay the low foothills, the pale, white sky. How hazy it all seemed! Like a picture left outside in the rain. The girl thought of the drab silhouette of the castle and shivered.

A few minutes later they were all the way out of town. The ground was brown and grey, the land fenced off into patches of stony soil. In the distance darkish birds swooped amongst the bow-legged pylons and splashes of yellow gorse scumbled the dark scree.

Mm, what was it the two old duffers were talking about? Deliveries, wholesalers, service charges. The girl didn't pay much attention. There wasn't much room in the cab and she felt like a cork in a bottle, liable to be shot out at any moment. Why had she got in in the first place? When the fella leant over to scratch his pits she was nearly squashed flat in her seat.

"Can we stop for a sec?" she asked.

The pair of 'em kept on nattering.

"Um, can we stop?"

"Oh, right, right."

The fella nodded and pulled over, stopping the van in a tight passing-point about three-quarters of the way up a hill. It looked kinda exposed, with just bare earth and a slight ditch, but the woman was already getting out of the van, saying that she needed to pass a little water too. Clara peeled herself from her seat and followed the wifey to the jaggy, purplish weeds at the bottom of the furrow, squatting as far away from her as possible. Trying to avoid sprinkling on her tights, she kept her eyes lowered.

"You all right, hen?" yelled the woman but the girlie didn't answer.

After a while they made their way back up the rise and the fella picked her up and placed her back in the van. None of this is good, thought the mannie; the girl's as white as a sheet.

But they kept on nattering about the fells, the plant, the weather, whatever was passing by out the window. Then they talked about the nearby village, their farm, their dogs.

Eventually the wifey started talking about how she'd first met her wee man, and here her voice turned soft and her expression became wistful; aye, everything about her seemed suddenly soft, her mug like a big round cushion.

Mm, it was easy to imagine what the wifey must have been like when she was the girlie's age, a big gal with beautiful black eyes, two deep wells shining in that big round face of hers. Was the young girl still there, buried under that flab, but the same essential shape? Well, who knows? When you're young, the life to come is but a shape half-glimpsed in the clouds, the pleasantest kind of daydream. Then the day comes when this shape is set in stone and it's all too heavy to lift. But no, let's not think of that now....

No, when the wifey was the same age as the pale-faced girlie, she was a red and healthy gal, a big-boned lassie, happy to help out, to fetch and dig and clean....

And she lived on a farm with her mum and dad and little sister, and liked her food and didn't mind getting her hands mucky or helping out in the fold-yard or doing bits and bobs about the place. Yes, she joked with the farmhands and flirted with the farm-boys, and her soul was as content as the cows in the cowshed, as solid and round as the potatoes in the field. After all, what did she lack? No, it was as if the worries of school had never happened. It was as if they had lingered as long as last year's snow....

And each night when she climbed into bed, her body was tired and her mind fully rested, her full tum planted in the bedclothes like a bulb in the soil.

"But one night, just after my seventeenth birthday," said the wifey, "a mysterious feeling came over me, right in the middle of the night, some kind of feeling I'd never felt before — something which woke me up, carried me out of bed and carted me off down the stairs."

Her face was round as an apple, and just about as red too.

"Oh, Missie," she told the girl in the cab, "When I got up, everything was dark. I tiptoed down the stairs and stood there in the kitchen, staring out of the window, though there was absolutely nothing there to see. To the right there was nothing, and to the left also. But somewhere I could hear a gate banging and one of the dogs was growling in the yard and I felt strange, so strange!"

In the cab, her mouth opened and closed unconsciously.

"I mean, what was I doing? Upstairs my mum and dad were asleep, and in the little bedroom my wee sister was snoring too, and there I was, standing alone in the kitchen, all sorts of odd things going round inside my head."

The wifey smiled in a distracted sort of way. Her head looked like a balloon with a face scribbled on.

"Well, this feeling, it just grew stronger," she said. "Not knowing what to do, I walked over and unbolted the back door and made my way down to the gate by the silage tanks, swatting at the midges and trying not to step in the mud and the manure. Ah, my dear – the night was as thick as oil, with blurry smudges smeared about the out-house and dribbled across the yard. The dog was still yapping but I couldn't hear the gate. And this feeling, it just grew and grew, as big as the world, as big as the night sky...."

What black eyes she had! Like two great oil wells in a desert. No, thought Clara, not oil, ink.

"Well, pretty soon I was wishing I was wearing something more than a nightie, 'cause it was cold and damp and my slip was looking all mucky and torn, but I kept on blundering on, till eventually I reached the barbed wire at the bottom of the plot. How cold I was! And how dark the night! Out there amongst the trees, the blackness seemed to drip and congeal."

Clara nodded.

"Then I heard a sound. I tried saying something, but my lips felt strangely numb. Something was out there though; I could hear it being dragged through the bushes. It sounded like a big heavy daub was being hauled through the undergrowth, a boulder or some such thing. For the first time that night I felt a bitty frightened. Oh Miss, the shape seemed huge! But when I tried to back up, my nightie was all snagged up on the wire and I couldn't get free. I mean, I pulled and pulled, but it wasn't going anywhere. And the thing was still coming toward me, a big black mark getting bigger, or a door maybe, or some kind of hole... I tugged violently but my nightie wouldn't even rip and when I tried to unhook it, my fingers felt clumsy and frozen, and all the time the door seemed to be opening and inside the door it was even darker... Oh, Missy! Tell me, ink, paint, night, what do they all mean?"

Clara shook her head and sucked on a stray strand of hair. It was orange.

"Well in desperation I yanked away and finally something gave. My nightie tore, my feet slipped and I was off! Aye, I tore myself free and fell head first into the muck. But what could I do? I scrambled on my hands and knees over to the compost-heap and somehow scraped my knee on a fence-post. Honestly, you wouldn't believe how dark it was − like every light in the world had gone out. When I tried to get up I cracked my head on something wooden and fell back down 'cause I was feeling kind of woozy and couldn't see my hands before my face. Well, not knowing what else to do, I got up and climbed inside this big wooden thing, figuring that had to be my dad's garden shed, you know, where he kept his tools and things, his pots. Tch, it was far too small though; there wasn't a thing in there and I thought to myself, this isn't any shed or hut. Still, I didn't know what else to do, so I stayed where I was — but pretty soon I really needed to go! It's true — my bladder felt just about ready to burst; but then it went quiet and the gloom seemed to settle a little and after a while I started slowly to come back to myself, my head not so sore and my knee not too bloody. Whatever was out there, it seemed to go off again and straight away the feeling inside my chest started to fade. Oh, Missy! I felt a little bit better curled up at the back of the wooden thing and slowly closed my eyes, my bladder not so bad and my breathing not so crazy. The box was no bigger than a man, and smelt awful strange, but for some reason, I felt kinda safe, and after a few minutes I closed my eyes and contentedly went to sleep."

In the cab, the wifey's eyes were shining and a smile played across her lips. Once again you could see the apple-faced gal of her youth, her eyes two beautiful black wells.

Clara glanced out of the window: washed-out fields, pale stone, bare black trees. But now the mannie sitting next to her was taking up the story and she had to drag herself back to the cab, her knees crushed up against the two stuffed crusties.

"You see, at the time," the fella said, his belly squashed tight against the steering wheel, "I worked for this removals firm over at the other side of town, and there I humphed stuff up and down the steep hills, 'cause, ah, I was young then and not quite so beefy."

It was hard to believe though; the fella was as fat as bacon. Just look at him, thought the girlie, wriggling in her seat. Like his airbag's gone off already.

"Anyhow," the fella went on, "one evening, when I was just locking up the depot, I spotted this pot-bellied wardrobe that'd somehow been left behind from another job. Full of clothes it was, but there was no kind of receipt or docket or record of it anywhere and straightaway I knew it was going to be trouble. Well, I rummaged through all the jackets and trousers in the thing and eventually found this scrap of paper with what looked like an address on it, a scribble really, or some kind of blot. Oh, well, I thought to myself, it's the end of the day and I don't want any trouble from my boss, so with great effort I loaded the big heavy thing into the back of my van, all the time thinking, Mm, well, at least it won't take long…"

The mannie smiled ruefully, his face expressing the eternal wisdom of sadness. His cheeks, though, were red as beetroot, and he looked as sturdy as a carthorse.

"Well, three hours later and there I was, still driving around these pitch-black lanes, tired and lost, and starting to doubt that the scribble was a place-name anyway. As you might imagine, I wasn't in the best of humours by then, so I thought to myself, Ah, stuff it, I'm off, and turned round to go home. But just then I heard this odd banging start up at the back of his van, a sort of steady drumming; thump, thump, thump it went. Well, by the time I'd pulled off the road, something was beating away in there to wake the dead, but when I opened the doors — nothing! I jumped in the back, checked the wardrobe, made sure it was still tied down, and then went on my way. How queer, I thought. But five minutes later — thump, thump, thump. Well, I stopped again, had another look, and, I don't know, it was the same all over again. Mm, well, on I went, still in the back of beyond, and … aye, thump, thump, thump, like the beating of a big bass drum. Ho, I ask, what is that? I stopped, shone my torch in the back, checked the fastenings on the straps — and when I got back into the cab my van was totally conked out, as dead as a door-nail."

The fella smacked his lips and blew out his cheeks to express his feelings. Clara half-heartedly shrugged. 'Where are we?' she thought.

"So there I was," he went on, "stuck out there in the middle of nowhere, just by the side of this dark, louring wood, not knowing what to do. But no, that wasn't exactly true: through the trees I could just about make out the lights of what I thought to be a farm-house, and since I didn't want anyone to nick the box, I chucked out some of the heaviest stuff, humphed the great lug up on my back, and headed off toward civilisation. Ah, Miss, what else could I do? Unfortunately, the wardrobe was so heavy and I was so stooped, all I could see were my own two feet and pretty soon it was so dark I couldn't see them either."

The wifey next to her was breathing heavily and Clara could feel her warm breath on her face. Like a cow, she thought maliciously.

"Anyway, after a while I thought, this'll never do, and so I put the wardrobe down, climbed on top of it and tried to get my bearings. Unfortunately, all was dark, with not a single star in the sky. And then, when I clambered back down, I must've somehow caught my foot in the wardrobe doors 'cause suddenly a great shower of shirts and undies went falling out into the mud and though I tried to stop them, tch, t'was to no avail. Well, I grabbed what I could and went on, but — O Miss! — I didn't get very far. I fumed and cursed and trampled on the stuff, but then I had to go on."

"The thing was," said the mannie, his bulk seeming to fill up the cab, "the lump was awful heavy and after a few more minutes of lugging the box up on my back I felt just about ready to scream."

"Not knowing what else to do I laid the great load on the mossy ground, sleepily knocked on the door, and climbed in for a quick nap, first chucking out all the jumpers and trousers and scarves to make a bit more room. Ah, but it was awful cramped; I'd only had my head down for a couple of minutes when I felt sore and stiff and so I got out and plodded on, the wardrobe back atop my hump and me none the merrier."

Had the fella been born sad? Clara tried to imagine him younger but kept coming up with smaller versions of how he was today. What a bloater, she thought. More of a sack than a man.

"Anyhow, I'd only gone a few more steps when all of a sudden I lost my footing and almost stumbled head-first into the brackish water of a trickling burn, nearly losing the wardrobe in the process. Picking myself back up, and trying not to dump the contents of the box straight into the murk, I balanced the great object atop a pile of flat stones and gingerly crawled across it, but as soon as I put my full weight upon the thing, the doors swung open again and most of the rest of the clobber — the hats and pyjamas and ties — were swept away into the slimy beyond. Ah, Miss, what could I do? I hauled the thing back up, set it squarely on my shoulders once more, and soldiered on."

He smiled his doleful smile, and rummaged about on his seat.

"By now I was in a right old roose and no mistake. When I came to a wooden fence, I just used the wardrobe as a battering ram and went on. And when I came to a stone wall I used the thing as a ladder and climbed on over. But I was awful tired; on I shuffled, over the smudgy greenery, over bits of spiky wire, on toward the blinking light. Of course, I couldn't really see properly; my eyes were bowed down to the murky ground and I couldn't see any further. And yet, and yet… I knew that something was out there. Thump, thump, thump, went the box, and I felt my own heart beating away at the same time. The night was dark, smeary, full of blobs and daubs and funny black streaks, and the shapes seemed to spill and seep, like thick patches of oil. What is this place? I thought. Whence does it lead? The darkness deepened, the night congealed … and then I saw them, right before me: toes, toes, little white toes, toes as white as teeth, like little white roots in the ground! Well, I dumped the wardrobe and made off as fast as my legs could carry me, over a line of tall, spiky things, and off to the tarry darkness. Ah, Miss, I wasn't going back for anybody! I ran and ran until I could go no further, my heart racing and my breath burning up inside my body.

"But as soon as I stopped I began to feel kinda foolish. I mean, what had I seen, really? Now everything was quiet. The darkness felt perfectly still. And slowly the thick black daubs all started to rearrange themselves into recognisable objects: bushes, tools, a fence. There was a farmhouse and there were some cowsheds and there I was, standing on my own in a neat-looking garden. Ah, what was I thinking? Cursing my own stupidity I went to look for my wardrobe amongst all the blots and marks stippled around the place, keeping one eye on the yard and the farm-house and another on this guard-dog barking just behind a wee wooden gate. And all the time I was thinking, Ah, you fool, what's got into you anyhow...

"Well, above me the clouds were just starting to part a little, and in the half-light I could just about see my tall wooden cabinet standing alone in a gooseberry patch. Well, at last, I said to myself, picking my way through the bushes. But all of a sudden I stopped; inside the wardrobe, I could hear breathing, snuffling, the unmistakable sound of a heartbeat. Missy, my cabinet was snoring! As if in a dream, I tottered toward it, my limbs trembling and thoughts all askew. And yet I reached out my hand, yanked open the door, and forced myself to look. And inside? A bonny bare girl, fast asleep, all huddled up in the box.

"Oh, Miss, such beauty! To think that my eyes should be hallowed by such a sight! And at that very moment, the cabinet fell to pieces like a magic trick and the girlie sleepily opened her eyes, her big, black, beautiful eyes, and it was like drowning in two deep black pools, drowning in two black pools at the same time. Oh, Missy, I was transfixed! 'My love,' says she, 'My love,' says I, and a year later we were married."

The fella beamed.

"And that's how we met."

Clara pursed her lips and eyed up the pair suspiciously. Tch, such a fairy-tale! But what were these things and what did they mean? The girlie pouted and picked at her skirt, feeling more miserable than ever. Just look at them, she thought, like two peas from the same pod. The wifey mumbled something affectionate and the fella took her hand, tenderly rubbing each of her fingers. In repose, her face looked like a jelly that had failed to set.

Watch the road, gramps, thought the girl, moodily staring out at the horizon. It was grey.

VI

After a while the fell-road stopped climbing and skivverd its way between the bumps and marshes that dotted the tobacco-coloured moor, roundy wee islands squatting amongst the bogs and bushes. The land was humped and spongy, with brackish water trickling between the tufts of heather like little brown streams of tea.

Through the window Clara watched unknown grey birds rise up from vicious-looking thorn-bushes, disappearing like wee puffs of dust into the air. The sky above them was incredibly pale and toneless and the wispy birds vanished as soundlessly as smoke.

"Don't worry, nearly there," said the wifey, and Clara felt her stomach tighten and twist.

But where were they? There were no trees or buildings. The crooked hills seemed to get no closer nor move any further away and the sky was whitewashed and blank. The van was making heavy weather, though; you could hear its blowers whirr and its engine strain.

"Are you nervous, hen?"

"Me? No, no," said the girl.

"Oh, right-o, just with the interview and all…"

Truth to tell, Clara didn't know whether she wanted to get to the plant or not. Flanked by the two bloaters, the cab seemed increasingly cramped and close, as if the last breath of air was being slowly squeezed out.

Still, the road was definitely descending; she felt the van change gear and the fat-bloke lean forward in his seat. Yes, the road dipped alongside a low stonewall, past some kind of tumble-down barn and a burnt-out car.

"Here we go," said the fella, his red-face bobbing.

Before Clara could reply the van pulled off next to a worn sign bearing a company logo, and then followed a badly tarmacked drive toward a cluster of dreary buildings. The land was artificially flattened, stony, strewn with bits of rubble. Many of the units looked abandoned or boarded up, and weeds poked up through the concrete and the blackened piles of scrap.

Was this it?

"Ah, Missie!" said the man.

A rusted metal fence seemed to surround most of the enclosure but its gates lay wide open, and the van followed the road to a broad, grassy meadow containing both the plant and its ancillary units, mostly grim, prefabricated offices. Four huge chemical tanks overshadowed these quarters, connected by enormous metal pipes to rows of plastic cylinders, lined up in neat little stacks in the yards outside. Alongside these, strange, contorted chimneys extended over a series of sealed vats, an unpleasant petrol smell pervading the entire area. Despite the chief product of the place itself, everything seemed bleached and colourless, the paint stripped away to reveal a leaden brownish-grey.

But rather than the buildings, the gal's eyes were drawn to the badly-kept grass which ringed the plant, an ill-tended meadow of weeds and rubbish; there, girls from the factory lay amongst the lustreless grass like pockets of wild flowers, some as red as poppies, others yellow like dandelions, their golden bodies scattered lazily on the pale ground. Most were idly smoking or drinking in little groups, but once in a while somebody would stand up to hoy a bit of sandwich at someone or toss a bottle in the air. Clara stared and stared. The buds seemed part of the landscape, brightly painted blooms growing wild in the bleached-grass. Reclining in the weeds they looked gorgeous, aflame; one of them stretched out luxuriantly in the long grass whilst another stared idly up at the sky, her hair unkempt and hairnet discarded carelessly on the ground.

Ah me, thought the girl: rest, rest!

As the van drove closer to the plant, Clara could see that far from being abandoned, the factory was in fact buzzing with life. The factory forecourt was awash with people — employees of the company by the look of their clothes — clustered around a line of tables and stalls set up on one side of the car-park. Refreshments were laid out on low benches, and there were games and races, and a sort-of mini-fair, with some guy on a makeshift stage selling raffle tickets. Clara's wee pouty mouth fell open. It looked like some kind of open-day or fête: sack-races, prize-giving, lines of hoops and bean-bags. There were hotdog stands, pitchers of lemonade, some kind of darts game. Guys in ties and women in tabards nattered happily, though Clara couldn't help noticing that everyone seemed to be standing rather awkwardly, knees bent and legs open, as if waiting to catch a ball. What kind of place is this? she thought. There were banners, streamers and lights, but also hump-backed old wifeys and bent-over duffers in coveralls. One guy over by the tombola was so bow-legged, you could have snapped 'em off to make a wish. No, I'm in the wrong place, thought the girlie. This isn't me! Everyone looked tanned, shaded, coloured-in. Their faces bobbed above their shirts and overalls like little gay balloons.

Meanwhile the van pulled in and came to a stop.

"Well, there you go," said the fella in the cab, looking over at Clara quite kindly.

He parked the van on the outskirts of the throng, near to an ice-cream stand, and picked the girl up out of her seat. Gingerly, the pale-looking thing climbed down from the cab, the roundy old couple helping her with her case.

"You see that building over there . . ." said the bloke.

"Mm, yeah, thanks." Clara made a face.

"Over by those drums."

"Mm."

"You know where you're going?"

"Yeah."

Embarrassed, Clara kept glancing in the direction of the flowers in the meadow.

"You see where I'm pointing?"

"Yeah, thanks, yeah."

"Oh, well, right enough then."

There was an awkward pause.

"Sure you don't want any fruit?" asked the wifey.

"No, no, really."

Clara looked at her watch. Half-past twelve.

"We'll be going then."

"Aye, thanks."

"Don't look like that, hen — you'll be fine."

"Mm."

The couple climbed back in the van and Clara could see them waving back from the cab. What a sight, she thought.

Load up the cattle-truck!

It's a hole, she said to herself and leant down to pick up her case, which seemed bigger and heavier than ever.

I'm not here, she thought. This isn't me!

But despite this she lugged her load through the noisy and boisterous crowd, bumping into folk and generally getting in the way. Strangely though, no one paid any attention to her at all. Nobody asked for her name, demanded to see a pass, or made any kind of move at all — no, it was as if she wasn't there. After a while she came to a pile of rough wooden pallets and hauled herself, case and all, to the very top. Once there, she lay down on the highest crate and had a good look around. From atop her case, she had a good view of the adjoining office blocks — which, if anything, looked even more washed out and dismal from this angle — as well as the rusted chemical tanks and piles of waste-barrels out back. Why had she been sent to this dump anyway? There was nothing here, nothing!

But at that very moment a gaudy line of pipers, bright and shiny as if they've stepped off a shortbread tin, appeared from nowhere and marched out onto the stage. What a sight! Clapping broke out in the audience and some older folk pushed forward to form uneven lines, little clusters of four or five. The pipers stood there in full tartan regalia – furry hat, sporran, the works. Then the one at the end gave a signal and they all started to blow, fast and loud, like a granny's record collection but played at double-speed. Hm, what a racket! And right away a big circle of folk joined hands and started to dance around the car-park, a long line of tabards, overalls and short-sleeved shirts, capering up and down the tarmac. Just look at those grannies, thought the girl, if that doesn't finish them off, nothing will!

Yes, off they went, biddies, wifeys, round little men, skipping gaily up and down the line, no matter how hunched or bent-over they seemed. Of course, most of the pipers were old codgers too, except for one young fella at the very end, who was fair, blue-eyed and kinda good-looking. What great knees, thought Clara: like a pair of hairy coconuts! Yes, she could imagine them hanging from a tree, little birdies pecking away at them. And meanwhile the dancers whirled and the pipers blew.

There they went, stripping the willow or some such thing, little toy figures, badly painted, like something pulled along on a string. From her vantage point, Clara looked down on them suspiciously.

How did I get up here? she thought.

Below, employees gambolled along past the tents and tables, never once looking up. Tch, why should they? The pipers played as loud and fast as they could and the oldies did their best to keep time, their little legs jerking up and down erratically. To the girl, they seemed as light as thistledown, and amazingly quick on their feet. Round and round they went, fast enough to make you dizzy — wifeys, old fellas, squat little blokes in overalls. And chasing them, a line of boiler-suits, garish ties and cheap slacks. But then the music abruptly ended and everyone was left panting and laughing, a pile of work-clothes heaped up by the stage. The reel was over and the folk stopped to catch their breath. Then there were cheers and whistles and the band took a bow and went off to get a drink. What now? Clara felt dizzy but still somehow managed to clamber down from her odd-little vantage point and wander over. She looked awfully wobbly though.

When she got there the pipers were all standing around by a big tent, chatting and drinking beer from plastic cups. Oh, the world of men, thought the girl. She felt the ground spin and dip.

"Are you okay?" asked the young guy as Clara tottered over, still clinging on to her case.

"Mm, yeah."

"D'you feel faint?"

"No, no, m'okay."

She tried to smile.

"Are you sure? Do you want a drink?"

"Oh, okay. Thanks."

The guy hopped down and took her over to a stand. He was pretty much her own age, strands of sandy hair sticking out from under that daft hat.

"A burger?"

"No, I'm fine."

"A can?"

"Oh, thanks."

He passed her one. She looked terribly pale and thin, absolutely nothing to her. The guy seemed very tall standing next to her, much taller than he'd seemed from afar.

"So, d'you work here?"

"Me, ah, no. You?"

"No, no."

"Oh."

Her belly let out a high-pitched whine.

"No, I'm just playing today with my da."

"Ah."

Her guts gurgled and seethed, and she tried folding her arms tightly around her middle.

"Yeah."

"Mm."

"So, do you live in town?" he asked.

She shook her head."

"I mean, I…"

The guy smiled awkwardly and Clara tried hard to suppress another gurgle. What was it with her belly?

"I mean, d'you want to go for a drink later?"

O-oo-oo-o, said her insides.

"I don't know…."

He was kinda good-looking she thought, you know, in a tartan dolly sort of way – but some sort of eruption was going on inside her.

"Ah, I mean if you want to…"

"I don't know…"

O-ooooooo.

"It's just that I…"

Something was welling up down below, and to disguise it she said, "Oh, okay. Okay."

"Great!"

He named a time and place but she was concentrating on her insides and missed it. What was happening to her?

"Is that okay?"

"Sure, yeah."

"So I'll see you later?"

"Aye. See you."

"Great!"

Was there something wrong with her tum? Clara felt giddy and hot.

She watched the fella's knees walk back over to the pipers, and then turned away herself, looking around for reception. Why wasn't anyone else taking any notice of her? There she was, dragging her huge swollen case past stalls and benches and wifeys having a rest, and no one so much as glanced at her. What am I, thought the girl, invisible? But then she didn't want anyone to make a fuss anyway. "I sure aren't sticking around," she muttered. Below the banners and the bunting she spotted a dilapidated sign and made her way toward it, dragging her case across the tarmac.

Reception was an ugly pre-fab stuck to the side of the factory. It seemed utterly empty, though; the desk was deserted, and so was the corridor to the rear. The little hall was terribly dreary, and you would never have guessed that there were banners and balloons and games just outside. She saw dusty plants, blank walls, a pile of unfinished paperwork. I can't do this, thought Clara, I can't.

Nevertheless, slowly, painfully, she lugged her case along a drab, monochrome passage, her luggage seeming to weigh as much as she did. From the first hall, steps led down into the factory proper, and there were more offices, a closed-off sanitation block, and then a long line of metal hatches. Clara pushed her way through a string of plastic strips, and wandered through to a dim room filled with row after row of bashed-in lockers. Hairnets, wellies and facemasks were lined up around the place. One locker was stuffed with a woman's magazine, some boiled sweets and a nest of hankies. What a life, she thought. Who could bear it?

At the end of the corridor were a pair of double doors, but she pushed her way through with her giant case. Come on, she thought. Come – on!

The next block couldn't have been more boring. All the ways into the main plant or to the laboratories which overlooked it were firmly locked and the girl could hear a constant humming and throbbing. The acrid chemically-smell had died away and now there was nothing there at all, just closed office doors, empty stairwells, an abandoned mop and bucket. And at the end, a deserted canteen, metal shutters over all the hatches.

Clara sat down at one of the wipe-down tables and rested her aching limbs. Her vitals seemed to be bubbling away like a pot on a stove. Such pains, she thought. The canteen was fair-sized but it was hard to imagine how all the people outside fitted in to it. Clara played around with the salt and pepper and tried to imagine sitting in here with all her fellow workers, pressed in on these little plastic stools, eating lasagne and chips. What was she doing here? From outside came the sound of cheers and laughter but Clara didn't dare look out.

Instead she thought of her mother — not her mother as she was now, but how she would have looked when she'd been Clara's age. And she had already been born then! Only my age, thought the girl, as if such a mystery had never occurred to her before. How could that be? She pictured her mother sitting in the canteen, reading a magazine, laughing with her friends, her eyes, her hair, the way she balanced her shoe at the end of her foot. How red her lips are, Clara thought, and such a strange shade to use! Clara's own face was so pale she was barely there at all. Then she rested her head in her arms for a moment, and let the world do with her as it will.

What a tick, eh? As soon as she closed her eyes, a gentle wave of sleep washed over her and the things around her seemed to mysteriously retreat. Pipes gurgled, sluice gates opened, vats filled up, but Clara could no longer tell if these things were happening inside her or someplace else. Then another gentle wave lapped around her chair, and she felt herself drifting away. The canteen seemed to dip and bob and Clara heard an enormous pump start up somewhere in the plant. Oh, why had she ever come here? A number of bells and buzzers were going off, but somehow far away, as if on another shore. Ach, who knew what they meant? The girl felt strange, disconnected.

Moving like a sleepwalker, she stumbled over to the window and looked out at the car parks and the grounds. Workers were starting to drift back toward the plant, but they looked like little coloured dots beneath her, or wee scattered flowers in the field. Such strange colours, Clara thought, as if they had nothing to do with her. And yet for all this numbness, something nagged away inside her. She rested her head against the window and tried to think what it was. More and more employees poured back inside the plant and Clara could hear voices, laughter, a low droning sound as the paddles began to turn. Was the holiday over? The games, the stalls, the rows of cheerful balloons — all were packed away now. Inside, the plant hummed and whirred. Great metal tubes were filling up with paint, an enormous pump was emptying out a concrete silo, wheels and machines everywhere grinding in endless motion.

And it was then that Clara knew – knew without even a shadow of a doubt, knew in a way unlike anything else she'd known in her life – that this place was a trap.

Yes, thought the girl, a trap! Immediately, she snapped awake. It was all becoming clear to her now — if she didn't get out before somebody found her, then she would never leave this place again. Ho, what was she doing here? But maybe it wasn't too late yet, maybe she could still get away. After all, what was the time? Clara picked up her case and started to run.

Unfortunately, her case — that wretched, stupid, impossible-to-shift lump – kept getting in her way. Whatever she did it was there, tripping her up, slowing her down, pulling on her arms. And such a weight! The poor girl was as pale as a snowdrop. Still, she dragged the big load along as best she could, its scuffed bottom seeming to stick to every surface.

The inside of the plant was blank and anonymous. On one landing there were barred double-doors and some kind of safety-cabinet, also securely locked. On the next, she stumbled upon a line of ladies loos, but didn't want to get any closer. Her tum was still bubbling and her case clattered down the metal steps like a freight train. What if people hear? she thought, but didn't dare slow down.

At the bottom was a mucky service-area filled with barrel-shaped bins, the surface of them all blistered and burnt. From there, a fire escape led to a foul smelling yard, blocked by a dirty great skip and a huge pile of bin bags. I'm off, she thought, angrily shoving her suitcase through. Clara was outside now, but her load seemed heavier than ever. Why this weight?, she thought, dragging the big daud across the yard.

At the end of the yard was a big metal door, topped with razor wire, and no visible bolt. The surface was corroded and stained and big scratch marks striped the rust. Clara put her shoulder to the door and shoved but it was firmly locked and there was no way through. She climbed down on her hands and knees to see if she could squeeze underneath, but that would mean leaving her case behind, and she didn't dare.

Instead she ran her hands along the scratched-out grooves and closed her eyes. No, there was nowhere to go. Nowhere, that is, until an orange coloured workman, his face the same colour as his safety-jacket, opened the door from the outside and seemed to look right through her. What was going on? It was as if she was so feint, he couldn't even see her. Instead the fella walked right past her with a bright blue trolley, wheeling it along as if nothing was amiss. Clara quickly squeezed past him, her case banging along at her side.

Outside, workmen were dismantling the stalls and kiosks, breaking them up to turn them back into pallets. Clara started to make up some kind of excuse as to what she was doing there, but there really wasn't any need; these too seemed to stare straight through her. When she walked past two fellas taking the banner down from over the stage they didn't even glance her way; it was as if the girl were transparent. She blew across the yard like the merest wisp of nothing, an inconsequential speck or dab. A forklift truck rolled past, and some guys started collecting up the pallets, but nobody was interested. Not a single soul approached her and the girl crossed the yard unnoticed. Then she staggered out through the main gates, past a weatherworn sign and out onto the road, her big bulky case tottering along beside her. Behind her, plumes of lurid smoke were being pumped out into the toneless sky. And that was all.

VII

Clara staggered along the tarmacked road for a while, hiding behind a wee grassy mound when a truck thundered past. The truck seemed enormous. Then, not really aware of what she was doing, she cut down across the moor and started to leave the road behind her, her little shape bobbing up and down amongst the rises and the hollows. It was very boggy there. She had to pick her way between the brackish puddles and sharp, slippery stones, concentrating at all times on keeping her footing. The mud was thick and treacherous but she managed to stay upright, and carefully followed the yellow-brown water down to the banks of a darksome burn. What would her mum say about her shoes? She didn't know.

To be honest, Clara felt kinda funny. At times her case seemed as light as a feather, whilst at other times it felt like a ton of bricks. Where am I?, thought the girl. She stumbled once or twice, down by the mire, but then followed a sodden path down through a mass of bracken and thistles. The mud was cold and tacky. When she came to the burn she used her case as a kind of makeshift bridge and gingerly clambered across. Then, when she came to a wooden fence, she used her case as a battering ram and went on through. But she felt tired, awful tired. On she shuffled, over the smudgy greenery, over bits of spiky gorse, away across the moor. When she came to a stone wall she used the thing as a ladder and climbed on over. But what a state she looked! Like some kind of dishcloth or rag. Occasionally little brown birds flew up from the undergrowth or something called out overhead, but Clara didn't seem to notice. The moor seemed daubed and smeary, full of blobs and spills and funny black streaks, but her eyes were bowed down to the muddy ground and she could see no further.

And yet...

And yet, for all that, she was slowly making her way back to civilisation.

Yes, after a while there were a few more fences around, stretches of barbed wire, even a sheep or two in the distance. Eventually the moor gave way to greener farmland, and slowly the descent wasn't quite so steep, nor the ground quite so uneven and sodden. If only she had eaten something at the factory! Her stomach still felt active and every once in a while her innards would let out a strange, strangled squeal. Never mind, though; now there were telephone poles, a lay-by, and the main road into town. And then the concrete units of an industrial estate, fenced-off areas, billboards, a railway bridge, a scrap-yard, and finally the whole mispainted jumble of the little town itself, the black smudge of the castle squatting over the town like a badly stuck stamp.

Clara dragged her case in a lumbersome daze, hollow explosions going off inside her tum. And yet her clothes didn't look as bad as she'd thought, her shoes not really all that mucky at all. Had she really walked back across the moor? Her limbs felt desperately sore and she couldn't believe that she'd dragged her suitcase all that way. But there were big red marks on both her hands and her arms felt ready to drop out of their sockets. How tired she was! All she wanted to do was to climb into her own bed and sleep. Alas though, her bed was very far away and her mother stood between her and it....

The sky was already starting to darken but Clara didn't feel well enough to go directly to the station and so ducked into a dingy wee café instead. There she bought a cup of tea and listened to the brownish liquid trickle gently inside her. The tea was very hot and strong but tasted good. How achey she felt! Her feet were awful swollen so she tried to rub some life back into them. What a long journey, she thought, I've never walked so far in all my life. And yet in another way she felt distanced from it, as if it had happened to someone else, like a story overheard on the train.

There were a few old wifeys dotted about, also drinking tea, but she didn't pay much notice; no, she was more worried about the state of her ankles and the pains in her feet. The girl glanced at her watch and lit up a fag, her face petulant and pouty. She spotted the waiter spying on her suitcase and stretched out one leg to make sure it was still there. Who's the wee daftie in the apron, she thought; and what does he think he's looking at? She could see him, right enough, peering out from behind the coffee-machine, a skinny wee fella with a long, gormless face. What was it the roundy old guy had said? The eye never has enough of seeing nor the ear its fill of hearing. But it wasn't true for her. Clara watched the lazy plume of smoke curl upward toward the stained yellow ceiling and slowly drank her tea.

VIII

The night was drawing in by now, the little charcoal town starting to disappear. Lights went out, pedestrians walked home, buses groaned and pulled away. But all this was ordinary and mundane. It was just a drab little market town shutting up shop, settling itself down for another quiet night.

The girl stared out of the café window and traced a line on the tablecloth with one delicate pinky.

Blimey, she's making that cup last a good time, thought Hans. What's she waiting for?

He wiped down the top of the counter, rearranged the condiments. He didn't know if he wanted the girl to leave or not.

In the square the last few stallholders had packed up and drifted away, leaving only the bare bones of the market in their wake. The tables were empty, the plastic sheeting wrapped away. How depressing it all was! Vacant, the wooden boards looked even more mournful, like the scene of a recent fire.

Yes, and in the café too, the customers supped up one by one and went home. Wifeys gathered their bags together and grannies wheeled their shopping trolleys out the door. They seemed to be waking from some kind of heavy sleep and looked awful reluctant to go, like sleepwalkers gently rocked awake. It was dark outside, the café lit by glary strips of light.

Once again Hans looked over at the sad, pouty girl. Should he go over and talk to her? His heart was racing and his mouth felt dry.

Her cup was empty and her little pink tongue was licking at the remains. Was she close to tears? he thought. Or just a bit fed-up? The girl rubbed the side of her suitcase, rather tenderly he thought, and once again he was plunged into confusion.

After all, who's to say that she needed help anyway? She sure didn't look very friendly. No, the girl sat there with her big long face and her big black case, and how was he supposed to know what she was doing here anyway? Or maybe she wasn't coming but going; one last drink before the train, which, given the state of railway tea and the lack of proper facilities, really wasn't that surprising. Besides, would she want to have anything to do with him? None of the other girls seemed to want to.

The girl sucked on a stray strand of hair and Hans picked up some odd bits of cutlery and slotted them away. Nearly closing time. The owner would be here soon and he still hadn't packed up all of the day's deliveries. Well, never mind. Sure, the girl looked sad and all but what was he supposed to do? Hans opened up the hatch and shuffled down the stairs.

Oh, why did women never want to have anything to do with him? There's no such thing as yellow blossom, he thought; only yellow leaves on the tree and wild flowers at the root.

It took him longer than expected to load up the boxes 'cause there was stuff all over the place and he kept finding things to do, inventories to check, bins to empty. When he came back up, the girl was gone, eighty pence left on the table. Hans walked over to the doorway, but there was neither hide nor hair of her; all that was left was her wee napkin lying scrunched up on the floor. O Missie, he thought!

The owner of the café was just parking his car opposite, a skinny old man with a hairy nose. What could Hans do? Reluctantly, he trundled out to meet him.

"A good day?" the fella called out.

"Ah sure, Mr Hemon."

He tried to look out into the square past him, but somehow the old fella always seemed to be in the way.

"Good, good… any problems, young man?"

Out the way, you old goat! Can't you see the girl has scarpered? But Hans just shook his head and smiled.

"No, no, everything's fine."

That hairy nose seemed to block off the entire street. Where'd she gone?

"Did Mr McGregor turn up with the crisps?"

Useless old codger; clear off willya? Hans suddenly noticed an enormous coffee stain on his apron.

"Oh, aye, I think so."

"Good, good."

"Mm."

Finally Mr Hemon turned round and, ah, well, it was just as he thought: the girlie was long gone.

Hans took off his apron and along with the owner, went back inside. After all, there was still the floor to do, and the till, and a lot more besides.

IX

But walking back home that night, Hans couldn't get the girl out of head. How had she even managed to humph her suitcase out of the café? In his mind, her bag seemed almost as big as she was. And where was she going, that girl and her luggage, like two people instead of one? What a melancholy, forlorn little figure! It was as if she had set out on a long journey without once looking back to land.

That night Hans went home as usual, had tea with his mum and dad, but seemed quiet and subdued, wrapped up in his own thoughts. What is this feeling? thought Wee Hans. Afterwards he watched telly for a bit and then went up to his bedroom. He brushed his teeth, read a few pages of his book, got himself ready for bed. In his mind's eye, the girl's hair was the gold-top of a milk bottle. She's certainly pale enough, he thought, even under all that make-up! And then he climbed into bed.

But it was no use; his pillow was hot, his feet cold, and sleep eluded him.

O, foolish youth! No, the fella couldn't drop off, the girl wouldn't let him be. Where is she, he wondered, and why the big case? He tossed and he turned.

No, sleep still wouldn't come. It was as if some kind of creaky old film were being projected inside his head.

At a loss, Hans got out of his bed and stared out of his window. Outside the house there was nothing, absolutely nothing: to the left there was nothing, and to the right also. But the longer he stared, the more a mysterious feeling came over him, some kind of feeling he'd never felt before – something which picked him up, lifted him out of bed and carried him off down the stairs.

Ah, me! he thought. 'Tis strange, strange, a mystery all...

Down there, everything was dark. His mum and dad were asleep, the dog too, and there he was, standing in the kitchen in his pyjamas, all sorts of odd and unknowable things going round in his head. Not knowing what else to do, he walked over, unbolted the kitchen door, and made his way out through the yard to the gate, trying not to step on anything sharp in his bare feet. The night was cold and draughty, a raw wind blowing in from the east. If only he had his waiter's apron, or at least some slippers on his feet! But this feeling, it grew and grew, until it was as big as the world, as big as the night sky. Well, there was nothing he could do now. No, this feeling, it dragged him along his street and onto the main road into town.

Even though the fella was in his pyjamas (and kinda scrawny to boot) he felt no sense of trepidation; no, it was as if he were just popping out for a stroll, a quick squiz round the block. Blithely, he cut down an alley between an evil-looking chip shop and a sour little newsagent (both closed) looking for where the girl was supposed to meet with Don, Don, the piper's son. And this feeling, it grew stronger, his pyjamas pulled along as if strung up on a line.

His little black feet traversed pavements and gutters, tarmac and cobblestones, but all he thought about was the girl, where she had come from and where she was going.

The girl! He imagined her peering in the window of the cheapo department store, pictured her pale, pouty face. Was it here that she was supposed to have met up with that guy from the pipe-band? Had he remembered to turn up? But the shop was closed and there was no sign of her pal. He could imagine some old goat watching the girl from the off-licence, an old wheezer with a bottle of cider and a scrunched-up packet of roll-ups. Miss, Miss, he wanted to yell, that fella's up to no good! And as if she'd heard, the girl didn't linger longer but headed off down a side-road, steering well clear of the offy. Oh Missy, he thought; this is no place to be wandering about on your own! But he was on his own too and so he quickly followed the girl past the shops and the flats and the bus stops — a little pyjama-clad shadow following in her wake.

Everything was empty and closed. All the shutters were down, doors locked, cars parked up on the curb-side. There was nobody about anywhere. It was like the whole town was asleep. Nothing stirred, not even a drunk.

Ah, but where would the girl go? He tried to picture her lugging her case along uneven pavements, through foul-smelling subways and over pedestrian walkways, but he kept losing sight of her and, besides, he was feeling a little cold himself. Miss, Miss, where are you? he thought. Despite the streetlights, the side-roads were as black as soot.

All the colours seemed to have disappeared too, and now the whole town was black and white, like an old movie on TV.

By the time Hans got to the station, it looked deserted too. A sickly light filtered out onto the dingy platform, but the ticket-office was all boarded up and there was nobody official-looking around to ask. Had the girl even been here? He tried to imagine her staring hard at the departures board, her feet hurting and her shoulders all knotted up and hunched. How was she feeling? Not so good, he guessed, not so good. There were no trains anywhere.

He imagined that the girl felt fluey and kinda unsteady, with some kind of thumping coming from her case. But why did it feel so heavy? A steady beating noise came from someplace deep inside it.

Had the girl phoned her mum? No, no, how could she tell her what she'd done? But she couldn't stay here and nor did she want to. Ah, what should she do? Go back to the plant? Look for somewhere to stay the night? But why would she want to do that? And as for the piper-fella, he'd probably forgotten her already....

Hans lingered by the departures board, his pyjamas untucked, feet the colour of coal. If only he'd said something earlier, but, no, it was too late now, just like always. What an idiot he was! O, you fool, the girl's long gone, he lamented; her train's pulled away and you weren't even there to see her off....

But just then he heard someone moving about in the ladies nearby, accompanied by some kind of splashing or a plop, and after that came a spluttering and a flushing and a smell so strong it made him catch his breath. Ah, it was bad! For a moment Hans thought he was going to heave and he stumbled backwards in mute horror.

Hans's insides lurched and jumped. What a stink! The smell in the place was making him sick and the sound gave him the skitters something rotten.

Then Hans suddenly looked down at himself and thought: 'what am I doing here? And in stripy pyjamas yet!' An astonishing stench was coming out the entrance-way and a blood-curdling flushing echoed across the concourse: 'time to go, time to go', he thought. Behind him the sound seemed to grow in volume and intensity and he backed away from the lavvy very carefully. 'What is this thing?' he thought.

'From whence does it come?' The loo gurgled and frothed and the fella legged it. 'What a reek', he thought. Whatever was coming, he didn't want to be there to greet it.

Hans ran out of the station precinct and out into the cold night air. Even the petrolly whiff smelt good. His heart was racing and his stomach seemed to twist inside him.

Ah, my soul, thought the young fellow; sweeter is the air than the earth! He looked down at his stripy bottoms, the terrible blackness of his feet. O, why had he ever left his bed tonight? There he was in his pyjamas, wandering about in the middle of the night, and for the first time that evening he felt terribly vulnerable and lonely. Unsteadily, he crossed the dual carriageway and retraced his steps toward the town centre. What a fool, he thought, why did I ever get up in the first place? Tomorrow's a work day; I've got to be up in the morning! And so saying he set off along another dark road, his scrawny figure as skinny as a twig.

After a while he climbed a hill by the steep stone steps near the castle and heard music coming from a pub at the top. By the sound of it the place was really heaving, but there was nobody near the entrance so he climbed up the steps and peered in.

One end of the pub had been cleared out to make up a rather dingy dance-floor, and there was a mobile disco installed on a table in the corner. The place was really packed though, as if all the inhabitants of the grey little town were crammed inside the one seedy snug. There were middle-aged folk getting steadily hammered, old crusties nursing their pints, hangdog couples, lonely bachelors playing the slot-machines; um, it's busy, he thought; no chance of a drink at this time of night! A gang of teenage girls jiggled about in the centre of the dance-floor, the cheap lighting effects turning them red, orange, green, yellow. Were those the sunflowers from the factory over by the loud speakers? No, just girls who looked like them, gabbing and laughing and passing bottles between them, their heads little halos of light under the glary display.

Should I go in? thought Hans. But then he remembered that he was still in his pyjamas and decided he'd better not. To be honest, he didn't know whether he wanted to anyway. There wasn't room to spill a pint and anyway the place was noisy, smelly, full of tanked-up guys and spoken-for lassies. The DJ cranked the music up and the waiter felt the vibrations penetrate all the way to the street, all the way through his body. Poor me, he thought, best not to get caught in one's pyjamas on a night like this! The girls kept changing colour as they danced and swayed, and Hans turned around and went. But the same thought kept coming back to him: maybe the girl with the case had been there tonight, maybe she had stood where he'd stood, thought the same things....

But girls were different, mysterious, otherworldly: who knew what went on in their heads? And yet if he'd just had the nerve to say something, give her a hand... mm, but it was all too late now. There was nothing to do but go home. All of a sudden Hans felt much more sorry for himself than he did for the pale-looking girl. He stuffed his hands down his pyjama bottoms and shuffled off up the hill.

Splashes of black sky dribbled down onto the pavement, thick oily shadows oozing across the shops and alleyways. But Hans was already thinking about tomorrow, about getting-up, checking the inventory, making sure that they'd ordered enough cakes, getting the milk in... he felt tired just thinking about it. And of course the whole time, Mr Hemon would be breathing down his neck, watching him like a hawk to see if he made any mistakes....

Yes Hans had his own problems: why go looking for more? But then the strangest, I mean the strangest thing, happened; out of the corner of his eye he spotted a second figure floating mysteriously up the hill, more of a shadow than a figure really, a smudge or a blur, flitting between the parked cars and the zebra crossing on the corner. Tch, was that her? His heart thumping, Hans, the waiter — though of course he didn't look like a waiter, 'cause without his apron or his white shirt or little bound pad, the mannie could have been anyone, just some skinny wee bloke in a pair of grey pyjamas — took chase, but as he rounded the corner, dodging out from behind a row of spindly sycamore trees, he realised that the figure was just some old Joe, a tiny wee scribble of a man, also dressed in his pyjamas, his head a great shaggy mane of white hair, his feet two little black dots beneath it.

So: somebody else was daft enough to be abroad on this dark and ill-starred night. But why would anyone want to traipse about the place clad only in their night things, unshod, their tiny wee stump exposed to the elements?

"Hullo!" he shouted, "Hullo!" But somehow his words didn't seem to travel. The old bloke paused for breath outside a boarded up dry cleaners and then moved on.

Not wanting to lose him, Hans tried to follow on the opposite side of the street, the two of them walking in exactly the same way, like twin shadows cast from the same source. The old fella kept disappearing though, his tiny frame always on the verge of being swallowed by a big black hole. What was he doing?

"Hey, old-timer, hold on!" Hans wanted to yell, but it was awful late and the street was very quiet. Then, as Hans crossed over by the bait and game place and the wee corner shop, the old Joe seemed to vanish entirely, his shape suddenly scrubbed out as if somebody had decided to blot out the entire scene. Hans looked this way and that but of the old fella, there was no sign: the night seemed to have swallowed him whole — thick mane of hair, tiny black feet, cornflower eyes and all. He raced over to the other side of the road but of the old bloke there was nothing, not even a speck. And yet he couldn't believe it; he'd been watching him so close, copying his every movement, staying so very close... But then he thought, ach, why bother? I mean, who cared? A great weariness suddenly seemed to descend upon him and all he wanted to do was go home. Who could be arsed anyway? In the morning Mr Hemon would be back clucking around him, moaning about the stock, the state of the counter, the crockery piled up on the tables... why should he go out chasing his own shadow? Who cared? His feet felt tired, his pyjamas cold and draughty. Worse still, his heart was as dark and empty as the night...

But even so, the feeling didn't leave him quite yet. Just imagine, he thought: imagine if the girl was also looking for him or if she needed help. The idea made him stop in his tracks. After all, why this feeling and why tonight? He thought about the girl sitting at the back of the café, drinking her tea and smoking her fag, and then he thought about dragging her suitcase along an endless procession of faceless, discoloured, streets, her case getting heavier, her feet moving slower and slower....

Yes, if the fella closed his eyes he could see her, make out her slender frame, her face and her little sore hands. Ah, but the girl wasn't looking too good. Her complexion was the colour of buttermilk, her stomach spinning and lurching, her breath coming in thin, ragged gasps. She flopped from side to side, and couldn't seem to keep her feet on the pavement. How white she looked! As pale as a winding-sheet. Inside her suitcase came the sound of a hushed, subdued, almost muffled drum. What is this feeling? the girl asked. She looked so white it was as if her face had been painted over. But even as she paused, stabbing pains rose from her insides to her backbone and she felt a dreadful weight press down suddenly upon her bladder.

"Please," she said, "please." She staggered over to a mucky stairwell and sat herself down, her body scrunched up into a little ball.

Yes, something terrible was happening to her. Her innards roiled and her juices bubbled.

Please.

X

And that was where the mannie found her, sprawled on the pavement between the low stoop and the cash-machine, her body turned in on itself and her case lying off to one side. He gently picked her up and carried her off as if she weighed no more than a rag. My case, she murmured, my case, so he bent down and picked that up too.

But who was he? Clara felt too ill to concentrate. Young? Old? A stranger?

The mannie checked the bruise on her head, wiped the muck from her skirt, and scooped her up into his arms. He's very strong, she thought, but it was getting harder and harder to think at all. All around her the streets seemed to merge into blocks of black and grey, whilst the speckled streetlights seemed further and further apart, like headlights disappearing into the void. Oh my head, she murmured, if only to herself.

Yes, she felt oddly insubstantial, as light as thistledown. She drifted in and out of consciousness, indistinct, fleeting, bodiless....

She was moving though, or being carried or driven or something. Everything around her seemed to hover or to glide. She was drifting away now. All the buildings seemed to be in the wrong position or the wrong size or somehow all jumbled up, but it didn't seem to matter – at least there was someone there to hold her up. If the fella wasn't holding onto me, Clara thought dreamily, I'd blow away altogether, disappear once and for all....

After a while they came to a halt outside a tiny little house surrounded by a circle of large trees. The trees were very green, but because it was night, everything looked like it was still in black and white. Still, the trees looked kinda familiar somehow and Clara felt a sudden wave of tenderness. If only she'd learnt the names of trees! Their branches seemed to hold up the little white house, as if to protect it.

But then they weren't outside any little house at all but rather inside a warm but kinda poky-looking flat. The fella switched on a light, carried her over to an old green couch, and scooted off to fetch her case. Clara struggled to focus. The flat was clean, tidy and well kept. There were pictures on the wall, and photographs, copies of a caravanning magazine.

After a few minutes the fella re-appeared with her case, and placed it beside her.

In a low, gentle voice, he asked her how she was: did she need a doctor, an ambulance, a phone?

"No", she said, "no."

"A cup of tea?"

She murmured yes and he switched the TV on and shuffled off to a tiny walk-in kitchen, where she could hear him fumbling about with mugs and a kettle.

The flat was very ordinary, but at least very warm. Then the fella came back in and handed her her tea in a big chipped mug with a picture of the Care Bears on the front.

"Thanks, that's really great," she said. "You're awful kind."

"No, no…"

"No, it's true."

She smiled at the fella and he handed her a biscuit.

"How are you feeling?"

"Oh, okay. A bit tired."

"You've hurt your head."

"That's okay."

The TV blethered away in the corner.

"Do you have any sugar?"

"Oh, aye, right, I'll get you some."

The fella jumped up and went back into the kitchen as her stomach gave out a high-pitched yelp. He came back with a big bag with a spoon in it.

"Thanks."

"You're welcome."

The girl's eyes had a dark, glassy look, and though she'd stopped shivering she was still scrunched up in a little ball.

"Ah, I've got a phone," the mannie said, hovering over her. "If you'd like to ring your mum and dad?"

Clara shook her head and took a big sook of tea.

"I mean, they'll be wondering about you and all…." He cast an inquiring glance over toward her suitcase.

"No."

The girl's mucky clothes had made a small round stain on the couch, and she gingerly laid her hand on top of it.

"I'm okay," she said, awfully quietly.

"Well, just to say that you're...."

"No, really."

The girl had a bright green caterpillar creeping down from her nose.

"Ah, is there anybody else? A friend?"

She didn't say anything, but took another sip.

"Oh, right, right enough."

The mannie was staring at her with such an expression of concern that she thought she was going to bawl there and then; but then some sluice gate in her innards suddenly opened up and she felt her belly fill up like a hot-water bottle.

"Ah, do you think I can use your loo?" she asked, kinda shakily.

"Mm, of course, it's just over there."

"This one?"

"Aye."

"Thanks."

She closed the door and peered apprehensively about the spartan bathroom. A few toilet things were lined up by the sink and an old towel strewn over the yellowing tub, but otherwise the room was stark and empty, lit by a single glary bulb.

Feeling dreadfully unsteady, what with the pains in her bladder and her abdomen and all, she sat down on the lavvy fully dressed, folding herself up to keep her insides in. Oh, such pains; they kept coming and going in random waves, sometimes sharp, sometimes dull. She could feel the bathroom starting to spin as the cramps in her stomach grew worse.

But she didn't want to stay on the toilet. Very wobbly on her pins, she tottered over to the fella's shaving mirror and examined her reflection. What a sight! She looked like a ghost already. So ugly, she thought to herself, so ugly. The girl rested her forehead on the glass to make it go away. Right above the mirror was a tiny frosted window, and by craning her neck she could just about see into a little wooded garden, its greenery somehow hushed in the grey light. A line of washing fluttered in the breeze, scanties, sheets and towels, and the girl watched them flap this way and that through the frosted glass, little melancholy flags.

I know this place, she thought, I know it.

Yes, a little green garden, overhanging trees, branches like arms...

This place, she thought, I know it....

But then, without any warning, the lassie broke wind with tremendous force. Ho, the sound! The windowpanes rattled and the bloke's stuff wobbled on the shelf: the volume was incredible! It seemed to explode out of her, a mighty eruption, a terrible emanation. Several shorter blasts followed in a descending scale, and the girl felt mortified, her face bright red. What a beamer, she thought. What if the guy hears? And, to be honest, unless the fella was as deaf as a post he would have heard every note.

However, all seemed quiet in the flat, and when she pressed her ear to the door she couldn't hear a thing. Maybe, he's gone back to the kitchen, she thought. Anyway, what could she do?

Still a bit groggy she stumbled bow-legged to the washbasin and ran some water over her hands and face. It was only when she'd finished and pulled out the plug that she realised that the pain in her stomach had gone, and her innards finally felt at peace.

So she thought: it was only the windies after all!

A feeling of relief immediately swept over her but she felt kinda empty too and staggered back over to the loo as if deflated. All she wanted to do now was sleep: everything else felt unpleasant and ugly and hard. Aching with tiredness she started to fall asleep right there on the throne, but eventually forced herself back up and dragged her lump back over to the bathroom door.

When she opened it the flat seemed strangely quiet, with the TV switched off and no sign of the kindly stranger. Clara padded into the living-room and footered about for a bit waiting for him to come back, but she soon felt exhausted and so lay down on the ugly green couch instead. If she could just stay here a while and rest... her brain kept telling her to go and get her stuff out of her case but she didn't have the energy and couldn't see it in the room anyway.

Everything seemed to be fading and dissolving: the couch, the pictures, the photographs. Half-recognisable voices drifted through the wooden partition wall and Clara thought for a moment that she could hear her mum talking to someone close by. Was it her? Well, it was time for bed now, her bedtime at any rate.

After a while someone (she didn't know who) came and carried her back to her little room at home, where all her bits and pieces were waiting for her. Yes, there were her posters and her smellies and her bits and pieces of jewellery, all carefully arranged. But she was so tired, so tired. It was very dark and voices rose and fell behind her bedroom wall, though the girl still couldn't tell who they were. All she wanted to do was sleep and be left in peace.

Somebody placed her on a narrow mattress and gently pulled the covers over her, tiny clusters of blue and yellow flowers printed on the bed-sheets. It was warm and cosy there, and once beneath the bedding her body curled in on itself, like a bud closing up for the night.

The girl murmured something but was too tired and it didn't come out right; instead she pulled down her pillow and nestled into it, breathing heavily.

Around and about, the shapes and outlines of the furniture began to dim and waver and the whole room flickered like a candle. The books, the toys, the ornaments all vanished, everything flying away into nothingness, fading back into the gloom.

Clara wrapped herself up in the flowers and gratefully turned over; then the last patch of light faded from the picture and she was gone.

In the morning Hans went back to work at the cafe. He swept the floor, switched on the coffee machine, lugged the crockery out of the dishwasher. When he was done he went and stood in the doorway; people were heading off to work, to the shops, to the bus stop. Empty, empty, all is empty, he said to himself, before going back in to clean the loos. But of course, he didn't understand a thing.

XI

The guide sighed and ushered us back. His back was bent and his eyes were black.

"The girl? Let her be, sir, allow her a brief few hours of respite; after all, tomorrow will have sorrows of its own. Oh, young Miss; what can we even know of her? No more than that foolish waiter, perhaps: no more than the sum of our own thoughts and suppositions and dreams."

The guide stared straight at us, his black umbrella the minute hand of a clock.

"No, my friends, all we can do is stick close together, eyes shut and arms out-stretched, until some shape appears before us, like a train of shadows, or a shoreline in the fog..."

That's right, we thought, a crooked line, a row of carriages, a black train racing through the night....

PART THREE

Homo Terminus

I

That's right, we thought, this train of shadows, our phantom ride. But where were we now? Somewhere a loudspeaker was squawking, and we could hear the clatter of trolleys, a squeal of brakes, feet echoing on a vast concourse. Then, as our eyes adjusted to the gloom, we began to make out shapes, forms — railway lines, long carriages, a tunnel darker than any hole, like a black picture in a black frame. Ah, yes, we thought, this place, of course. And then we could make out the station itself, a huge cavernous space, commuters and passengers everywhere, all of 'em running from platform to platform, and lugging heavy cases. "Stay together, ladies and gentlemen," intoned our guide from beneath his moustache. "It is awful crowded and our time is short…"

We pushed our way through the throng and made our way over to a long row of benches, all lined with bundles of dozing clothing, great mounds of coats, kagools and plastic jackets. One fella in particular, a sleepy wee bloke, skinny as a minute to midnight, lay curled up on his seat, and we squeezed in right next to him, practically sitting on the fella's lap. His drowsy features looked kinda familiar to be honest, his dreamy expression somehow known to us. One of the party leaned in to ask him something, but the tour-guide shook his head, a long white finger held to his lips. "Not yet, Madam," he whispered, "let the fella be…"

The mannie's expression seemed strangely preoccupied, his eyes fixed on the tracks ahead of him, like a ladder leading down a well. It was as if he were searching for someone or perhaps some other thing, his gaze falling on wave after wave of travellers, his wee eyes blue, as blue as the known and unknown sea….

II

Well, this little yellow train pulled in and released all its passengers, but I couldn't see my parents anywhere. I was sitting on a bench just beneath the arrivals board and starting to fret, to be honest, 'cause my mum and dad were over an hour late and their train hadn't even made it onto the screen yet. Instead more and more coaches kept shunting in and dumping passengers onto the cold, hard concrete, and I felt kind of sad for some reason, watching the folk elbowing their way along the platform, squeezing their luggage through the ticket barrier as if their lives depended on it. I strained my neck to see if I could spot a frail, elderly couple carrying a large bag of fruit, but then I started to feel a tad peckish myself, so I decided to, you know, go off for a quick snack instead.

Anyhow, after hovering around outside one of the bakers for a bit, I finally sauntered over to this chicken place and settled down with a plastic tray by the window. My heart wasn't really in it though, 'cause it was a pretty desperate place, full of casuals and drop-outs and drunks, and when I opened up my polystyrene box the chicken was all flat and gritty, like it'd just been run over by a truck. I chewed on the gristle for a while, but this strange feeling, it just wouldn't leave me and I couldn't even face my second pail of nuggets; instead I wandered back to the main concourse, full of worries and anxieties and broken-heartedness.

Alas, well, there was nothing to be done, so even though my lunch-hour had run out long ago and I was sure to catch hell from my boss, I plonked myself down on the same hard bench and resumed my former position staring up at the computer screen.

Now I'd been perched there for less than a minute when this fella traipses up and flops down next to me, collapsing onto his seat like a glove puppet with the hand pulled out.

Huffing and puffing, the fella crosses his legs in an exaggerated manner and then starts to tug at one of his well-buffed shoes, gritting his teeth as he does so.

"Grrrr," the fella says.

Well, when he spotted me looking at him he nodded dolefully in my direction and then went back to worrying his shoe. Ach, he was twisting and turning it till it looked like his whole foot was about to unscrew — anyhow, I felt kind of embarrassed and was just about to get up and go when the bloke suddenly groaned, toppled forward, and plopped head-first onto the linoleum, his hand wedged in his shoe and his sit-me-down stuck up in the air.

Well, of course I looked the other way 'cause, ah, my parents were due any minute and I didn't want them to slip past me in the crowd — I mean, what if they missed me entirely? — but eventually I got up and went over to help the poor guy. He was a funny looking fella, not so much wearing his business suit as wrapped up in it, and when he mumbled something from beneath his flat face I spun him round like a tortoise and asked if he was okay.

Well, the bloke gave me this look containing all the sadness in the world and nodded morosely toward his shoe; you see, somehow he'd managed to get four fingers stuck between his leather tongue and his great sweaty hoof, and now his back had locked into place to boot, all because he'd fallen asleep in the waiting room with his feet up on the radiator, his nippers swollen up to jam both shoes. "Howl, howl!" he said, his face turning red.

Anyhow, I couldn't just leave him there, so I hauled and haled and finally wound up on top of him, trying to shoo the fella like a horse. By this time a small crowd had appeared, though mainly composed of small boys and girls 'cause, um, everybody else was skating 'cross the concourse, heading off to who knows where.

"Chop it off! Chop it off!" chanted the boys.

I tried to shoo them away like a great gaggle of geese, but they kept on coming and clustering round us, poking and pointing, and it was all I could do to roll the bloke over to a quiet corner of the station.

"Don't worry, pal," I told him. "I'll have you out of there in a jiffy."

We pulled and tugged, squeezed and yanked, until finally I grabbed hold of his tongue and managed to squeeze his great paw free. "Ach, such feeling," he yelled. After that he tried to get some feeling back into his fingers by squeezing and rubbing each one in turn, and then he slowly straightened his hump, unclenched his mitts and let out a deep and resonant sigh. His feet, alas, stayed stuck in his steaming shoes, but he thanked me in a cheerless sort of way, and asked if I'd care to join him for a quick snifter in the snug across the way. Now of course I was still worried about my mum and dad 'cause their train was terribly late by now, but I said yes and we made our way across the slippery concourse, the smell of his sweaty pads accompanying us.

Anyhow, we went into this bar on the other side of the station, and the bloke ordered a vodka and Irn-Bru and got me a Diet Coke, and then we retired to a quiet corner of the lounge, the mannie limping a little as he went. It was a pretty rough place though, the bar awash with hard-liquor and windows the colour of ashtrays; a few hard-men with nicotine-stained teeth and beady, wino eyes sized us up as we walked in and I thought to myself, mummy, daddy, where are you? — but by then we'd sat down and the fella was gloomily bevvying away.

Close-up, he looked in a pretty disreputable state, with several days worth of growth on his chin and big sweat marks under his pits. And his suit! On the platform it had looked pretty snazzy, but now seemed occupied by a fitful collection of bulges and lumps, the lining all mucky and torn.

He sucked lugubriously on his glass and asked me if I fancied another.

"No, no, I'm fine."

"Something harder."

"Oh, no, don't fret."

"Go on."

"No, really."

The bloke was so tired-looking it was hard to guess his age; a pair of heavy eyelids drooped over two red sores, and his soft mouth sagged down into his tipple, sleepy bubbles forming at the edges.

"A little drink."

"M'okay."

"A nip."

"Honestly."

We went on like this until I agreed to buy him another. Then he told me his strange and terrible tale, all the while fixing me with his awful, sorrowing gaze.

So who was he? Well, it seemed that the fella was a railway-man who travelled the length and breadth of the network, checking on punctuality, cleanliness, the standard of facilities and so on, ticking off boxes in a vast yellow pad. This pad of his resembled an enormous yellow brick, a monumental wedge of papers, unwieldy as a suitcase; he seemed to carry it with him like a snail carries its shell, a great yellow lump. But who am I to say? After all, that was what the fella did all day: ride trains, note down delays, poor facilities, customer complaints. But tell me my friend, and tell me now: why was it he looked so bad? I mean, once upon a time he too must have splashed on after-shave in the morning, given his pits a quick spray with some kind of smelly, chosen a crisp white shirt, a tie, maybe a wee pin in the shape of a train, and then out of the door, hair combed, suit pressed, pens arranged by size in his inside coat pocket. And then I could picture him clicking open his briefcase, arranging his inventory, doing businesslike things in a pad...

But how had he got from there to here? "What went wrong?" I ask him, trying not to breath in the vodka fumes emanating from his end of the table.

"Oh, the usual," the fella replies.

"The usual?"

"Mm."

They keep upping his completion quota, extending his hours, tightening the deadline. More and more pads had to be filled, more boxes ticked, more targets actioned. And in the meantime it was getting harder and harder to get home; every night the train was late, the line was blocked or services cancelled — and the state of the carriage, well, it was a disgrace! Rubbish scattered across the floor, scratches on the table, big rips gouged out of the seats. And all the time things were just getting steadily worse, each train arriving later and later, every last lump of chewing gum, scribbled graffiti and torn reservation stub needing to be noted down, listed in the fella's voluminous yellow ledger. I mean, what was the bloke supposed to do? Cracks on the line, broken door handles, wobbly luggage racks — and in the meantime, the mannie's own train was going slower and slower, the dingy little carriage growing more and more crowded with every stop. Yup, people were crammed in everywhere: squeezed in by the loos, squashed in doorways, crushed on top of anybody who'd actually managed to find a seat. And all the time the fella was scribbling in his thick, yellow pad, his nose almost touching the page... But what was it he wrote? He fixed his terrible blooded eyes on me and then carefully handed over his curled up jotter, and slowly, reluctantly, I began to read...

The lights, which had flickered spasmodically for the past few hours, gave up entirely when we entered the tunnel. There were a few moans, but for the most part people stayed calm. All anyone could hear was an odd whistling and the sound of the carriages creaking like old bones as they rattled along the endless track. Were we lost? Although the train was still moving, we felt becalmed, adrift, swallowed up by some kind of greater darkness. But I had to go on!

Cautiously, I made my way along the coach, clambering over all the fallen luggage.

After a while there didn't seem to be any people around. The next carriage seemed eerily deserted, abandoned almost, filled only with the bags, cases and satchels which always seemed to dog my path. Only the loos seemed dimly illuminated, their doorway outlined by an eerie green light. I advanced toward it, my insides churning. Hm, I really needed to go! But when I tried the door, I was greeted by a dank and terrible stench beyond the grasp of mortal speech.

I felt my brain reel, my soul tremble and my limbs go rigid where I stood; but still I forced myself to advance, flinging open the portal to the hideous chamber within. And within? No paper, no water, a busted tap. Litter was strewn over the damp and sticky floor and paper-towels filled the sink. But what of the pan? Alas, my heart failed me and I could go on no more. A strange and terrible wind was blowing through a crack in the window, enveloping the entire cubicle in its icy grasp. I was near the loo-seat now; someone pounded on the toilet door but I did not turn back. Instead, I looked down into the bowl, and then, and then...

And then what? Ah, me, what lay within?

But at this point the fella snatched back his note-pad and slumped back down into his drink. He was starting to greet now, tears running down his mug; I mean, he hadn't been home for weeks, sleeping in waiting rooms and on parcel trolleys, eating processed food from sticky plastic containers... "But why?" he bellowed. "Why this toil?" Well,

I have to admit that I looked around kinda nervously at this point 'cause, ah, this wasn't really the type of place where you wanted to draw attention to yourself, if you get my meaning, but luckily the snug was pretty quiet and when I looked back it turned out that the fella had conked out under the table, pouring his drink all down him. What an alkie! I thought. What a clod....

When I was sure the fella was out like a light, I pried open his mitts and pulled out his yellow notebook, which was big and sticky and about the size of a small desk. Then I looked down at the fella, who was face down in a puddle, and said to myself, "No sir, he isn't going to be going anywhere for a while," and started to flick through the pages, reading the entries written in his odd scratchy hand. Unfortunately, it was just then that I noticed one of the hard nuts at the bar casting evil skegs in my direction, so I half-inched the book and tiptoed out of there, leaving the mannie asleep on the floor. Got to go, got to go, I said to myself, drying the book's cover on my sleeve. My parents were waiting and I didn't want to miss them!

Hm, what's that? Didn't I feel bad? Listen: the fella was sleeping like a baby, a look of blissful contentment plastered all over his mug. Look, you tell me, what harm was I doing? Ah, if anything I was saving him from himself, delivering the fella of his burden. I mean, without his book, he could finally go home, kiss his wife, get some proper food inside him... or at least that's what I told myself, anyway.

III

But when I emerged from the grubby wee bar, I thought I'd wound up in a different station entirely. Tch, it was only when my head started to clear I realised it was just that the concourse was so incredibly packed, with more and more commuters pouring in all the time, like apples down a chute. And what about my mum and dad? I pictured them tramping up and down the endless plaza, searching this way and that, Mum in the lead and Dad following on behind, crooked, bent, weighed down with great bags of fruit. But what is old age? I reflected, flicking through the newspapers on a stand. Nothing but an old bent branch on an old dark tree. Such a fate! I imagined someone bumping into Dad and tipping him over, his big bag of fruit rolling off down the track... or Mum pausing for breath and a passing porter loading her onto a little yellow trolley, carting her off to who knows where....

Well, feeling down, I immediately popped into this nearby burger joint, hoping that a bite to eat might make things look a little better. The place smelt of grease and cleaning fluids and there was a very dubious puddle of something all over my table, but of course, beggars can't be choosers, and besides my tum was really grumbling by now ... Anyhow I plonked myself down and propped open the fella's book, peeling apart some of the damp yellow pages to do so. *Below my seat,* I read, *there came a terrible rumbling as if from the bowels of the earth. T'was as if the very wheel that turned the world were slowly grinding to a halt....* I flicked on a few pages and read of *a sleeping carriage, full of nameless shapes, absence, darkness, things which are not....* But just as I opened up my bun and was about to take a bite, there was a loud commotion out on the concourse, and when I looked up, I saw the guy from the snug roving up and down the station in a state of great agitation, his eyes all red and fearsome like. Well, straight away I slid down in my seat and hid the book on my lap; I mean, was the fella looking for me? His pad? O, you fool, I wanted to shout, you're free, free! but instead I hid under the table and tried to disguise myself with the plastic container.

But how was I to get past him? Choking a little, I finished off my fries and made a run for it across the plaza, planning on losing the guy between the vending machines and the flower stall. Luckily the fella was searching in one of the waste-bins so I ducked down behind a bucket of lilies, breathing hard all the while.

To be honest, it was pretty hard to make out anyone — I mean, there were people everywhere, on top of each others' feet and in each others' laps, an indescribable avalanche of passengers that seemed to go on forever. But then, just as I was about to scuttle across the plaza, this woman appeared as if from nowhere, bashing her suitcase hard against my shins.

"Hey, pick 'em up, pal," snapped the dame. "Coming through!"

The gal was quite a formidable size herself, and was hauling the biggest piece of luggage I'd ever seen in my life.

"Move it or lose it," said the gal, breathing hard through her nose.

As she trundled her case past me, I could see that one of its wheels had come off, and that the whole contraption was wobbling dangerously from side to side. Not that it slowed her down, though; the woman rolled through the crowd like a bowling ball through skittles.

"That's some trunk," I said as she rumbled by. "What have you got in there anyway, a body?"

The woman blew a few strands of sticky hair from her eyes and fixed me with a hard stare.

"Look, give a lady a hand, will you? I'm not pushing this thing for my health, you know."

The woman was squat, red and perspiring heavily. She was wearing some kind of nurse's smock that looked like it had been stitched around her, with a shock of curly blonde hair sitting on her head like a mop.

"Um, over here?"

"That's it. Hey, watch the handle will you? That thing's worth more than you earn in a year."

Together we shoved it over to a line of metal bins, and there we rested on top of it. The gal was breathing hard, and great sweaty patches had formed under her arms. Close-up, she seemed to have no neck at all, her head poking out from the top of her nurses' smock like the end of a sausage roll.

"Well, thanks," she said, suddenly scrunching up her face. "It seems like I've been crossing this station forever."

"So what is in this tub?" I asked, banging its sides and dangling my feet over the end. It really was huge, you know, about the size and weight of a small wardrobe.

"Oh, samples, products — bottles and bottles of stuff."

"Stuff?"

"You know — cosmetics. Anti-aging creams, exfoliates, rejuvenators... top of the range stuff."

"Ah! Lotions and potions!"

"Mm. I gotta deliver 'em today, but I can't see my train anywhere. And just look at all these people! I mean, where's everybody going anyway?"

It really was wall-to-wall commuters in there, a solid mass of squabbling humanity. One poor guy's face was as flat as a frying pan and when he bent over to tie his shoelaces he abruptly disappeared from sight.

"So, whatcha doing?" she asked, eying up my big yellow book.

I shrugged and made some kind of half-hearted gesture. "Um, I'm waiting for my mum and dad," I said. "You haven't seen them have you? She's about so high, in a funny green hat, my dad falling on behind, a little bent over with a sad-looking moustache."

"Mm," she said. "Your mum and dad, you say? Well, if I see 'em..." She looked around her but the concourse was so packed by us you couldn't have fitted a pencil in unless you'd remembered to sharpen it first.

"They're coming for a visit, and to, you know, bring me something to eat. To be honest though, they're getting on a bit, so I said I'd meet them here, though, um, I really should be getting back to work, 'cause if my boss finds out, then..."

At that moment strange electronic crackle echoed across the vast enclosed space, but neither of us could make out what it said. The woman sighed and shuffled around in her apron pocket. "Listen, if you want to make yourself useful, pop to that shop and buy me a sandwich will you? A gal can die of hunger you know..."

The woman was about to fish something out of her purse but I said, "Ah, madam, this one is on me," and she said, "Well thanks, fella — last of the big time spenders, huh?"

What a dame! When she smiled her mouth seemed enormous, a great suspension bridge between her cheeks.

Well, when I came back with a couple of rolls we munched away in silence for a bit, and the gal stretched her legs out and rubbed her swollen ankles. In fact, to be honest, she was one big lump all over, but she let me eat the tomato from her sandwich and we chatted amiably about the size of her bunions and her varicose veins and how she was going to get her sample case onto one of those diddy little carriages.

"Don't worry," I said gallantly, "I'll give you a hand," and so saying, I made an elaborate gesture with my hands.

"Mm, you're a doll," said the gal. "Where've you been hiding out on me?"

I smiled flirtatiously and we chatted a bit more about the state of her feet and what she might put on them, and then I told her about my mum and dad coming to stay and how they were bringing a big bag of fruit from their garden, though, you know, I did worry about Dad's back, what with humphing that great load around...

"Yeah," said the gal, "I know how he feels..."

"Listen," I said, "let me tell you about how they first met. You see, one day Dad cycled into town to buy himself a new suit and went straight to the first shop he came to — only it was this great big department store and soon he found himself hopelessly lost, blundering this way and that down the aisles, ending up in haberdashery rather than gentlemen's outfitters. Anyhow, he wandered around, saw all these multi-coloured bails of fabric, and (plucking up his courage) went over to this shop-girl and asked her for something to wear. 'Well, strip down to your vest and pants and jump up flat on the table', says my mum, 'and we'll see what we can do.' When to her great surprise he did, she immediately leapt to and cut out his gangly silhouette from a roll of dark fabric, snipping all the way around him with lightning speed. Some of the other girls were giggling and pointing over to one side, but my mum had a gleam in her eye and a smile on her lips and after he'd gone she held up the material and thought, 'well, that's the shape for me!'"

"Mmm," said the woman, eyeing me up cautiously.

"Mm, what?"

"Mm, nothing. Just trying to read the information board, is all."

"Oh," I yawned. "Anyway I remember another time when I was just a little kid and the three of us went for a picnic in the woods, and on the way there we came upon a whole tangle of bramble bushes, so quick as a flash my mum hauls up her skirt and starts filling it with sticky red fruit, and my dad says, 'What do you think you're doing? D'you want the whole world to see?' and my mum says, 'See? See what?' and Dad says, 'Your bare knees!' and Mum laughs and hitches her skirt up even higher, and the funny thing was her pretty pink knees looked just like fruit too, two big red raspberries, and then my dad hitched his trousers up too, and his roundy knees looked like two hairy gooseberries, and I wanted to do the same but I was wearing shorts already so straight away I burst into tears…"

The gal tucked a strand of sticky blonde hair behind one ear and stretched out her sturdy little legs.

"And this was when?"

"Oh, a long time ago. I'm supposed to meet them today on the central plaza, but, um, I've kind of forgotten the platform…"

"Yeah, well, you're a prize calf aren't you?" she said, smiling at me now. Her mug was incredibly round and red, like a hot plate on a stove. "Why don't you just find the arrivals board and be done?"

"Arrivals?"

"Sure! You've never been in a station before? Just find the right screen and… say, what's happening over there?"

Some kind of scuffle had broken out by the ticket-barriers over at the other end of the station but I couldn't really see. All I could make out were bodies, bags, and trolleys, all piled up in a great heap.

"What do you think it is?" asked the gal, busting her nut to see.

"I dunno, but it looks like trouble. Let's stay where we are. Anyhow, there was this other time when Mum was making up jam in a big pot…"

"Something's up," said the gal, her head bobbing up and down. "Some kind of ruckus…"

"And Mum's stirring this pot and…"

"Is that a train going out?"

"A train? Um, no… no. Anyhow, she got out her roundy wee

spoon and…" but the gal was already clambering down from her case and starting to elbow her way through the crowd.

"Look, keep an eye on this while I go see, will you?"

"Um, are you sure that that's a good idea? I…"

"Just for a sec, okay? I'm just going to go and have a look…"

"Listen, I think you ought to stay here, 'cause…"

But with that she was off, pushing her way through the throng like a swimmer setting out to sea. I set off in hot pursuit but her case was so heavy, I was soon left behind, gasping and panting, my arms practically falling out of their sockets.

I mean, why did her case have to be so heavy and clumsy anyway? And why was there always somebody in the way, bod after bod, and all of them weighed down with luggage of their own? I mean I tried to manoeuvre it between them but the dame was off, disappearing amidst a sea of bags and faces.

"Ah, lady," I said, but then I suddenly froze. Right in front of me was a guy from work — in fact the guy from the desk right across from mine, truth be told — and we both did a kind of double take, like actors in a silent film.

"Hey!" the mannie shouted. "Hans! Is that you? What are you doing here?"

I shrugged and tried giving him my most innocent smile. He wasn't buying it though.

"Don't you know that everyone's looking for you? Where have you been?"

"Ah…"

"There are people everywhere. The whole office has come to a stop."

I tried smiling again, but the guy didn't look very impressed.

"Have you got it? The report?"

"Report?"

He seemed to be eyeing up the fella's weighty yellow pad suspiciously.

"Hans, what have you been doing? The boss is going mad…"

"Um, hold on…."

To be honest, I didn't have a clue what the fella was going on about.

He was wearing a very natty suit and tie, but had a kind of distressed look about him, as if he'd just got dressed in a great hurry.

"I don't believe it! What are you doing here? Is that your case?"

"No, no, listen, this woman…"

"Woman?"

"Um, listen, it's not what you think…"

The guy's features started to twitch, and he looked like he was about to burst out of his suit.

"A woman?"

"Ah, I can explain."

"I don't know what you're playing at Hans, but everyone's out looking for you!"

A cracked electronic voice boomed from the tannoy, and the feedback crackled across the square.

"Do you know what's happened?"

"Listen, I've got to go," I said. "I'm awful late and it's my mum and dad, you see, I…"

The guy's eyes started to bore their way right inside me. But I really had to go…

"No, really, I'm sorry, honest…"

I tore myself away from him and tried to lose myself in the massed throng of bodies. What a loon, I thought. What's the fella babbling on about? But even so, my throat was clammy, my heart racing ten to the dozen. I have set foot, I realised, in that part of life beyond which one cannot go with any hope of returning. But what could I do? Feeling tired, I slowed down and stopped by an old underpass for a minute to catch my breath.

A rather ragtag-looking Salvation Army band had set up their instruments in a space near by, and I eyed them up suspiciously, trying to steer clear of the wifey and her tin. Now I admit that I wasn't looking too smart either, but the band seemed to be about on their last legs, everything about them just incredibly decrepit.

Keeping one eye out for the guy from the office — and my mum and dad, and, come to think of it, the fella with the red eyes too — I carefully examined my pad, which, to be honest, was more than a little creased in the crush. Here we go, I thought, watching the band get ready. What an absolute shower....

But when they started to play it was beautiful, beautiful! I'm not kidding! I'd never heard anything like it — so this is what music is, I thought. The brass wailed and I felt myself stumble and sag. Such beauty! I'd never heard such loveliness, such solemnity. But why was it so sad? Their lament spread over the whole concourse, swamping the station in grief and sorrow, tugging at one's soul. Ah, all the sadness in the world, I thought – it made you forget about the runny-eyes and veiny-legs, the crooked backs and sagging middles, it caused the plaza to waver and vanish, lost amidst the plaintive notes, it annihilated everything until all that was left was the hymn. And beyond that? What then might come into being?

Ah, the same old question: and then?

Listen: the old fellows blew and the band wailed and I no longer knew anything, the pain was too much. But when it stopped and the tin was passed round, my soul still felt ragged and lost. Where am I? I thought. Why this grief?

And that's when it occurred to me: hey, what ever happened to that girl's case?

IV

But by now it was all too late. I mean, people were crammed into every inch of the concourse, and there was no way I could fight my way back to where I'd started from, even if I could have remembered where that was.

No, I felt lost, adrift, mislaid. I let myself be carried by the crowd for a little while, passed to and fro by the buffeting waves, until eventually I ended up outside a shabby-looking waiting room, alongside a great mass of people pressed up against the glass. Inside it was even worse; I tried to force my way over to where the seats were but the benches were several bodies deep and the room stank of bad air and stale clothes, everyone squatting in a big pile of misery, just longing to be somewhere else. Tch, my poor feet, I thought, but nobody was willing to budge. And just look at these bods, I sniffed, stuffed into every nook and cranny, with yet another little yellow train just pulling in. Passengers grumbled and moaned, but while every train brought in another load, nobody on the concourse seemed to be going anywhere, like a pot being filled to the brim.

Alas, there was very little I could do. Unsure of myself, I flicked through the fella's crumpled yellow pad and leaned back against the guy behind me. Was that the guy from work outside the window? I tried to peer out through the pages but there were too many passengers so I quickly turned back to my book.

You see, the next entry started off with this kid going away to see his girlfriend, only he was too cheap to buy a train ticket and planned to hide in the loo. I mean, what kind of a plan was that? How could anybody be so dumb? Anyhow, when the ticket-inspector came along, the lavvy, of course, was occupied, and so this young guy found himself stuck outside in the corridor. Well, with no time to lose he rushed over to one of the doors, fiddled with the window and flung the thing open. Then, with no one looking, he hopped out onto the metal couplings between carriages and shimmied up to the roof, his limbs shaking and his teeth all-a-chatter.

What a jerk! Why couldn't he just have bought a ticket like everybody else? But no, he couldn't be bothered and now he was shivering up there on the roof with his jacket flapping and his nose all red and frozen.

"Brrrr," said the fella.

You see, it was desperately cold up there and the wind was blowing like a bastard. The fella could scarcely stand to open his eyes, and the sky looked vast and threatening, just this endless expanse of nothingness. Uh oh, he thought to himself. I have crossed that line between this world and the next.... But just as he started to look for a way out, a flurry of arms pulled the door back and the window slammed shut behind him. What a clod! What a fool! He scuttled back over to the door but by then it was far too late.

What now? he thought. What now?

You see the fella was well and truly stuck there, pinned beneath the weight of all that sky. No horizon, no features, just this roaring that would not cease...

Who writes this stuff? I thought to myself, pushed into a hot and smelly corner of the waiting room. Why such terror? But then I thought about the fella writing it, his eyes red and sore, his shoulders hunched, the mannie bent over his pad as if his life depended on it...

Clouds raced past, the rains came down, the wind never slackened – but what could the young man do? He watched the day turn to night and slowly turn round again.

His hair grew long and his teeth became sore and dirty. Eventually, the man too became old and tired, his limbs withered and his hair white. And in all this time, the carriage never slowed and the train never stopped; rather, it seemed as if like the tracks went on forever. Just once, on a grey, characterless day like any other, the train started to slow and in the distance the man saw a black solitary signal. He strained his eyes and stared before him. Was that another train, roaring through the nothingness toward him? And would, perhaps, someone see him there, pinned atop the carriage?

When he looked he saw an old woman's face, pressed hard against the windowpane, a face he did not recognise. As the two trains drew closer, the woman began to wave, jumping up and down with great excitement, and the fellow, emaciated, doddery, the merest shell of a man, climbed to his feet and waved back. With every little leap the woman seemed to get younger again, more familiar. What is this thing? asked the fellow. But then the train was past and the man could see no more.

123

I put down the book and suddenly, desperately, needed to go for a wee. Feeling a tiny bit panicky, I pushed my way out of the room and took off in search of the necessary facilities. I've got to go, I thought, find the path, even to the very bottom....

Unfortunately the lights down by the underpass were very poor and the walls all smelt of pish. I shuffled about for a while but there really wasn't much to see: a few obscure posters, a pile of old paint-cans, one horrible bench. To the left was nothing, and to the right also. Such strangeness, I thought. The blackness seemed all sticky and congealed, covering every inch like ink, like glue. And no sound either, as if the volume had been somehow switched off above. But where was I? I stumbled half-heartedly through the tacky nothingness and then my feet stopped at the border of what seemed to be completely empty space.

See how it gapes, I thought. Like a door lying open....

Down here the darkness stuck to everything, like tar, like paint, but the space in front of me was somehow different, though how exactly I couldn't really say...

Like a door or an opening, I thought. Or some kind of window, open to the night....

I dangled one foot over the edge and felt a kind of vertigo or nausea, as if my head were filling up with gas; but at the same time some voice inside me told me to go on, to take that step, finish the fall that had started so many years ago...

A window, I thought, A window that opens out....

But just as I was about to take that final step, to stride out into the void, a hand reached out from nowhere and gently pulled me back.

"Sir, sir," said a voice. "I wouldn't if I were you..."

Behind me was some kind of guard, a pair of dusty-looking spectacles on his nose and what looked like a stuck-on moustache pressed to his mug. Lit up by his torch, the fellow stared at me, kinda sternly.

"Sir, sir? Down there isn't for the likes of you. That's it sir, back from the edge. That space is dark, sightless, made up of all that is not. No, there's no reason to press on here, to cross that final line. Ah, sir! Take my hand if you think it'll help – the way is slippery here, darker than a clod of earth."

I wavered slightly and then started to retrace my steps. I was still slightly shaky, though. After all, who was this fella anyway? Although the mannie was dressed up as a railway man, atop his noggin he sported a clownish top hat rather than the regulation cap.

"That's it sir, over the cables and the service hatch. Watch your feet sir; it's like one long urinal down here! But look, there's more light again and therefore things to see. An ancient cigarette machine, a rusty looking fire extinguisher, a pile of old buckets stacked up against one wall. What's that, sir? Yes, the mundane things of a mundane world. And yet in some ways it seems a kind of miracle that these things exist at all."

I nodded and followed the fella back through the gloom and the murk. There were gaps in places, and deeper pools of oily pigments, but for the most part it was like wading through a kind of sticky nothingness.

"What do you think sir? For some melancholy souls, a thing is only real when its shape is already gone, and all that is left is its outline, the merest shadow of a memory. But I tell you, nothing is not the same as something, no, not even a hundred times nothing…"

What a strange shape the guy was! From behind, his hump and his cloak made him look like an old black crow.

"Right this way, sir, watch your trouser slops! The way back up is awful steep, and there's broken glass and spillages everywhere. Ah, that's more like it, mind how you go: the steps are treacherous and the handrail is kind of loose. What's that sir, this place? Just some kind of maintenance corridor, full of abandoned boxes and pallets and the like. Look – the passage is coming to an end, and the ancient service escalator awaits. Don't be nervous sir; that noise is entirely normal, just that the mechanism has seen better days. There now, the tunnel is opening up before us, though all the tiles are smashed and the lighting has been vandalised, it's true…"

But as I stumbled onto the escalator I felt one shoe get stuck between the steps, and heard the mechanism grumble and whine.

"Why this feeling?" I asked. "And why now?"

When the guard turned round, I saw that his eyes were sad and his 'tache was once again starting to peel off.

"Ah, sir!" he said. "The wheel that turns the world is still working, and with it the day and the night. Listen, can you hear? The sounds of the station above carry even here, containing within them the essence of the workday above…"

I whimpered and tried pulling at the sole of my shoe but it was well and truly stuck. The escalator rumbled and groaned.

"Excuse me, sir," I said, tugging plaintively on his sleeve. "It's just that… well, I was wondering if you might have seen my parents. I mean, I was supposed to meet them what seems like hours ago, but, well… um, my mum's about so high with a green hat, and my dad is following on behind, a great bag of fruit on his hump…"

The guard stared off into space as if considering the matter thoughtfully.

"About so high, you say? Well, maybe, but…"

Somehow the laces of my shoe were caught in the metal grooves, but I tried to keep the panic out of my voice.

"Do you know them sir? They're not as young as they used to be but my mum still hops from foot to foot like a bird, whilst Father is much more sober, his moustache the saddest shape in the world…"

The guard nodded and patted down his own 'tache with one simple flick of the wrist.

"Mm, now you mention it," he said, "I do remember a couple just like that, you know, the woman so high, the fella with his droopy moustache, but ah sir, that was years ago, many many years before…"

"What do you mean?" I asked, trying to worm my way out of my shoe. Above me, the tunnel looked like one great hole. "All this happened years ago?"

"I'm afraid so, sir," said the guard. "On that day, the whole station had been all cleaned up, everything swept and brushed and washed, and there was whitewash on the walls and flowers poking out from every box, and — ah, sir — there were people everywhere, all flushed and excited and frisky, and a trestle table set up with little plates of meat and crisps and a whole table of drinks, row after row of little glasses, with some kind of dessert spooned out into wee china bowls."

The guard smiled and tugged at the brim of his hat.

"And when the train pulled in, everybody suddenly rushed forward and the band played 'Love Divine' and there were whistles and cheers and bells, and the crowd, they picked up the newly-weds and plonked them on the carriage, as if they were dolls, sir, as if they were little kids, and there they were by the doorway, the two of 'em, pressed together like the first and last pages of a book, and everybody was yelling and cheering and shouting 'goodbye, goodbye' as the couple began to wave."

I nodded and then looked down at my great sweaty hoof. Around us the tunnel seemed to go on forever, a strange round space, like the inside of a chute.

"And then?" I asked, my throat feeling kinda sore.

The guard's back was dark and enormous, an archway or some kind of hatch.

"Well, sir, the carriage itself, it was looking pretty packed, and as the train set off you could see 'em wandering up and down the corridors, checking their tickets over and over again. And then, when they found their seats, the compartment was absolutely jammed, it seemed, every last seat taken. Luckily, though, when the other passengers finally spotted the girl's long white dress, they shuffled over and made room, and then the great grey canopy of the station was ceremoniously rolled away, peeled back like the opening of a can..."

I tried to catch his eyes, but he seemed to be staring off into space. "Well, I don't know," I said, trying to remove my foot from its sock and listening to the escalator grind and scrape. "I mean, all this was years ago, you say?"

"Mm," said the guard, his gaze seemingly fixed somewhere between this world and the next.

"Or perhaps in some kind of second life, a dream life, like that between the pages of your torn yellow book..."

With a pang of fear, I suddenly realised that we were nearly at the top now, and the metal jaws of the final step hungrily beckoned.

"But where were they going?" I asked, watching the moving walkway start to disappear. "And what happened next?"

"Oh sir," said the guard, "the fields were grey and featureless and the tracks seemed to go on forever. But after a while there was suddenly some kind of a bang and a clatter and then a great commotion started up, somewhere toward the back of the next coach along. 'What's this?' asked one of the passengers. 'What horrors now?' Well, after a few minutes the whole carriage started to sway erratically from side to side, and the passengers all stared at each other apprehensively, but the couple, mm, they just nestled closer, practically curled up in each other's laps."

With the end of the escalator coming closer and closer, I finally freed myself from my shoe just in time to see it savagely swallowed by the awful machinery below.

"Mum and Dad?" I asked, practically gasping for breath. "Oh sir, what then?"

The guard lowered his voice and we both stood on solid ground at one end of the concourse, me without a shoe, of course. There were still commuters everywhere, milling about in odd groups. But what was that going on behind the railway guard's shoulder?

"Listen: the engine faltered and banged and when one of the passengers got up to investigate, an old man suddenly appeared in his place, the old fella dressed in a railway uniform and carrying a clip-board and pen. Well, the old wheezer looked around, checked his pad, and then strode over to where the fella was clinging to the soft warm bump of his wife. 'Sir?' The fella coughed and tapped his pad. 'Sir, if I could just have a word...' And as soon as the young guy opened his eyes, the fella had him up on his feet and was leading him off down the corridor, past a whole host of sleepy, surprised-looking passengers, their arms full of all kinds of wood and lumber. 'Just this way, sir,' says the guard and the guy didn't even have time to nod. Instead, the passage echoed to the sound of sawing and chopping, bits of furniture tossed out from every compartment. 'If you please,' says the guard. 'No time to lose.'"

And on the station, more and more passengers were pressing in all around us, seeming almost to pick the fella with the moustache up and start to cart him away.

"Mister, Mister!" I cried. "Tell me, what happened next?"

The guards voice echoed mysteriously across the concourse as the crowd lifted him up on their backs.

"Well," he said, "it seemed as if all the passengers were busy hacking chunks from all the rear carriages, chopping them down for firewood, and then lugging everything along to the cab at the front. I mean, don't ask me why; the guy was handed a stiff pair of boots, a bright orange vest, and an axe, and then his name was ticked off from a great long list in some kind of a yellow pad. When he got to the last coach, huge gashes had been hacked into the walls and a large chunk of the roof was missing, the carriage like a man without a cap. Above him the night sky looked like one enormous hole. What a night, he thought. Less like space than the grave...."

By now the guard seemed almost swallowed up by the mob, but I could still hear his voice, and pushed my way through to find him.

"And then?" I cried.

The guard's moustache criss-crossed the plaza, but his 'tache seemed to go one way whilst his hat went the other.

"Listen," he said. "Around a pile of splintered wood, there were several guys playing cards and drinking tea. 'Some job, eh?' said one, beckoning him over to sit down. 'I mean, just look at the state of these facilities.' All around them passengers were methodically demolishing every side of the carriage, loading everything onto barrows and trundling them off down the train. 'One big balls-up from start to finish,' said another. 'Who's in charge of this shower anyway?' Then the fella was handed a cup of tea, and the guy with the pack of cards dealt him in, and all the time more and more cracks were appearing, in the walls, the floor, great jagged fissures opening up as the fixtures and fittings were violently, randomly, stripped away.

"At that moment an evil-looking guy with apple cheeks and a little round tum, suddenly appeared next to him. 'Something harder?' he asked, proffering a wee plastic bottle above the fella's mug. 'No, no, m'okay,' said the fella. 'Ah, c'mon. Time for a quick one!' says the mannie, and our fellow starts to falter. 'Well...' 'On a night like this? C'mon, don't be silly. Sit yourself down; the train might be falling apart but this night goes on forever. Hey what do you say? Join me in a wee nip?' And the fella grinned an idiot grin and sidled up closer to him, a bottle in one hand and a dirty, torn sack in the other. 'I mean, just look outside,' said the strange wee man, pointing to where the great black sky was tearing itself into pieces, a huge dark canvas coming apart at the seams. 'Might as well sit on your arse, warm your cockles, play some cards... what do you say, pal? Join me?'"

"And the fella thought, Oh my love — what has overtaken me?"

But with that the guard completely disappeared from view, his top hat sinking fast beneath the sea of people.

Ah, me! But, you know, it didn't really matter, didn't really matter at all, 'cause by flicking through the yellow pad, I could finish the story all by myself.

"You see," I told a passer-by, the station seeming to close in all around us, "by now more and more refugees from the rear carriages were being pressed into every available space and all of the compartments were full to bursting point, with all sorts of folk slumped outside in the corridor too."

It was so noisy in there, I practically had to yell into the guy's face.

"Listen," I said. "When the gal woke up all she could see around her were bodies. Somebody asked her to hidge up and she found herself squashed tight against an armrest, her bustle crushed and her hem caught beneath the seat. How crowded the carriage was! Like the pages of a book all crushed together. She felt another fella squashed up against her and it was only then that she noticed her wee mannie was gone, replaced by a throng of people she'd never seen before in her life. But where was he? Confused and sleepy, she gathered up her wedding train and pushed her way out of the compartment, her dress awful creased, her headdress squew-whiff. 'My love, my love,' she whispered. 'What has o'er taken you?'"

I too was picked up by the crowd, but didn't let that stop me.

"You see," I told the people all around me. "Near to the front of the train a seemingly endless queue of customers were filing into the dining car and the place was packed out with hungry bods shouting and jostling for service. As soon as she entered the woman had a tabard plonked over her and was placed in charge of the food — laying out the pastry, adding a dollop of filling and then humphing the whole load over to the ovens.

"'Listen,' she said, 'there's been some kind of terrible mistake. I'm looking for my husband — a tall fellow with a droopy moustache, like so,' but alas, nobody was listening, so she had to roll up her sleeves and get stuck in, her tabard resting awkwardly on her wedding dress. It wasn't long before her arms were aching and her burnt hands felt terribly sore. And pretty soon her dress was smeared with grease and juices while all the time more and more hungry passengers kept on pushing in.

"But truth to tell, the rest of the train was in an awful state too: windows broken, latches smashed, big scratch marks gouged along the walls. In the corridors light fittings hung loose, doors dangled off their hinges and a chill wind blew through dark gaping holes in the husk.

"And the sound of the wind was unbelievable! In the packed compartments folk shivered and sniffed, wrapped up in all the clothes from their suitcases. 'Such terrible facilities,' whispered one old dear, squeezed up against a draughty window. The heater gave off a hiss but no warmth, whilst the lights flickered and dimmed."

I felt my clothes starting to rip, saw my last shoe carried off one way, and one sock the other.

"And as for the carriages at the rear — well, by now they were almost entirely gone. Every last scrap of kindling had been smashed and used up until only the dull steel bogeys remained."

My voice felt tired, my throat hoarse and sore.

"In her break, the woman watched the navvies lugging the lumber down the swaying corridor, the big hulking guys straining under the weight. She listened to the sawing and the banging, the clacking of the wheels and the howling of the wind; her hair was streaked white from the flour and she looked old and pinched. Some hoary-haired old fella wheeled a wheelbarrow full of kindling down the corridor and she moved aside to let him pass. His gait was uncertain and his shoulders hunched but they didn't recognise one another and the gal went back to the dining car and back to her pots and pans."

My arms felt bruised and I felt a sudden pain in one of my knees.

"Ah, me!" I said. "By now only the bare skeleton of the train remained, and on it went, huffing and puffing, barrelling its way through the infinite, ceaseless, night."

My heart was breaking, breaking!

But what did the yellow notebook say? *Bags and cases spilt out from the luggage racks, blocking the corridor and filling the train. Beneath these were horrible old clothes and scraps of fabric and cloth. And beneath those? Skin and bones, the remains of the departed, the sediment of the dead.*

And so saying, I closed my eyes. The crowd carried me this way and that, a great sea of passengers and bodies, before depositing me back where I started, abandoned and bereft, lying in a great untidy heap by the benches. I have been abandoned! I thought, eyes screwed up into little black dots.

V

Anyhow, after that things happened pretty quickly. Just as I was starting to drop off, I felt this sudden blow to the small of my back, and when I turned round I caught another one, right in the nuts. Stars exploded above me and I felt a sharp pain spread out from my gut. When I looked up, the fella from the snug was louring over me, his eyes red and crazy, his face that of a monster.

"Bastard," he shouted. "Bastard!"

I tried to answer but had problems getting air down my windpipe. I mean, what had gotten into him? The fella looked like some kind of loon.

"Where is it? Where's my pad?"

He was really having a go at me, you know. Kicking, shouting, punching...

"Give it back, give it back!"

I murmured something pitiful and tried rolling up into a ball. "Ayghh," I might have said.

"Where is it? Where is it?"

Ah, it hurt! Shooting pains raced from my limbs to my head.

"My pad! My notes!"

I felt his boot going in, and my body flop back.

"Where is it? What have you done with my book?"

I tried to say something, but no words would come out.

"My book, my book!"

The kicking went on for quite some time and after it I felt a pair of sweaty mitts going through my pockets.

"Take it, take it," I tried to say, and at that very moment he pulled something away from me, legging it away from the concourse, the great yellow book in his hands.

"Urrr," I said, but the fella was already out of there, his shape fast disappearing across the plaza.

Yes, the mannie was gone and I was left lying there. What had happened to him I didn't know. The fella pegged it out of there, but whence I could not tell.

And me? My back hurt, and my head and my knees but no one seemed to pay me the tiniest bit of notice. All the passengers simply stepped over me and I decided to stay there for a while, letting the world do as it liked. I mean, I suppose I cut a kind of pathetic figure lying curled up there on the floor, but to be honest, I could have stayed there all day. I mean, why not? All around me commuters were scurrying to and fro, dashing this way and that, and I just lay there in a broken heap, feeling — oh, why try to deny it? — a kind of blissful peace. Ach, is that so hard to understand? I felt my eyes droop and my muscles start to relax. I mean, it wasn't as if I had finally given in to laziness or lethargy or anything like that. Rather, it was as if the day's work had finally come to an end.

Listen: a kind of fog seemed to creep across the scene, and I could hear a strange hissing sound in my ears. It was as if the station were still there, but muffled somehow, as if everything were taking place behind some kind of wall.

Mm, what's that? Yes, everything seemed to be fading and dissolving, the waiting rooms, the benches, the computer screens. Half-recognisable voices drifted across the partition and for a moment I thought I could hear the woman with the suitcase saying my name, but then I thought, hey, how does she know my name anyway? All around me, parts of passengers wobbled and fell apart, their shapes breaking up and their outlines starting to blur. At one stage I was sure I caught sight of my boss and a gaggle of co-workers from the office, but then they too passed over me, like a kind of cloud formation above my head.

A hundred times nothing is still nothing, I thought to myself. And, lo, a thousand times more...

And after that? Well, I wasn't feeling too clever. My limbs ached and my clothes stank. I moaned and I sweated. After a while a gang of kids came past and spun me on my back like a tortoise, and by the time they were finished I didn't know where I was. Well, this is it, I thought. At last I've reached the end.

But it wasn't — or at least it wasn't just yet. You see after being spun round and round like a fly-wheel, I looked up and saw a bank of monitors I'd never clapped eyes on before, a whole wall of screens which had somehow escaped my notice.

Yes, times, destinations, platform numbers...

And that's when it happened — that's when I suddenly realised my terrible mistake...

You see, it was all so simple! If only I hadn't been distracted by the fella with the yellow pad, if only I hadn't started to read it, filling my head with all sorts of fancies and nonsense...

But there it was right in front of me, as simple and straightforward as any thing could be.

Yes — all along I'd been gazing up at the arrivals board when I should have been looking out for departures. What a fool, what a clod! I mean, how could I have been so wrong? I followed the line of figures along the top of the screen and there was my mum and dad's train, as clear as a sunny day.

Of course — departures, departures! All sorts of crazy thoughts suddenly started rushing through my head. I mean, what had I been thinking about? I wasn't here to meet them but to see them off. What an idiot I was, what a fool...

But maybe there was still time. Picking up my bloodied limbs as best as I could I ran toward the ticket-gate, elbowing people out of the way and pushing my way through as if my life depended on it. No time for politeness, I thought, I've got to run, run.

Tch, how could I have been so stupid? Departures, departures, how could it have been anything else?

But the crowd was solid, hard, a great heaving mass which permitted no ingress.

"Out of my way, out of my way!" I cried.

And there was the platform — the right one this time — and there was the little yellow train with its little cargo of people. But it was all too late. A fat grinning fella with appley cheeks grabbed me as I tried to straddle the ticket barrier, and whilst we struggled I watched the signals alter and the wee yellow train slowly pulling away.

"Stop it," I yelled, "bring it back," but the crowd bunched around me and I felt the wee fella with the idiot smile wrestle me to the floor. His hair was crazy and his eyes looked hollow and sinister. "Who are you?" I asked, but the fella was terribly strong and swiftly pinned me to the ground, his short, stubby fingers clenched around my throat.

"Don't let it go," I mumbled, but now it was all too late. Behind him the little yellow train was edging its way out along the platform, its lights flickering and disappearing one by one.

"Mum and Dad!" I yelled.

But the train was already vanishing from my sight and there was nothing I could do.

"Yes," said the guide. "On the train, the old couple checked their tickets and hunted up and down for their seats, finally settling in this grubby little carriage away near the guard's-van. It was kinda chilly in there though, 'cause the heater seemed to be up the spout. It sputtered and hissed but failed to give off any warmth, and a thick pool of oil leaked all over the floor. In fact, the whole carriage was a complete tip. Graffiti had been scrawled over all the tabletops and broken glass littered the seats.

"Not very nice, is it?" said the old man."

"He struggled with their heavy leather bags and tumbled into his seat as if someone had let the air out of him."

The view from the window was of an ugly sprawl of warehouses, scrap-yards and empty sidings. It looked dark and unfriendly, utterly devoid of life. A terrible wind blew across the whole dismal scene and it smelt of petrol and smoke.

"Love, love? What is it?"

The old woman shook her head but didn't answer.

"My love?"

She sniffed and laid her head on his shoulder.

"Shh," he says kindly, "don't worry."

He put her hand in his and started to gently rub her fingers.

"It's all right."

His voice was tender and soothing, and she nestled in a little closer.

"It's okay."

I see them there, all frightened and old, and something breaks inside my heart.

"It's okay."

"Mm."

"Shh. Don't cry. Look! Look out of the window! The sun is shining and the day is singing a little song. There, look. Can you see? There's nothing to be worried about. There's a meadow showered with red poppies and blue butterflies, and wee blackberries grow amongst the hedgerows, all plump and dark and sweet. There now. It's okay. Close your eyes. Close your eyes and you can see better."

The woman nodded but there were big ugly tears rolling down her face.

"Don't be scared. Don't be scared. Look, we're out in the fields again. Put on your new dress and your wellies and come with me. Go on, it's okay. Why not climb on the back of my bike? If we fall off, the ground is soft and we're both still young."

The old dear stroked his bony hand and wiped her nose on his sleeve.

"And look, look! Even the trees are waving."

And do you know what? The trees were waving! Blossom showered down from their blackened branches as they waved goodbye, goodbye.

The feint sound of hammering and banging filtered down the corridor, but by then they were both too deaf to hear it.

VI

Was this the end? Even as we stretched out our arms, the picture was already fading, the crowd breaking up before our very eyes, turning themselves into blobs, daubs, tiny motes of dust. A hair flickered across the gate, the image jumped, and for a few terrifying seconds we were plunged into a great and fathomless darkness, a terrible blindness, black as the bottom of a well. Ach our poor hearts, we thought, what has befallen us now? We shuffled to and fro, holding on to our bags, tickets, each other. What were we supposed to do? We couldn't see the guide and it was as if we'd been abandoned too, left to fend for ourselves under some black and limitless sky.

"Where are you?" we cried. "What shall become of us now?"

We didn't have to wait for long however. Inexorably the dimness began to clear and we could begin to make out some awfully familiar sights — grey hills, grey stone, grey shops. And next to the grey chemist was a grey travel-agent, and a grey card-shop, a grey offy, and then there was a row of grey tenement buildings full of grey little flats, and in the tiniest of all these flats, right at the very top, an old man sat waiting for his soup, a tiny little fella, half the size of nothing, neither whit nor scrap nor jot, wee Hans...

Yes, all tours must end at the same place that they began, and we knew then that this tiny little fella, his beard as long as a staircase, must somehow hold the key to everything. After all, we muttered, there had to be a reason why we kept returning to this place – the gloomy tenement block beneath the castle, the drab wee town that seemed to exist only in black and white. Aye, there had to be an answer here, an answer to all those girls, those suitcases, this feeling...

O my friends — grannies, bairns, ladies and gents! We stared up at the old man and felt a sudden gust of wind blow through us, a wind that made our coats billow and our scarves flap, a wind that carried with it a sinister malodorous smell....

PART FOUR

The Sleepwalkers' Ball

I

Truth to tell, the old fella didn't feel so good. I mean, his back hurt, his knees throbbed, his feet were like two blocks of ice. My life's grown so small, he thought, my poor eyes can't see it. It was the middle of the night and there he was, still footering about, heating up some soup in a pot. Ah me, he thought, looking for his little roundy spoon; why this hunger, now? His belly growled and his joints ached, but for all that he blew loudly on his pot, splashing his whiskers orange. Such a tiny little man! No more than a smudge on a page really, shuffling between the kitchen and the lavvy, searching for his slippers. Listen, old man, they're under the sink! No, no, just over there. Ah, but it's no use telling him anything; I mean, just look at this place. It's dark and cramped and smells of wee.

The pot still bubbling, the old fella picked up a newspaper, folded it up, and shoved it back under his chair. Old man, old man, what about your soup? But by now he was sitting at his writing desk and waving his spoon about like a baton, making funny little squiggles in the air. The spoon was tiny, like a little kid's, and covered in coppery rust. He swung it, tapped it and used it to rub the end of his nose, turning the tip as orange as his soup. Then he stared off into space and started to hum a little tune, his moustache twitching as he did so. His spoon trembled, his cloudless blue eyes sparkled, his whole body seemed to vibrate like a tuning fork. But what was the little old man looking at? It was the middle of the night and outside of this room there was nothing, absolutely nothing: well, nothing you could see anyway. When you looked up, the sky was a big black hole, and when you looked down it was just the same. Ah, there must have been houses, blocks of flats, parked cars, street-lights and so on, but it was hard to imagine them. No, it was as if this little shoebox theatre were the whole world. Still, the old man seemed to be looking at something, 'cause after a while he gathered together some bits of paper and picked up his pen.

"My dearest Memling," he wrote, "How the devil are you? In fact, who the devil are you? Frizzy perm, glass eye, heavy make-up … that isn't you at all! Madam, hand over this letter immediately, or else I shall be forced to … ah, that's better! So Memling, who's the gal? And what are you doing letting her open your mail? I worry about you, carrying on at your age, when you of all people should be getting some rest."

It was cold in the flat and the old fella's radiator was on the blink. The soup was still bubbling away in its pot though, and the burner gave off a little heat.

"Ah, Memling, my oldest friend. I'm sorry that I haven't written for quite some time, but, you know me... all you want to hear from me are frolics or jokes or racy stories and instead I've been having problems with my boiler and my knees and the rent. Tch, who needs such realism? Memling, you've never been one for the real world, but — mm — old age is such melancholy slapstick. All this falling down and forgetting things and knocking things over. Listen, can you hear? The bones in my leg make a funny sort of knocking noise whenever I move. What a state; I'm skinny as a pencil stroke and they still won't hold me up. Still, I could write, 'Memling, I'm fit as a fiddle, and my legs are two steel springs'. In fact I think I will: Memling, I'm fit as a fiddle and my legs are two steel springs! See old friend, there's hope for me yet..."

The old man shivered and seemed to retreat inside his pyjamas. What a beard he had! Like a fresh fall of snow. And the rest of his thatch wasn't too shabby either...

"Oh Memling, I can't sleep! And that means I can't dream. But funnily, I seem to sort of doze all the time, which makes it all the more confusing. And that isn't the worst of it! I'm always rubbing my knees and now I've worn a hole right through my pyjamas. What's that? You too? Well, I can't say I'm surprised. We're old, Memling, old! But don't worry, I'm not about to go all maudlin on you. No, it's just that I've got to write this letter right now, smack in the middle of the night, because tomorrow I have to get up, make myself a cup of tea, go out to buy a spot of fish, perhaps take a turn around the park, and before I know it the whole day will be filled. So, to save time, I've decided to leave all my crossings-out — all the doodles and scribbles and smudges. Do you see? Now hold on Memling, it's cold and I have to find my dressing-gown."

But for some reason the old man opened the front door of his flat instead and paddled off along the corridor and down the stairwell, still holding the writing paper under his chin.

"Old friend, though it's been many years and the distance between us very great, I often think of you. Sometimes I picture you doing perfectly ordinary things — sitting in a café, reading a book, waiting for a train — and the picture in my head seems more real to me than my own life. I look around at my little flat, or the supermarket or the post-office and think, Ah, all this is but a pale copy of, well, something or other. Do you ever think the same? And then when the rain falls it makes everything look grainy like in an old film, and I think to myself, Why is everything in black and white? Oh, Memling, imagine that, everything in black and white! And yet, and yet... when I peer in my shaving mirror and stare intently at my own two eyes, they're cornflower blue, as I'm sure some woman told me, oh, many moons ago. Ah, I thought that would get your attention, Memling! Yes I too have known something of the vicissitude of love... And I've kept a good head of hair too; a deep drift of hair, Memling, a mighty avalanche of hair! Hm, are you jealous, old friend? Sure, I may be tiny and as thin as the rain, but my mane is my crowning glory as you can plainly see..."

The old fella drifted down the stairwell, an animated pair of pyjamas. Rather him than me, I say, wandering about in the dead of night! There was no light, no handrail, nothing to stop the doddery old fool from tumbling down the stairwell. I mean, just look at his feet, blacker than the coal-man's balls! Hm, what's that? Wasn't he cold? No, the old fella hardly seemed to notice. Down, down, down he went, his little white head and stub-end of a body. The doors on each landing were locked and silent, not even a crack of light spilling out from beneath them.

At the bottom of the steps the fella had to skip over a pile of old paint-cans and the decrepit remains of a bicycle wheel, and there were all sorts of other shapes, impossible to make out in the gloom. But the grey streetlight beckoned and suddenly there the old guy was, standing outside, squinting in a rectangle of colourless light. He looked up and down the road, picked up his pen, and continued to write, stopping every couple of feet to rest his pile of paper on a low wall.

"Memling, I'm walking up my road past the phone-box and all

the rows of bins and, ach, it's depressing! The tenements look tired and forlorn, the cars abandoned, the newsagent locked up. It is a world without sound, without colour. Everything here — the earth, the trees, the people, the water and the air — is dipped in a monotonous grey."

The little man, strangely delicate, tiptoed along the street. There was almost nothing to him, just a little grey snowflake or a speck of ash. "It is not life but its shadow," he wrote, keeping his paper pressed flat against one bony knee. "The world in negative, badly printed, silent as the grave! Yes, a world stripped of all sound, voiceless, mute. Listen, I'm jumping up and down now and there's not a thing to be heard. What do you say to that, old friend? Up and down I go and not so much as a thud, not so much as a slap. But I can smell the breweries to the west and the refinery to the east, so I know this is really happening. And I feel better out in the night air, somehow younger, as if I've got my second wind. Yes, that's it! Tonight it's kind of peaceful, beautiful almost; I can feel my gloom falling away from me like a cloak of old rags. Well, let's go, let's go!"

The old man trotted up the steep hill, past the bait shop and the dry cleaners and the snooker hall on the corner. Two guys in T-shirts were lying sprawled out on the pavement, fast asleep by the look of them, and the old fella waited till he'd tiptoed warily around them before going back to his page.

"Tell me Memling, do you ever think of me shivering in this grey northern town, no decent bus-service and no picture-house for me to while away my old man's hours? But, you know me Memling, I couldn't live anywhere else. I am dour of heart and grey of soul; this wee charcoal town suits me fine. If I were to jump on a plane, race over the sea and the mountains and the plains and plonk myself down in some sunny *piazza*, I'd expire in a second. I'm not kidding! I'm not made for the heat. Anyhow, who wants to see an old man's goose flesh, as hoary as his hair? Ach, just look at this beard, old buddy, as white as a sheet. No, I belong here, Memling, though the cold is turning my fingernails black and the drizzle plays havoc with my knees. Where else should I be? In the morning I lean out of my window and feed the wet birds. Tell me Memling, is it hot or cold where you are? I'm

144

sure you told me but I forgot."

The old man in his pyjamas tottered across the main road, but tonight no traffic roared past, or even pootered along by the traffic lights. No, the only cars in sight had come to a stop at the edge of the kerb, their drivers fast asleep at the wheel.

"It really is peaceful, you know," wrote the old man. "Like the sound's been turned off. Hold on, my pen won't write at this angle, let me sit down."

The old guy wandered over to a traffic island and looked up and down the street. Despite the fact that it was just after chucking-out time, there was no movement anywhere, the world soundless and still.

"Memling, I don't know what's going on, but there's nobody around at all – no alkies, no casuals, no glue-sniffers. It's like the whole town is asleep. Even the sky has its eyes tight shut."

He scratched the tip of his nose with his pen.

"Ah well, let's see what we can see."

The old man walked toward the old town-centre, occasionally passing a prostrate figure or a sleeping lump stretched out on the pavement. But he was right: the whole town was asleep. Nothing stirred, not even a drunk.

"What a town this is, Memling! Charity shops, bargain shops, boarded-up shops, and tartan knick-knacks for the tourists! Still, I can get everything I need at the little corner-shop, and anyway there's a chemist and even a post-office at the top of the road."

The old man's stick figure hobbled along beneath the streetlamps, its shadow even thinner than he was. Less a puppet than a string! Below his great hairy head, his pyjamas were pale and worn, his feet two pencil-stubs.

"What's the name of that pub I'm thinking of? You know, the one with the pool tables upstairs. Was it that one or another which served chips? Well, it's late and probably shut. Too late even for the kebab shop! Anyhow, enough of filling my face... let it go, let it go!"

It was windier up by the precinct, but the fella didn't seem to notice. His long white hair was streaming like a comet, his frosty beard streaked with soup.

145

"Listen, old friend, it's awful hard writing on the hoof since your pen goes straight through the paper. And it's hard to find a good, solid surface to rest on, 'cause it's tricky to write and watch where you're going at the same time. I mean, just look at my handwriting, it's all over the place! But I'll persevere for your sake 'cause something is up tonight, a mystery or some such thing. All the world's a-bed, but here I am, footering about in my pyjamas in some funny little pantomime… Memling, I've just thought! What about my soup?"

The old man stared back the way, his blue eyes watering. Stop thinking about your belly man, your soup'll all be boiled away by now! The old fella turned around and made an eccentric motion with his pen, but just at that moment the wind blew up out of nowhere and his page flew off, dancing away down the street. The little sheet took wing and suddenly shot up into the sky, passing first a street-light, then a road-sign, and finally a bus stop; then it blew up into the black sky before drifting back down to earth again, turning left by the bank, a white square, flapping. The old man broke into a little trot and tried to grab it, but the page turned left by the estate agents, starting to pick up speed again. Quickly, man! The old fella jumped to and chased it down an alley, coming onto the back lane leading up to the castle. There the paper spun and swirled, sucked up into the night sky and scudding along by the old stone wall. The fella, by now looking none too clever, hobbled after it, rounding the corner just as the wind started to drop again. He looked left and he looked right, straining his eyes in the half-darkness, but there the paper was, lodged between a line of green and sticky railings, and he ran to grab it, puffing like a steam-train out of fuel.

"Memling, Memling, I thought I'd lost you! I'm too old for this chasing around, I tell you. My knees, my knees!"

The old man sat down on the steps and gave his knees a quick rub. In places his pyjamas were thin and faded and you could see his little frame shudder when he breathed in and out.

"O Memling, O Memling! But my heart is feeling better now, so I can tell you where I am. I'm on a steep, cobbled hill near one of the old snickleways, the steep steps covered with dog muck and broken glass, and from here I can see right into the windows of the nearby

146

houses but, ah, they're all terribly still, not a squeak from any of them. In one I can see a whole family slumped senseless in front of the telly, mum, dad, kids, dog, and the mannie on the telly is sleeping too! Well, I'm not surprised; after all, it's late and tomorrow is a working day. In fact, Memling, I wouldn't mind nodding off myself..."

The fella climbed up the steps and came out by the cannons on Castle Hill. There he rested his little legs on a council bench.

"From up here, you know, the town doesn't look so grim and foreboding. Even the shapes in the gloom seem sort of gentle: the steeples, the multi-storey, the distant monument. Oh, and the silhouette of the hills, broken-backed and weary. Yes, there's a softness to the night... what's that you say, before the hills? A few farms and the half-built enterprise zone, the lazy coils of the river, the old town bridge. But even this weariness seems beautiful, a kind of restfulness... Look at that, Memling: even the cats and the dogs and the birds are asleep."

Funny little fella, smaller than the dot of an i. He turned over the piece of paper and started to scribble in all the margins, pausing once in a while to rub his knees.

"Just look, my legs don't even reach the ground! Of course, when you see what's down there, that's no bad thing. Ah, well! I remember reading somewhere that there are only two ways of looking at things: as if for the first time or as if for the last. And we both know where we are, eh, old friend? Yes, there are more things missing than there are to find! But for all that, there's something different about tonight, something grainy and speckled and blurry. And that's not all — listen, Memling, all this soup I eat is playing havoc with my system! Honestly, you wouldn't believe the sounds that rise up from my insides. And yet, when I go to the lav, nothing at all! No, really; I must be filling up with soup by now. Where does the stuff all go?"

The guy's pages were pretty full by now and he turned the paper this way and that, his scratchy handwriting covering nearly every line. Wait, old man, what's that behind you? Turn around, Old Fella, there's someone there! But no, he still couldn't hear us; he was too busy scribbling, his mug pressed tight to the paper.

"Memling, Memling, disaster! I've been whittering away to you about nothing in particular and now I've run out of paper. Oh, my friend, what have I done? Wasting your time and my last few spaces with next to nothing: O, forgive this foolish prattle! There's nothing worse than a yapping old fool with time and ink on his hands. It's true what they say, Memling; without a stick, old age is lame! But what to do, what to do? Memling, I'm writing this line very small to fit it in, but even the line 'I'm writing this very small' is taking up precious space, and this line too! And even the words 'and this line too', are swallowing up my page, in a kind of vicious circle. Oh, if only I hadn't gone on about my soup ... but even now I can see the end coming, the last few empty inches: Memling, Memling, I'm at the end! Hang on, I'll have a look in the rubbish bin and see if there's any paper..."

The old bloke rummaged through the litter and the plastic bottles, virtually climbing into the bin. Such a funny little fellow — only half a shadow at best. Behind him some kind of figure glided up the hill, an insubstantial wisp of cloud; but before the figure finally vanished, the old man straightened up and rubbed his 'tache.

'Wait,' thought the old man. 'What is this thing?'

He rubbed his eyes and the figure reappeared, crossing the road between two parked vans.

A spectre, he thought, An apparition abroad in the night. Then he turned back to the bin.

"Memling," he wrote, "I'm writing this in the margins of a *Daily Record,* so you'll have to follow what I'm saying round the borders. But listen: cross out what I said earlier about this not being a dream! A young beauty has just walked past, dressed in negligée and flip-flops, and is heading up to the castle. A disgraceful dream for an old man to have, but Memling, what can I do? She keeps disappearing in the shadows by the Thistle hotel, but I can see the top of her head and the edge of her nightgown, and you'll just have to imagine the rest. Yes, that's right, a girl! Now hold on a sec, my sentence seems to have curled up round an advert. You'll have to follow this over the newsprint I'm afraid; that's it, second column down, keep going! Right, where were we? Memling, the girl is taking off! But I'm tailing her, old buddy, following as best as I can..."

The old man in his pyjamas scuttled after her, still trying to write on his folded paper. His sentences were all over the place and his pen kept going through the paper.

"I'm alongside the old town cemetery, but — alas! — I can't keep up. Hey, it's not my fault, Memling! These cobbles are awful hard and I'm not so nimble on my pins. Oh, my friend, what if she turns around and yells? An old man out in his pyjamas in the middle of the night... ah, there's no dignity in any of this! Maybe if I went home, finished off whatever might be left in the pot, pulled back the bedclothes, made myself cosy... what do you think?"

The girl in the nightdress looked like she'd blown in off a washing-line, a slip of a thing. The old man too was as white as a sheet, his feet two little black dots.

"Miss! Oh, Miss!" he yelled.

She reappeared from behind a row of spindly trees and made her way up the hill. The old man followed, hobbling on the cobblestones.

"Hullo! Hullo!" To be honest he wasn't sure that any sound was coming out. The girl's scanties were very white, her head a black peony.

"Memling, I'm at the top of Castle Hill, near to that last turning, and, well, hold on, I'll draw you a diagram to show you where I'm going."

The old man scratched a few lines, but found it hard to jog and sketch at the same time.

"Hm, this is harder than it looks; it's next to impossible to get all the roads and buildings and signs in the right position. Just look, that corner's all to cock for a start! But, Memling, listen, I've spotted someone else! Some other fella, short, skinny, wandering around in his night things... Memling, is that you? Wait, old friend, wait for me! I'm rounding the last corner now."

The figure, however, vanished as quickly as he'd appeared, and though the old fella lumbered past the restaurant and the museum and the little painting gallery, there was neither hide nor hair of him.

"Memling?"

Suddenly the old fella realised that other shapes were making their way up to the castle, and the tired old man paused before the esplanade, gathering together his messy pile of papers as best he could.

"Memling, where are you? I'm near the top of the hill, near all those tourist kiosks that you used to complain about, with their postcards and their flags and their tartan pencil-cases, all shut-up now of course. But listen, we're not on our own up here! There are other folk standing around, dressed in pants and pyjamas and nighties and sometimes naught at all. And that's not all; right by the gate to the castle there are trestle-tables with snacks and drinks and dance-cards, and a bunch of uniformed bods letting people into the castle-grounds. What's going on, Memling? Everybody looks a bit sheepish and a bit sleepy, but people are starting to drift inside, and I'm walking with them, pocketing a handful of crisps and sipping something fizzy, and we're over the drawbridge, and everything is lit by little lanterns, and a sign reads 'The Sleepwalkers' Ball', so that must be where we are."

The old man gazed up and down the courtyard. People in their night-attire were everywhere.

"Was that really you Memling? I didn't see long enough to tell. But Memling, if you can see me, I'm over by the ticket kiosk, the little fella in the faded pyjamas. Look, I'm jumping up and down and waving! But maybe I should just keep on writing; hold on, I'll rest this by the old well and fill in my last page."

Inside there was quite a crowd. Most of the somnambulists congregated in a second courtyard before the great hall or else spilled out into the little rose-garden, where there were refreshments and games and stalls selling tickets. Overhead, the sky was dark and empty.

The old fella peered over the edge of his paper: nightclothes, bed shirts, gowns, nighties, greyish pairs of pants. The guests stood around uncertainly but with little sense of embarrassment.

"How beautiful our little town looks from here," said one woman in a polyester nightie and curlers, and those nearest to her looked over the ramparts at the little orange street-lights below, like stars, only upside down.

"It's hard to believe," said one old gentleman, dressed in some kind of romper suit, "that somewhere down there lies our ordinary houses, our ordinary bedrooms, the whole waking world. How small it seems from here! Get up, get dressed, go to work; the desk behind which one's life disappears. Yes, it's a strange feeling…"

"D'you know I can't even see my block of flats," said this young guy with nothing on. "It's like it's vanished entirely."

"What a dump! Let it go, I say," said a teenage girl at the back.

The woman in curlers shuffled closer to the edge, trying to spy her house.

"Y'know, I'm sure I left a light on," she said, "and it's an early shift tomorrow…"

"Careful," said the old gent, averting his eyes from her backside that was poking out over the edge.

"I can see my window!" she yelled. "There it is, all the way over there."

"Big deal," said the girlie, who was rolling the bottom of her T-shirt up and down like she needed the bathroom.

"Which one?" asked the guy in the romper suit.

"There, by the cooling tower."

The bare young man followed her finger across the skyline, but still couldn't see it.

"There, there, the next one down!"

"Which, that one?"

"Aye, the one with the lamp on. That's my window!"

And the whole crowd (even the young girlie) stared at the little prick of light, a tiny spot in the darkness.

"Ah!" said the old gentleman, holding onto the turret.

A breeze rustled through all the nightgowns and bed shirts, causing them to billow and twist.

"Yes, that one's mine," said the woman, climbing back down from the battlements.

The old gent helped her down.

"Watch your step, down you go…"

The little group looked very pale and flimsy against all that darkness, their underthings like wee torn rags; when the wind caught them it was like there was nothing inside at all. But for all that, they nattered away quite cheerfully, and some played around on the cannons or by the old dungeon steps like they were little kids. Just look at them;

like washing that's been blown off the line! And all the while waiters kept bringing snacks, and waitresses in little black and white outfits wove their way through the throng. What service! The old man already had two drinks but this waitress swiftly plonked another one between them.

"Whatcha writing?" she said, saucily. She was a kittenish thing with a streak of gravy down her apron.

"Oh, just a note to an old friend," he said shyly. "Nothing very exciting. But tell me," and he leaned in confidentially, "Miss, the night, dreams, sleepwalking, what does it mean?"

"Hey, I just work here," she said, shrugging. "Could you hold this tray for a second? My feet are killing me."

"Ah, oh, sure." He put down his pen and paper and took the tray on the crook of his arm.

All around him people were drifting from stall to stall, some of them carrying the things they'd won.

"You're a pal." The waitress stretched like a cat and then started to fiddle around with her shoe. "I'm sure I've got something stuck in here," she said, peering into it and rooting around for a while.

"Long shift, eh?" said the old man, who was already beginning to struggle with the tray on account of the fact he was a very tiny fellow.

"I need the money, you know? I'm buying a bike. A big one," and she seemed to push her whole arm into her delicate little shoe.

"You're buying a motorbike?"

"Yup. To upset my folks!" The waitress beamed at the little old man. "Wait till they see me on it! There'll be a terrible scene and my dad will keel over on the spot. Or else I could buy something really ferocious. There's this guy down by the park who sells dogs, um, no questions asked."

"A dog, you say? What kind would you get?"

"Any. My dad's allergic. Say, can you see anything in my shoe?"

The old guy peered in.

"Well…"

"One of those dogs with big slobbery tongues. What are they called? The ones with the funny eyes, you know… hey, are you okay with that tray?"

"Well, maybe we could just rest it on the grass for a bit."

They both sat down on the lawn and the girl stretched out and yawned.

"These double-shifts are murder," she said. "I'm sure my feet are swelling up. And I'm getting funny veins all up and down one leg."

"Would you like one of your drinks?"

"Thanks." She took a big slurp but because she was lying down most of it went down her chin. Then she examined the ball of her foot. "Something's gone right through my tights you know and they're new on tonight."

The old man nodded in sympathy. "It's very late…"

"Look at the sky," said the girl, "there are no stars at all, not even one. It's just a big black hole. Hey!" She rolled over to have a look at him. "You're a tiny little fella aren't you?"

"Ah…"

"I've never seen such little feet. And such a great long beard!"

A group of guys in pyjamas were playing tug of war in the middle of the rose-garden, whilst other guests — in long johns, dressing gowns, slip and pants — clustered round the coconut shy and the darts game and the pin-the-tail-on-the-donkey.

"I went out with a little guy once," continued the waitress, toying with her shoe. "A fantastic dancer! You should have seen him in the clubs, he was great! He only came up to your chest, so when it came to the slow ones, all the girls were too embarrassed to dance with him. Luckily I'm as flat as a pancake so I didn't mind."

The waitress helped herself to another drink.

"Keep an eye out for my boss will you? If he catches me skivving again, I'm for the chop."

The girl curled up on the pale lawn, forming a languid S-shape.

"Wooo, I'm sleepy!"

The grey grass went right through the old man's pyjamas and pricked his legs. He tried rolling over onto the other cheek, but his knees and back were all complaining. I'm not sure I can get up from here, he thought.

"I don't know why I ever bought these shoes," the waitress

complained, yawning. "They're squeezing my foot into one giant toe. Look, see!" But the old man didn't want to get too close. "Pass me another drink would you?"

The rose-garden was starting to empty out now as guests drifted across the lawn and courtyard in the direction of the great hall; a couple of sleepwalkers lingered down by the old coaching-houses but that was all. Meanwhile a sudden breeze ruffled the old man's snowy thatch and a few stall holders had to grab hold of their wares.

The waitress slung her shoe away and it landed in a thorn-bush off to one side.

"I should really get back to the kitchens, you know," she said taking another big gulp. "But I can't get the hang of piling up those plates. Every time I take a step I get something down me; custard, soup, gravy, you name it!"

"Really?"

"Yup, everyone says I'm a messy pup, but what can I do? This job's rubbish, you know…"

The girl finished off his other drink. Someone was going round snuffing all the candles out, one by one.

"I only took it 'cause I need money to get my bike, you know? Then, I'll roar up to our house, rev the engine, and when they come outside, I'll yell, 'Mum, Dad, it's the open road for me!' Yep! I'll snap the visor shut and away I'll go, like a rocket! Hey, it's the open road for me…"

In fact her haircut already looked a little like a motorbike helmet. The wind couldn't budge her fringe at all.

"Oh, fella, what do you say? My folks are getting smaller and smaller and I'm shouting 'stand aside old-timers, I'm coming through!' And off I zoom…."

The old man looked thoughtful. "Ah, Miss," he said. "If only that were true…"

"You're a pal," said the girl with a smile. She let her glass drop and looked a little vacant. The rose-garden was pretty dark by now, lit only by the lights in the castle proper.

"Miss, we seem to be getting a little left behind," said the old fellow, looking around him. "Miss? Can you hear me?"

Yes, everyone was trooping off to the inner keep, shirttails and nighties flapping. Meanwhile, the girl was looking awful sleepy.

"Should we go in?" asked the fella, looking behind him at the gathering gloom. "I mean, with the others?"

In fact, the girl was flat out, and curled up on the grass.

"Ah, Miss?"

She seemed to be breathing awfully heavily, mainly through her nose.

"Miss? Look, everyone's going, we'll be left all alone in the dark. Miss? Oh, Miss?"

But the little 's' rolled away from him and the old fella found it hard to get up.

"Miss? I have to be going..."

Alas the waitress had passed out entirely, her bod lying down, 'pon the darkening ground, her tray lying there beside her. Looking around him, the old man leaned over, fished around in her mucky apron, and removed a sauce-stained pad.

"Memling," he wrote, flicking to the first blank page. "Everyone else has gone and it's time I was in there with them. Listen, can you hear music? I don't want to miss whatever's going on."

He looked at the girl's tired face.

"No, no, she'll be fine. Look at her! She's purring like a cat."

Old man, old man... ah, but he'll find out soon enough. What a tiny little man! Skinny as a pencil stroke.

"Memling, I'm sure the dancing's starting," he wrote, scribbling on his messy pad. "And there might be more to eat! Well, I better make a move. Really Memling, I don't want to get left behind. Don't pull a face, let's go..."

So saying, he left the waitress snoozing on the grey grass and followed the grey gravel path across the courtyard, her shoe still dangling from the thorn-bush as he tiptoed by.

II

"Memling, here I am passing through the old barracks, where there are more drinks to be had and a table where you can hand in your dressing-gown, and here I am passing through a smaller courtyard near to the armoury, and now I'm going up the steps to the great hall. That's me there, with the mass of white hair, walking up through the double-doors, past all the officials in yellow jackets and the men in their vests and the girl with rags in her hair. And here I am in the hall itself, with tables set out for dinner before all the dancing. No more drinks for me, Memling! My head is fuzzy and my heart all a flutter."

"Did you ever come here in the old days? Or was it all too touristy? It's been so long since I've seen you, I've forgotten what you thought. Where are you old friend? I'm standing under some kind of banner, looking up at the swords and the pikes and the axes, can you see me? For some reason there are candles everywhere but the lights are on too, making everything look kinda bright and glary. Memling, I'm looking at folk in their scanties and I can see everything — the bumps, the hairs, the bony and the bloated. And reflected in that funny-shaped shield, I can see myself, skinny as a walking stick, topped off by a heavy fall of snow. That's me, Memling, the old fool waving!"

"And this is me being seated in the middle of a long table, opposite a sad-faced young man drinking heavily, a baldie-bane in a pair of checked pyjamas, and some blowzy old dame in a slip. Hang on Memling, somehow I'm writing on my napkin instead…"

"Whatcha writing?" asked the blowzy woman, scraping out the inside of her melon. She had enormously fat arms, like toothpaste squeezed up to one end.

"Oh, just a letter to a friend," said the old man. "Nothing too exciting, I'm afraid. But tell me, Madam, what are we all doing here? Why this ball? Why tonight?"

The woman studied the little guy's reflection in her spoon.

"Ach, I'm always the last to know," said the woman, slurping up her melon juice. "But isn't it nice to be out? I mean, I don't know when was the last time I was out all night. And there's to be dancing, too!"

She poked the old fella in the ribs.

"You one for the discos, eh?"

"Oh, my knees gave out a long time ago…"

"No, give over! I bet you were a devil when you were young."

The old man bowed modestly, which made him look even tinier.

"Me? No…"

"Ah, c'mon, don't come that one with me…" and she swiped him with her melon spoon. What a dame! The woman had a fantastically wobbly face but the most beautiful mouth he'd seen in his life.

"It's true; I've always been the quiet type," the old guy said, though he deliberately made his eyes sparkle, the Romeo.

"Well, I don't believe it! I bet you're writing to some lady-friend right now, eh?"

She hidged up closer to have another look.

"No, there's no lady-friend," said the fella. "Who has the time at my age? You see, tomorrow I've got to have my breakfast, go to the fish-shop…"

A harassed-looking waiter squeezed between them, collecting plates.

"Mm, I don't believe a word of it! You remind me of this guy I went out with, oh, years ago. I mean, to look at him you'd say he wouldn't say boo to a goose. That's 'cause he was little and skinny and had a kind of timid expression on his face, like this."

Ah, this woman! Her mouth seemed enormous, like a great red boat.

"So, when we'd go to the club he'd sit right at the back and stick close to the loos, never once going near the dance-floor. Hey, I'd say, we've paid our cash, let's see those feet of yours, but he'd shake his head and look real sad and, ah, it broke your heart! Well, this one night, right after the dance, my fella went to get my coat from the cloak-room, but like I said, he was only a half-measure at best and no matter how high he reached, his little arms couldn't reach the peg. You could see him getting more and more embarrassed, because of his height and all, and there he was, hopping up and down with me fussing over his shoulder, getting more and more het-up, his face growing redder and redder, till eventually he got one arm stuck in his sleeve, twisted the other round his back, and suddenly realised that he was stuck there, like a cat in a bag. Ah, dear; he started to struggle but only managed to bring the coat down smack on top of him, turning round and round as he tried to make his way out from under it. Round and round he went, speeding up and slowing down, and it was something to see at that, really. I mean, he took my coat by the waist and spun it like a top and, oh, what I wouldn't have given to have been in it! Him and my coat went round and round and I thought, Ah, if only it was me in there...."

"Oh, that's not me, I'm afraid," admitted the old man. "I can dance neither the tango nor the twist nor the lindy-hop..."

"You're kidding! Look at those legs, they're made to dance..."

"These spindly things? Oh, I think not!"

The woman's face beamed.

"Ah, c'mon! Don't be bashful — I bet when you get going... Listen, you remind me of this other bloke I went out with..."

The next course had arrived by now – some kind of chicken in a white-wine sauce — and the little old fella tucked in, his beard practically in his supper. Funny looking fella! His little blue eyes peered out from under all that hair like forget-me-nots in a meadow.

"Once upon a time I went with this bloke to the pictures," said the woman, wolfing down her grub, "and on the way back we got stopped by this gang of yobbos hanging out by the bus station. Well, they started to make fun of my man on account of him being little, but when I told them where to get off, they just got more and more mad 'till one of 'em smacked him in the head, so of course I yelled at them all the more and another one punched him on the chin and then this other bloke started to go through his pockets, and when I really told 'em what for they punched my mannie black and blue. Honest, it was awful! Every time I came up with another name — pow! I gave 'em a tongue-lashing and — thwack! My poor fella was looking much the worse for wear by now, his nose all bloodied and sore. 'Hey mates,' he said, 'she doesn't mean it, leave off,' and after a while they started to tire, but I kept on cursing and yelling, till eventually one of them said to my mannie, 'Hey, enough's enough pal, tell her to give over,' and though they kept giving my man the occasional clout, you could tell their hearts weren't in it, 'till one said that he was going home and all the others started to follow, 'cause, you know, it was getting late, and tomorrow was a work-day at that, but I shouted 'Hey! Where do you think you're going?' and even though they looked completely knackered, they had to chase us down this alleyway, though of course since my wee man only had little legs they soon caught up with him. But, ah," said the woman, "he was lovely!"

The old man eyed her up over his mashed potatoes.

"Hm, I don't think that was me," he said. "I'm not much of a fighter…"

"More of a lover, eh?"

The dining-hall was very bright, like a bleached postcard left too long in the sun. And all the figures looked arranged for a camera too, albeit a bit fuzzy at the edges.

"I fear, my dear, I'm too timid for either."

"You? I don't believe that for a minute, you rascal."

"Oh, I'm humble man with much to be humble about," said the old man, flexing one leg. "And much too bashful in love."

The woman nodded and swallowed a green bean.

"Aye, well, the world is full of timid suitors. I remember when I was at school and I went for a walk by the river with these three boys who were all, mm, madly in love with me. It was a beautiful day so after a while I turned to them and said, 'Okay, who likes me enough that they're willing to jump in the river?' and straight away two of them took a running jump from the bank whilst the other says very solemnly, 'Oh, Missy, I've just had my uniform cleaned, I can't jump in'. 'Well then,' I say, 'who'll swim across the river and back to prove that they love me?' and two of 'em do but the third says, 'Are you kidding? There's barbed-wire and tyres and all sorts of crap in there, I'm not going in,' so finally I say to these three boys, 'Right then, who'll carry me to the other side on their shoulders?' and the two guys in the water start to fight for the privilege, whilst the last one says 'C'mon, look at the size of you and the size of me! I'll never make it!' and so the three of us splashed across, and there we were, messing around on the bank in the sun, just fooling around and having fun, and this fella looked awful sad and forlorn, and kinda cross too, watching

159

the three of us messing around on the other side. Well, he grumbled and sighed, muttered and groaned, until finally he too started to wade across, still whining about his uniform and looking like he was about to grizzle any minute, but then one of the guys shouted 'leg it!' and by the time he got to the other side we had gone, and all that was left was some wet clothes and a pile of shoes..."

The old man's blue eyes looked thoughtful.

"Aye, that might have been me," he admitted, shyly. "But you're much younger than I am, my dear..."

"Oo, he's a charmer," giggled the woman. "What did I tell you?"

The old man's moustache looked all rakish and jaunty, though it had bits of food stuck at the edges.

"Ah! If only that were true," he said.

"O, look at those bright blue eyes."

"Mm."

"Cornflower eyes!"

The old fella looked kinda bashful, and stared down at his plate.

"Well, this chicken's very good," said the old man, his chin poking over the tabletop. "Is it cooked in soup?"

The woman's big red mouth seemed to beam.

"Dinner at the castle! And not even the veg is soggy."

"No, not at all..."

"And lovely roasties..."

"Mm..."

In fact, the food seemed to be disappearing in double-time, like a speeded up film. Old man, old man, it's the middle of the night. Think about your poor insides, you glutton! And you with your pot still bubbling on the stove... but it was hard to imagine that his pot and his stove and his flat were still there. No, the castle seemed so bright and the town so dark, it was as if they were impossibly distant, like the distance between the earth and the light from a star.

The hall was packed by now, with sleep-suits, long johns and unmentionables squeezed together round the tables, like some kind of refugees after a fire or flood. The mood was bonny though, and all the folk nattered away happily no matter how undressed or dishevelled their neighbours were. Yes, there seemed to be a lightness, a strange unreality... At one end of the hall a band were setting up their instruments on a long wooden stage, four guys and a biddy, checking the microphones and tentatively peering out at the crowd. They seemed kinda elderly though, and their old fashioned uniforms — big blue jackets, brass buttons, peaked caps — hung from them, as if they'd got dressed in a hurry. One old wheezer struggled to mount the steps, whilst this bloke at the back examined his trumpet like he'd never seen one before in his life.

Tsk, what a shower! To be honest, the crowd looked none too impressed. The young guy, deep in his cups, shook his head in disgust, whilst Mister Baldie-bane fastidiously cleaned his glasses. Without his specs he looked like some kind of nocturnal animal caught out when the lights came back on.

The woman suddenly belched and said, "Oops, pardon me."

"Better out than in," said the little fella, nibbling at his chicken breast.

"Are you going to finish those potatoes?" asked the big old gal, eyeing up the bald guy's plate.

The fellow's large round eyes opened and closed, like some kind of sloth in a zoo. He barely seemed aware of his dinner and gazed around the room as if in some kind of trance, his eyes two red bruises on either side of his nose.

"Hello? Can you hear me?" asked the woman, scooping up some of the fellow's veg.

"Mm?"

"Are you okay?"

"Oh, I'm sorry my dear," said the man, looking down at his plate. "I thought for a moment I was dreaming a dream which I wasn't even in." He placed his glasses back on his peepers, which looked awful red and tired. "Please go ahead, help yourself..."

"Aren't you hungry?"

"No, no, it's too late for me; besides I never eat out unless properly attired." The woman tucked in and regarded the fella philosophically.

"Mm, it's funny to be here in just your night-things," she said.

"How strange it makes everything seem. Look! There's a guy over there in a pair of plastic pants."

The bald fellow looked down at his pyjamas as if he'd never seen them before. "It's like all our night-things have turned up to this ball, and we're just the things that brought them here. Or perhaps we're all just washing flapping on a line — it's hard to say! And yet, I feel somehow lighter tonight, as if something has fallen away from me. Do you know what I mean? As if I'm being buoyed up by something…"

The woman nodded and polished off his plate.

"Yes, it's odd," she said, running her lips over that great mouth of hers. "I mean, my house is miles away from the castle but now that I'm here I don't feel tired at all."

The old man imagined the woman crossing the little grey-town, her slip huffing and puffing across hills, roundabouts and subways, her beautiful red mouth floating a few inches above it.

"When do you think there'll be dancing?" the woman asked.

"Oh, soon, soon. The band is just tuning up."

"Hm. Doesn't look too promising does it?"

"Well, one never knows. I'm sure whoever has organised tonight's festivities knows what they're doing…"

The band were making a number of odd, and distinctly unmusical, sounds, and several people seemed to be dragging their chairs away from them.

"Mm, d'you think?"

"Why, yes! We've seen the castle lit up and the amusements and this dinner. And now the ball itself."

"Ah, a real ball! Well, I'll better pop to the ladies first. Keep my seat warm you two!" and the woman winked as she got to her feet, her cheeks all flushed and shining. For a moment, she looked years younger, almost like a teenager.

"Ta ta!"

Ah, what a dame! She skipped between the tables as if she were swimming through choppy water, a plump bathing beauty glowing with rude health. And look at that mouth bobbing about on her wobbly face… her whole face seemed to beam.

"Watch my chair!"

The two guys waved goodbye. They looked kinda funny sitting next to each other, one tiny with a great crest of hair, the other a tad portly without a hair on his head.

"Ah, 'tis a strange night," said Mister Baldie-bane, folding up his napkin. "And I'm sure these pyjamas aren't even mine...."

"Mm," said the old man, watching the wifey take her leave and drumming his spoon on the table. "She's some woman, eh?" he said, waving his cutlery in the direction of the fast-moving figure. "Like an open window, with the world streaming in!"

"Well, something like that," said the second fella, rubbing the top of his nose.

"It's true!" said the little guy. "An open window, the smell of cooking, a pot bubbling on a stove. Ah, me!" He rubbed first one knee and then the other. "I wonder where she's from and what she does... I mean, apart from tonight."

"Well, it's hard to imagine what all these people look like during the working day." The hairless fellow looked around the hall and shrugged. Dessert was being served, and several nightshirts were clustered round a big tray of puddings. "Never mind what strange compulsion brought us all here tonight; 'tis all a mystery, a thing imponderable."

The old man nodded and picked some broccoli out of his teeth.

"It's hard to imagine that there'll even be a tomorrow," said the bald guy, his big round pate gleaming beneath the shields and the armaments. A loud squawk came out of somebody's accordion, followed by the sound of something heavy and metallic rolling off the stage. "And even if tomorrow comes, do you think we'll remember anything of the night's festivities? I mean, the people, the food, the castle itself?"

"What do you mean?" asked the old guy, keeping one eye on the puddings.

"This night! The Sleepwalkers' Ball... when the morning comes and we have to go back to our ordinary lives, will any of this remain in our heads? I mean, the lanterns in the courtyard, the games and the amusements, the hall decked out for a feast... No, no, I fear not." He patted down some imaginary hairs and started to fiddle with his napkin. "No, it seems to me that the only people who will remember anything are the waiters and cleaners and stewards who work here, and for them this was just another night, another shift to be gotten through."

The old guy stared at the candle, its flame nearly invisible under the glare of all those lights. "D'you think so?" he mumbled through knitted brows, "That this is all there is?"

"I'm afraid so," said the fella. "In the morning we'll look at our black feet and food-spattered pyjamas and wonder what on earth we were up to last night. But this too will pass; then all that'll remain will be the working week. I mean, think: can you remember even how you got here? Your route or your means of locomotion? No, already your passage seems vague and insubstantial, a thing of fog and mist. It's true, my friend, everything fades towards morning…"

The little old man tugged his beard. In the bright light, his mane almost seemed to glow.

"Well, you say that, but listen: I'm writing all this down in a letter to a friend." And here he brandished the pad he'd swiped from the sleepy waitress. "You see, it's all here; a bit scrawly it's true, and with all my crossings-out and spelling mistakes left in, but, ah, as good as I can get it, given that I had to write it as I was going along… And when my friend receives it, in only a few days, dependent on the post, he'll be amazed, no, more than amazed, astonished! And given what I know about this friend of mine, he'll write straight back, so that in a week's time I'll be opening up an envelope and there we'll be, right there on the page, having this conversation. What do you say to that? All this will be saved, the castle, the ball, even that blowzy dame on the way to the ladies…"

"Do you think?" The baldie-man smiled, but rather condescendingly. For a moment, his eyes seemed to contain all the sadness in the world…

"Yes, yes, my good friend Memling. If I know him, he'll be in touch straight away. By return of post, I imagine."

But the bald fellow's eyes still looked tragic.

"Your friend, you say?"

Old man, old man, put down your pen! Look, the tables are being cleared and the band is about to play. Do you want to miss everything? Put your pad away and listen! The crowd are standing up, the lights are being dimmed, the waiters are moving out of the way. Yes, the guy at the front is shuffling forward...

"Yes, Memling, my friend..."

Shhh! Old man, listen! The music is finally starting...

And it was beautiful, really beautiful! No, really — even though the band looked ancient, with their uniforms all tatty and their instruments bashed in at best, the sounds that came forth were pure, sweet, like the opening of something long ago jammed shut. Hm, who would have thought that they had it in them? Oh, the wailing of the brass, the sighing of the strings! Even the old biddy's accordion sounded strangely moving, its black and white teeth gleaming in the candlelight. What were they playing? Some kind of reel? Swing? Stomp? The trumpet blew and the others followed. And suddenly, everything was forgotten — the runny eyes, the veiny-legs, the crooked backs and sagging middles... yes, all were vanishing, growing lighter and lighter, each note inflating the hall like some vast balloon.

Listen: when the bearded fella blew his trumpet a kind of shimmy passed through the bed jackets and nightshirts, making the nighties flap and the pyjamas spin. And all at once, the bedclothes starting to circle in a vast spin-cycle, a great eddy pulling all the rags and scanties, polyester pants and see-through slips, up out of their seats and twirling to the centre. Nighties billowed, nightgowns gyred, enormous Y-fronts started to reel; it was like the whole washing-line had torn free, casting underthings here there and everywhere.

Then the tempo picked up even more and people were falling over one another to get onto the dance floor, jostling with the waiters who were trying to clear all the dinner-things away. You could see guys in shirt and ties struggling with long tables, and waitresses grabbing tablecloths and cutlery, all sorts of pyjamas and gowns getting in the way and getting tangled up in the process, a sea of ill-matched clothing. Everything fluttered, flapped and spun; even the castle itself seemed to be revolving

But the little guy hung back. He could just about make out the beautiful red mouth of the woman in the slip, three extra puddings cradled to her bosom, but didn't dare get any closer. He should gambol with these knees? The woman looked beautiful, though. Her bosom heaved, her cheeks glowed, and her lips were as bright as a strawberry. Suddenly she spotted him in the crowd and started to wave, but then she too was swept away, picked up by the dancers and carried this way and that, one more figure bobbing about in the chaos. Round and round she went, only getting closer to her table if the music slowed down or if a particularly forceful bunch of waiters made a space.

"I've got some puddings!" she yelled, but the old man could only hear the music, the wailing of the trumpet and the sawing of the strings. So loud, he thought.

The blowzy gal made it three-quarters of the way across the dance-floor before two waiters carrying a trestle table headed her off. By the time she came round again, a spiralling mound of washing — long johns, camisoles, and pantalets — blocked the way.

"Some ball, eh?" said the old guy, idly fiddling with the elastic of his bottoms.

"It's very lively," agreed the baldie-man, who had been watching the festivities through his little roundy glasses. Their table had been picked up and carried away, the silent young man with it.

The old man nodded. "It makes my knees ache just to look at it."

Mr Baldie-bane leapt up as his chair was whisked away. "I don't think my poor heart is up to it, to be honest…"

As they watched, the woman in the slip shrieked and lost her grip on one of her puddings.

"Just look at all the people! My poor wee feet will be crushed!" said the old Joe, pulling on his beard.

"And I can't afford to lose my glasses," said Mister Baldie-bane, mopping his brow in sympathy. "No, I think it's better if we look for a place of safety, someplace where one has the space to think…"

Indeed it seemed like the revel was getting out of hand. More and more folk were pushing their way onto the dance-floor and the circle of flapping night-attire seemed to be getting ever tighter. Still, people laughed, sung and whistled, stamping the floor as best they could in their slippers. Blooms of light spread across the picture, and the dancers jumped, flickered and jerked.

"Can you see her?" asked the little old man, his little blue eyes scanning the chaos. But then the woman's beautiful red mouth triumphantly emerged from the sea of laundry, two large puddings carried proudly before her.

"Did you hang onto your spoons?" she asked.

How terrific the woman looked! Like a big dollop of ice cream herself.

"Oh, just use your fingers then. Ah, it's hot in there; my slip's sticking to me like a new coat of paint."

She wasn't kidding; her bosom parted the waters like the prow of a ship. The old fellow looked around for a chair and a little bit of space, but he was awful close to the dance-floor.

"Okay," said the woman, "who wants a dance? C'mon fellas, don't be shy; who thinks enough of me that they want to bop?"

What a gal! Like an ice-cream sundae with a big strawberry mouth at the top.

"Ah, my dear!" said the old man. "I'm only a little fella. If I tried to step in there I'd be crushed to a pulp. Besides, I still haven't finished my letter and I've got nowhere to put my pen."

Behind him the music started up again, causing the crowd to stir. There was movement, laughter, yelling...

"Hey, old-timer," said the woman, her red mouth bobbing up and down. "This is no time to be scribbling. I mean it! Put down your pad — you know you're not so backwards. C'mon, let's go! The floor's filling up and the band's already getting up a good head of steam."

The last bit was right. The band had launched into another number, and as the old man surveyed the tangled laundry – the flapping nightshirts and jitterbugging slips — his blue-eyes shone.

"Oh, madam, if only I could! But this letter has to be finished tonight and posted first thing tomorrow. If not, then I might lose everything — the castle, the lights, the ball itself... oh, my dear, though I would dearly love to, I must decline..."

"What do you mean? If you feel like dancing, dance! C'mon fella, a girl can die of waiting you know."

The underthings whirled, a giddy mass of cotton and winceyette, but the guy's cornflower eyes said no.

167

"I'm afraid my dancing days are past," he said sadly, pointing down to his knees. Go, go, enjoy yourself; I just have to take some things down in my pad." And then he turned his beard to the first blank page.

Old man, old man, can't you hear? The music is filling the room, occupying every space, blowing into every corner. There's happiness and light and music; the very air is intoxicated! But still the fella scribbles away regardless.

"Well, I guess it's you pal," said the woman, grabbing hold of Mister Baldie-bane's arm. "Hey, let's go! I don't want to miss the next number too..."

"Oh, Madam..."

"C'mon! Just follow me."

The fellow started to say something but the woman pulled him off into the merry-making, the two of them swiftly entwined amongst the spiralling nightshirts and bed socks. His bald head seemed to slip in and out of focus and his slippers moved in double-speed, but from time to time he came back round, a rolling barrel tossed from shore to gleaming shore.

The old man watched the revellers for a while and he took out his pad. *Don't say a word, Memling,* he wrote, *let's go, let's go....*

And yet still his pen lingered, his hand making a series of slow circles in the air.

"Memling, I need to find somewhere quieter, somewhere where I can tell you what has been on my mind for, oh, these many years. No, no, this racket will not do; I know you seek only jollity, Memling, but there's something I have to tell you. Let the revellers be: if they want to dance, then dance! But Memling, it's not for us..."

Even so, he stayed there for quite some time watching the laundry revolving around the woman's red mouth, the music filling his soul and making his heart pound, ten to the dozen.

III

The old man crept out of the hall and padded across the yard, his little white knees clicking on the flagstones. It was incredibly dark out there, like every last stone had been painted black. Ah me, he thought, so late, so late! His head looked like the top of a paintbrush, his body the thin stick behind it. A little light escaped from the windows of the great hall, but not much; all he could see were outlines, cross-hatching, spilled paint. At the end of one walkway, he found a garden littered with sleeping sparrows, a soft, brown lawn of feathers; no, not here, he thought. Then he retraced his steps and crossed an even smaller yard, this one piled high with black bags of rubbish, like clumps of enormous plastic mushrooms. How quiet it all seemed! His ears were still ringing from the ball, but otherwise he couldn't hear anything at all.

By now he didn't know where he was. Every wall felt like a solid block of black, as if his head had been dipped in a pot of black paint. But even here, down amongst the darkness, there were people working, toiling, slogging away. Yes, the endless toil went on! In a little alcove he heard somebody roll a barrel down a chute, followed by a distant thud and creak. The little old man made his way toward it, his pyjamas a kind of smudge against the darkness. Maybe here, he thought.

Opening a small side-door, he was surprised to find a wee snug, with a roaring fire, kitchy knick-knacks and Scottish country dancing playing on tape. Inside a barmaid was sketching something on a piece of paper, her quick brown hands running up and down the bar. The only customer was the sad-looking youngster who'd been sitting at his table earlier, sucking on a pint-glass, his face a perfect picture of misery.

"Ah, Missy, I just won't do it," said the kid, shaking his head at the gal behind the counter. He was dressed in his boxer shorts, and looked kinda peaky, even under the snug's dim lights.

His thick black beetle brows frowned.

"But you'd be perfect!" said the barmaid, pointing to her sketchpad and shaking her bangles in his face. "Listen, here's what I'd do. First I'd chop your head off and blow it up to double size. There now, do y'see? And this head of yours would be fashioned out of broken beer bottles, but I'd put all the labels on the inside so that if you wanted to read them you'd have to put the head on, like a diving helmet."

"Mm," said the young guy. His eyebrows looked like two black birds, resting.

"And this helmet would be perched on top of a mighty duvet, like a heavily lidded eye, just peering over the sheet. And emerging from the duvet, as if from roughly hewn stone, would be the naked human form, plucked from the womb…"

"I don't want to take my pants off," said the morose young fella, shifting anxiously on his seat.

"Oh, you don't need to worry," said the barmaid, smiling. "The body I'd make from bits of rubbish — takeaways, newspapers, a packet of cigarettes with one ciggie poking out. And the torso would be so distorted it would seem like a shower of rubbish, like it was raining paper and beer-mats and chocolate wrappers…"

The young guy looked kind of anxious. "She wants to do a sculpture of me," he said, turning blearily toward the little old man. The old fella seated himself on one of the barstools, his little legs dangling high above the floor.

"It sounds very ambitious," said the old man.

"All you need is enough paste and a good long stick," said the barmaid, her hair a great black minaret above her head. She was very striking looking, with dark, heavily lidded eyes, coffee-coloured skin, and pierced nose, lips and brows.

"Tell her I won't take my pants off," slurred the dreich young man, his face practically in the old man's beard.

"If I can get the body to stand up, then I can tack the duvet to one side and rest the eye on a pike," said the barmaid, swilling out a glass. Her piercings kept catching the light, a tiny constellation of stars. "The paper bod emerging from its cocoon; it'd be great! Now what can I get you?"

Her hair was enormous, a tall black tower; in truth it made the old man dizzy just to look at it.

"Oh, I'm not much of a drinker," said the old fella, modestly. "A Coca-Cola would be nice."

"I'd call it *l'endormi*, in French." Her dark eyes were the colour of chocolate. "The eye would have a lid made out of beer-mats, which you could open and close on a string."

The old man looked down at her sketch, and pulled on his beard.

"Ah, I see…"

"And that's a model I want to make of Mr Frimpong, the guy who changes the barrels. The torso would be this huge barrel on top of a big old wheel, and I'd fill it full of soil and tar which would dribble out of wee holes here and then collect in little rubber gloves, and when you turned the wheel the gloves would start to fill and pop up and wave, getting fatter and fatter, like udders, or little black flowers, waving."

The barmaid squirted some fizzy stuff into a glass.

"Very artistic," said the old man.

"Mr Frimpong doesn't mind at all! He's awful good to me…"

The young guy didn't look convinced.

"I only came in for some crisps," he said.

"But you'd be just right! Look, let me take some measurements. What if I just get some material and cut around you, like a flag or a night-shirt or something, and then if I attached this long pole, it would be like a wind-sock, a ghostly sheet…"

"I don't want to be a sheet…"

"But you're so pale already! C'mon, what's the harm?"

Ah, the girl looked so mysterious! A mountain of hair, skin like cinnamon, the vague aroma (to the old man's nose, at least) of other, more pungent spices.

"I see your face made from folded cardboard, all the writing rubbed off or smeary."

"Those crisps look nice," said the old fella, skinny as a rake. "Do you mind if I…"

The young guy offered up his packet but just then the three of them heard the sound of someone footering about in the cellar beneath them, a general banging and knocking and crashing about.

"Oh, that's just Mr. Frimpong," said the barmaid. "He's down there, fixing the pumps. D'you know, once I was doing this construction called 'Study in Geometric Form' and he let me take all his clothes off and break his body down to its constituent parts. No, really! I used bits of foam, paper-mâché, and the plastic containers the ready-meals came in."

The girl's bangles clattered and clapped.

"I can remember him saying 'Oh Miss, the other deliveries can wait. I give myself up to you!' and so I moulded his great belly there and then, because, um, we didn't have many customers at the time and no-one minded one bit."

"Hm," said the young fella, sprawled out over his stool.

"You don't know the first thing about art," said the girl, huffily. Her bangles clacked together like castanets. "By the time I was finished with him, he was beautiful, beautiful! It's true what they say, you know. When a thing is perfect, it is eternal."

At this the barmaid smiled enigmatically. Her pupils glowed like a torch at the bottom of a well.

"Ah, but you should have seen him! The curve of his back, the bulge of his tum, his two meaty thighs; all I had to do was move the lines around a bit and a perfect Frimpong emerged, an immortal Frimpong!"

The old man sucked on his fizzy drink, his eyes looking sad and thoughtful. If only that were true, he thought: imperishable, undying! The girl's hair looked like a great black tree with little jewels perched in it.

"Tch, it's a lovely piece," said the barmaid, mopping the bar. "And even though I couldn't get all the paper-mâché to dry, and the plastic bits wouldn't bend and kept snapping into funny shapes, each bit was just right, each bulge and blob in just the right place, which is to say, the only way things can be."

The barmaid rested her elbows on the bar and stared off into outer space.

"But then Mr Frimpong's such a terrific model. I mean, when the guys came to empty the fruit machine right next to him, he didn't budge an inch. 'Lads, lads', he said, 'you are in the presence of a rare and beautiful thing', and even when his boss phoned up to see where he was, he refused to come to the phone. 'We are dealing with the eternal', he hollered across the bar. 'Now, Miss, how do you want me to stand?'"

But across the way, the young guy regarded her gloomily. "I'm not taking my pants off," he said.

The barmaid's bangles shook like a rattlesnake. "Listen — a few pencil-strokes, a bit of posing…"

The young guy's brows came together like thick black curtains. "Ah, Missy, I'm just not in the mood. Why not sculpt the old grandy instead?"

The old man looked casually over his shoulder. "I'm sorry?"

The fella pointed at the funny little gnome. "I mean, just look at him! Long beard, tiny-wee hands, bandy-legs — he'd be perfect."

More crashes rose up from the depths of the earth, and the old man shifted uneasily on his seat.

"Oh, I don't think…" He tried to slink back on his stool, but the barmaid was already eying him up and down, her brown eyes flashing like torches.

"Ah…" said the mannie, the wee fella the size of a half penny. The barmaid leant over and took hold of the old man's beard, her big dark eyes growing wider.

"Mm, what do you say?" she asked. Her breath was hot and fragrant, like a curry or some such dish.

"Um…"

Truth be told, her black hair, towering over his, scared him a little. From this angle he couldn't see the top of it.

"I'd get some kind of kneebone, carve your face at the top and make a little spoon at the bottom. Then I'd prop this up in a big bowl full of tiny white hairs, like a little shaving bowl."

"Mm…"

"Only this bowl, it wouldn't be a normal bowl, it would be your little legs curled up, wrapped round like a sleeping dog. Hold on, where's my pad?"

Memling! thought the old man. ''m in the presence of a crazy woman!

But then the three of them were again distracted by the sound of someone sloshing a bucket and mop around down below, somebody huffing and puffing, breathing like a steam-train.

"So does Mr Frimpong work at the castle?" asked the old man nervously whilst the barmaid looked for more paper. Under the big bright light her skin almost looked golden.

"Deliveries, repairs, stock-taking. But he never complains. Once I saw him lugging two great crates of beer, one on top of the other, and it was such a magnificent sight I immediately ran home for my brushes. But by the time I got back Mr Frimpong had gone to have a bit of a lie down and the thing was lost forever."

"Hm," said the old man, his blue eyes sparkling. "Sounds like this Mr Frimpong has taken a shine to you…"

The girl smiled, dreamily. "No, no, 'tis all for art. Do you know what he once said? 'The shape of things are but windows on the ineffable, encumbered by curtains and drapes and material things…"

"He said that?"

"Well, words to that effect."

The old man sucked noisily on his straw but the barmaid ignored him. "Once he said to me, 'What does it matter if I miss a delivery and my boss yells at me, or I'm late for my dinner and my wife crowns me? These missing moments, those absent minutes, are neither extinguished nor lost, but doors, windows, openings to someplace else…'"

Below the bar, something was being slowly, laboriously dragged across the cellar-floor.

"Sometimes it seems to me that my Mr Frimpong is like a huge wardrobe, some kind of box or open door, and the shape of him leads from here to somewhere else…"

"Ah", mumbled the old man uncertainly.

"So what happened to your sculpture, eh?" asked the spotty young-man, proffering his glass for another pint. "Where did it end up?"

"I found the perfect place for it between the cigarette-machine and the Gents, but the manager said that it got in the way so I gave it to Mr Frimpong, as a present, a gift. 'Show this to Mrs Frimpong', I said. 'Let her look upon such beauty too.' But his boss wouldn't let him take it back on the van, so he had to take it home by push-bike, loading it up on his hump like a snail, with a second upside-down Frimpong on his back. Mm, what a sight! All the pub regulars lined up to see him off and away he went on his bike, the two Frimpongs like Siamese twins, joined at the hump."

The young guy looked at the old bloke and shook his head. The youngster's bleary eyes were red and blood-shot.

"Unfortunately the cobbles by the castle were awful bumpy though, and he'd only gone a little way when a few of the pieces started to fall off. 'The shell may be fragile,' roared Frimpong, 'but the form is immortal!' and so saying the two Frimpongs pressed on, one staring down at the cobbles, the other looking up at the sky."

The barmaid had got hold of her sketchbook by now and was making strange, flowery doodles on the cover.

"Well, down by the park a police-man clocked him and flagged him down suspiciously. 'Ah, officer', said Mr Frimpong, 'Why do you stop me? Look at this statue; though parts may fall from me, their passing points to what has always been and always will be.' But this police-guy, he wasn't impressed and asked for his name and address, writing everything down in a little black note-book.'

"Ah. And then what did he do?" asked the old guy, sucking on his lemon.

"Well, just as he was writing everything down Mr Frimpong took off, clouting him on his helmet and pedalling away down the hill, his double juddering about on his back. 'The law deals only with what is', he yelled. 'Art owes no such allegiance.' And off he went, a kind of mirror-image, twin Frimpongs escaping over the hill."

The young guy rubbed his chin as if he didn't believe a word.

"Unfortunately by then it was starting to rain, and by the time he got over the bridge and back to the ring-road it was really tipping down. Though Mr Frimpong pedalled as hard as he could, the paper-maché slowly started to dissolve, dripping all over him, till by the time he reached home there was not two Frimpongs but one, a monstrous shape, all white and melted, like an ice-cream cone upended in the street."

"And what did Mrs Frimpong say?"

"She yelled and cursed and led him to the tub. 'What have you done, you old fool?' she cried. 'What mischief have you got yourself into now?' But my Mr Frimpong was unrepentant. 'Oh, my dear,' he said. 'Even when the work perishes, its ghost is left behind, like an outline of the possible. It's true, I tell you! Once created, nothing fades.' 'Get to that tub,' she said, 'you foolish old man.' But her voice was tender this time, and her eyes much more kind."

175

"And the statue?"

"Mm?" whispered the barmaid, dreamily.

"Nothing was left?"

"Well, not nothing." The bangles around the barmaid's wrist jiggled mysteriously and her piercings seemed to wink. Then she carefully reached down behind the counter and produced a large round dome of moulded plastic. "The Belly of Frimpong," she whispered breathlessly, whilst the sad young man and the little old Joe took a look at it.

"Ah."

"Mm."

"Yes, very artistic," said the old man, as if an art-expert. "Like the cupola of an old church, the very dome of heaven..."

The little old man made his eyes shine angelically, but then there was another, enormous crash from down below, followed by the sound of falling barrels, breaking glass and some kind of strangled cry.

"Mr Frimpong? Mr Frimpong, is that you?"

The barmaid immediately leapt to her feet and flung open the trapdoor.

"Mr Frimpong, are you alright?"

Stuff seemed to be spraying everywhere and there was a terrible smell of booze. The hole beneath the bar looked terribly dark and forbidding.

"Ah, Miss," they heard a deep baritone voice intone, "I seem to have tripped and lodged myself 'neath the barrels. Come quick, my dear, come quick! Fountains of beer are gushing every which way, and the pumps are all twisted and bent."

"Oh, Mr Frimpong!" exhaled the barmaid, her dark eyes burning with exotic fires.

"Ah, my dear, come see; my feet are in two crates, boxes lie about me, and a barrel of beer crowns my head."

The barmaid looked like she was about ready to burst.

"He's so sweet to me," she said to the old man, with genuine emotion. "The kindest of men..." Her skin glowed like burnished gold, as if she were a statue too. "Wait there," she hollered, standing above the trap door, "I'm going to get my pastels..."

"Oh, my dear! There are bubbles and froth everywhere and the cellar seems to be filling up…"

His sonorous, bear-like voice seemed to emanate from the bottom of a mine.

"'Tis like I'm adrift on a sea of beer…"

All a-flutter, the barmaid raced through a backdoor. "Stay still!" she cried. "Don't move an inch!" Everything about her seemed to shine.

"I'll be right back," she called out to the pair in the snug. And with that she disappeared off-stage, her light suddenly switched off.

The two fellows, young and old, looked at each other uncertainly. Then they climbed up on the counter and looked down at the big trapdoor, a kind of black hole, or pool of black paint spilled on the ground.

"Well, she's a live one," said the old fella, sagely.

The young guy turned the pot over, the belly of Frimpong, and it made a perfect bowl for his crisps.

"S'right," he said, finishing off the crumbs.

"Do you think we should go?"

The young man looked around at the bar and stretched. "Hm, why not? This place is a dump, anyway. Let's scram whilst she's busy…"

Down below there was a sound of splashing and a series of odd bangs.

The old fella nodded in agreement. "Yes, let's away. We've tarried too long as it is. The hour is late and we still have much to finish…"

He climbed down from his stool, swiping the barmaid's pad on the way down. The pages were thick and slightly curled.

"After you my boy!"

More odd noises came from the hole — drips, crashes, a low rumble.

"Let's go, let's go!"

The old man felt light, giddy almost. It was as if the night was picking him up and using him as a paintbrush.

Shush, Memling, he thought. Can't you see that I'll get to you in a moment?

The old man blew out of the wee snug, the sullen young guy

177

following on behind. What a pair they made! Like two shadows cast from the same source.

"Yes, let's be off," said the old man. "After all, even this night can't last forever…"

Behind them, the upturned pot on the counter resembled nothing so much as a turtle's shell, smooth and round and perfect. Such a roundy pot! And yet one could imagine it filled with soup, or a little bowl of vittals, bubbling away on a stove.

IV

Well, what had happened to the kid was this: after he'd got back home, tired and forlorn and full of broken-heartedness, he fell into his bed, vowing never to wake up again.

Such sadness! he thought.

But the kid wasn't allowed to rest. No, something that night picked him up and carried him off, sweeping him across town as if he were no more than a crumb. How light he'd seemed! Like a spot, a fleck, the merest scrap of nothing.

But all that was many hours ago. Now, as he followed the old man across the courtyard, it was as if the two of them were wading through an inky pool, the pair of them up to their chins in the blackness. It's true! The two fellows, one as white and skinny as a candle, the other no more than its stump, sallied forth through the nothingness, little circles of light in the midst of all that gloom. And ho, what a pair – the young fella pale and waxy, the old man's beard an unlit wick, like the New Year seeing out the old...

"So, what happened?" asked the old man, his knees clicking mournfully on the cobbles.

"Oh," said the kid, "the usual — loneliness, laziness, sadness..."

You could still hear the music from the ball, but muffled now, as if deep underwater.

"There was this girl that me and my friends were all crazy about and, ah, grandy, you should have seen her! It wasn't that she was especially pretty or anything — if anything she was kinda plain — but she was pale and interesting, with this long oval face and a beautiful curved neck, which drooped like a tulip. And, grandy, she just drove us nuts..."

The top of the old man's head nodded.

"You see, she was always so sleepy. She worked in the library, and we'd spot her dozing on the issue-desk, or staring wistfully off into space, a big red mark where she'd tried to prop up her head. What can I say? It was as if her head were too heavy for her neck, or else her neck was too long because of her long oval face. Once I found her curled up by a book-trolley, her mouth a perfect 'o' and her long white neck tucked up under her, like a swan. Such a thing — who wouldn't have tried to wake her up? When she was reading she'd lick her inky fingers and pinch the corner of the page, leaving a little smudge like a lip-print. And when she picked up her stamp she'd play with it dreamily, sometimes stamping the desk and sometimes her arm and sometimes your hand…"

The young guy held out his paw and the old man nodded. How strange the night was! He still held the waitress's pad in one hand and the barmaid's sketch book in the other.

"Ah, grandy! It was as if her eyes were fixed on some far away thing, a thing the rest of us could not see. Listen: one day we found her asleep on the photocopier, her face resting on the glass, a death-mask atop the pile of papers, features all dark and strange. Her eyes were black and her lips a mysterious shadow — tell me, grandy, what did it mean?"

The wind blew and the fella's pants billowed soundlessly around him.

"Ah, son," said the old man. "How little we can know about anything…"

"Luckily," said the young fella, "there was this girl at the canteen we all really liked too, so we often used to go there, trying to put the librarian out of our head. You see, the girl at the canteen was shy and sweet and kind of a large portion herself, with masses of blonde curly hair and a great red face like the sun. We never knew if her face was red 'cause of the fryers or because she was shy, so we used to tease her something rotten, though secretly we all had a thing for her, 'cause she gave us extra chips and because of the bright red beamer on her face…"

The old man rubbed his beard and nodded. It really was pitch-black in the courtyard, but he could make out different kinds of black, from tar to pencil to ink. In between there were little black moulds of nothingness, waiting to be filled.

"But one day we saw her with some fella and they were so close it was like they were wearing each other as coats. And we imagined her cooking him something in a big pot, a great vat of something, hot and bubbling, and then we imagined the gal taking off her tabard, and mm, how lost we were! Tell me old fella, why is it that some people are made for love and somehow others just aren't? I mean, there were rumours that the librarian read Poe to her boyfriend in bed, her underwear blacker than the raven wings of midnight, and all this made us feel sad and lonely and we thought, Ah, if only that were me, though of course it wasn't and there was nothing we could do."

"My lad," said the old man. "Such are the vicissitudes of youth." The old fella pulled on his beard and tried to look wise, though in reality he was trying not to fall over in the darkness.

"And then there was this girl in our class who was really fit and sporty, mm, she could run a hundred miles without a single drop of sweat, and she always wore these shorts and an awfully tight T-shirt, but everything about her was so clean and fresh, she seemed to emit a kind of light, a sort of ruddy glow. D'you want to go with me round the loch for a jog? she'd ask, and we'd all say No, no, we're just off back to watch TV, and then slink off to our rooms all round-shouldered and sad."

The old fella nodded. By now his eyes were starting to adjust to the gloom and the black of the sky seemed separate from the black of the earth, whilst the darkness in front of him was different to the darkness to one side. Yes, everything was in its place. There were walls, battlements, even some type of tall tower, surrounded by scaffolding and old bits of wire.

"No, the world doesn't belong to the timid," agreed the old man.

"But what's the use of all this chasing about? I mean, where does it get you? And yet, one day after all my classes were finished and I didn't know what to do with myself, I wandered down past the old music rooms, and even though the music department had been closed down years ago, you could still hear people playing there from time to time, a kinda lonely sound if truth be told, and I wandered past the gloomy grey building, thinking about nothing, when I heard someone playing some kind of instrument, a violin or a cello or something, and because I was in a sad mood and because I didn't know what to do with myself, I stopped to listen, and, ah grandy, it was beautiful! So sad and fine and full of such feeling. Tch, I thought to myself, just think, somewhere in there a girl is playing that and she feels just the

181

same as me! And then I thought, well, maybe this girl's been locked in and she's waiting for someone to come and let her out. Or maybe she knows that I'm outside and she'd seen me walking along the path so she's playing just for me. And if I went in and opened the door she'd lay down her bow and her papers and this girl, she'd be shaped just like a musical instrument too, long, strong neck, supple body, big round bum, and all the other girls, they were just sketches for this one, just scribbles…"

The old man nodded. They were standing before a low stone building, just before the tower, the kid a kind of smudge upon the lens.

"But then I thought, what if I'm wrong? What if it's just a record someone's playing and there's no girl at all? Or maybe there's a whole music class in there, and it's not a girl but some old wifey, what would I do then? What if I burst in and it was all wrong, not what I'd thought at all?"

The young guy's pants seemed to float mysteriously on the night air, the last part of him that could still be seen.

"I don't know grandy, maybe it was better to leave well alone. Ho, what if there wasn't any music and it was all in my head? Or what if all this happened many, many years ago, and all this is just an echo, a kind of repeat…"

The guy's pants were a smudge, a ghost, a tiny scrap of light.

"And then I thought, tch, the music's so sad though, so blue and lonely, I don't know. And the more I listened to the music the sadder I became, and then I realised that there was no girl in there at all, and that music, that was me, and there was nothing I could do. And yet, you know, when I think back, I can't recall a note, not even the tiniest little bit…"

How groggy the kid's voice sounded! Like he was half-awake and half-asleep, one foot in this world and one foot in another. The kid sighed.

"Well, I left the music rooms and went on back to my room, and straight away I crawled into bed and thought well, that's it, I'm not coming out for a hundred years. That's exactly what I thought — 'I'm in my bed and not coming out for a hundred years. But, old man,

182

something picked me up and brought me here and it just won't let me rest..."

The pants billowed and flapped and his voice seemed to blow away too.

"Oh grandy, why this ball and why tonight? But this feeling, it came over me and then it picked me up and carried me here as if I were no more than a rag..."

His voice wavered and waned.

"Like I was a rag, a dot, the merest speck of nothing."

Yes, everything was fading.

"That's all I was — a blemish, or a hair or mote..."

The lad was no more than a spot, the tiniest grain.

"A wisp of a thread..."

"Kid, hey kid!" hissed the grandy, but with that the kid had fallen fast asleep, curled up on the cobbles in a little heap. Not knowing what else to do, the old fella hauled him into one of the little stone alcoves, pushing the young fella into the wee black space. There were a few bags of something composty and a bit of old sacking, so the grandad made up a kind of rough and ready bed and left the young fella to it.

"Memling, shhh," said the old man. "Time's running out and we'd best go on. Don't worry, the lad'll be fine; but there's something I must tell you and I don't know how much longer this old body will keep on going...."

The area around the tower was covered in scaffolding and the wee man had to climb through a tight little gap in the wood, past a fenced-off area and through a tiny ramshackle door.

"He's okay old friend, just let him be. I've got so much to tell you, and besides I've still got to write down about tonight, the ball and the music, the old gal with the wobbly face and everything...."

Just through the door was a storeroom filled with workmen's tools and a row of hard-hats and bits of rope and wood and wire. Next to that a narrow spiral staircase led up to the tower, its tiny stone steps incredibly steep and treacherous.

"But you know, Memling, that other fella, whatsisname, was right; already it's starting to fade – how I got here, who I was dancing with, what I ate...."

He rested on one of the little bare landings, the tiny arrow-hole looking out onto nothing.

"Yes, it all fades toward morning… but I can still hear the music from the ball, so somewhere there's still dancing and feasting and all kinds of frivolity. Yes, somewhere life goes on! And though I would like nothing more than to find my chair and watch the lights and the dancers and the band, there's something I must do tonight, something I must write…."

Old man, old man! Listen to the music, go find your seat – there's still drinks and nibbles and who knows what else? Ah, old man, why do you persist? D'you think all this can be saved? But the old fella, he kept on climbing higher.

"Ah, Memling! This night, it's such a strange feeling."

He passed the second landing now, his little grey pyjamas padding their way up the tight little stair-case. He had bits of paper stuck in his pyjama bottoms, sheets stuffed down his front and a wee pad in each of his tiny hands.

"Hold on, old friend, nearly there…."

From the third floor, you could see the lights of the great hall, the last point of illumination in a vast sea of nothingness, and then the old man came to a little wooden door, and pushed it open.

The little room at the top looked rather like the old fella's flat. Yes, a low table, a scrunched up newspaper, even an old gas-stove, with a pot of something sitting on the top. There the old man sat himself down at the table and stared off into space, humming a little tune, his moustache twitching as he did so. His pen trembled, his cloudless blue eyes sparkled, and his whole body seemed to vibrate like a tuning fork. But what was he looking at? It was the middle of the night and outside of the room there was nothing, absolutely nothing. Then the fella traced a squiggly line with his pen, spread out his ragged collection of papers, and slowly began to write.

V

My Dearest Memling,

How the devil are you? In fact, who the devil are you? Frizzy perm, glass eye, heavy make-up... that isn't you at all! Madam, hand over this letter immediately, or else I shall be forced to... ah, that's better! So Memling, who's the gal? And what are you doing letting her open your mail? I worry about you, carrying on at your age, when you of all people should be getting some rest.

Listen, old buddy: has old age claimed you yet? I seem to be getting smaller whilst my beard keeps growing longer — who knows where this might end? Ah, Memling, it's like a spell or a curse. Every morning I comb my whiskers and find something else — a crumb, a speck, a spot of breakfast — and I think to myself, Yes, something of yesterday is still here, though, of course, it's hard to know exactly what. Is it true that your hair keeps on growing even when you're in the ground? Maybe that's what's happened to me and nobody has told me yet. One day I found a pea in my beard and the next a spider; who'd have thought that my hair would end up so mysterious? Still, it's my crowning glory, my halo, my mane; trust me, Memling, not everyone has got a mighty fleece like mine! And as for my beard, well, I don't like to boast, old buddy, but it's like blossom, a soft white carpet cascading down my chops, and the gals round here, they can't wait to run their hands through it....

But I have to be careful. Mrs McTavish in the flat opposite keeps threatening to take a pair of scissors to it and when she spots me she flies across the hall with a towel and a bowl. "Come here old man," she yells, "quick cut, quick cut." I tell you, she's a crazy one that one, brown and wizened as a conker. But what should I do? When she sees me she beams like it's her wedding day. "Snip, snip," she cries, "snip, snip." I tell you Memling, this great fleece of mine, it drives the widows crazy! Mrs Dombrovsky once told me at the butchers that she had a dream about my beard and the very next day it had snowed; tell me, old buddy, who else has hair that old biddies dream about? And then there's Mrs Bremner at the launderette; her face lights up like a Christmas tree even though my laundry is terribly drab, grey pants in a grey wash, grey collars on grey shirts, not to mention all the spills and leaks and drips. And yet whenever I see her she glows like a light bulb. "Such a head of hair!" she sighs. "Like a cloud come down from heaven...." But Mrs Bremner isn't my favourite auld wifey. No, my favourite is old Mrs Murray who comes down from the sheltered housing to do her shopping at the precinct. Hum, she's tiny, the woman, like a button. "Let me help you with your heavy bags," I say to her, and she says, "Help? You're much older than I am — mind your own business, you old fogey," and if I say, "Ah, give me your shopping, look how you're bent," she says, "You with those little legs? They hardly reach the ground, you old fool." Yes, she's quite a gal that one, older than Sarah and narrow as a clothes-line....

But I know what you're thinking, Memling: all these women and not a man in the neighbourhood? But that's the way things are, old pal; I live in a world of women, a feminine world full of grannies and wifeys and gals. Okay, there's a little lad who kicks his ball against the bins in the yard, and I see various fellows hanging around if I go all the way to the post-office, but on my block, not one. Why is that, Memling? They can't all be pushing up the daisies can they? There was one old fella who lived in the flat under mine and from time to time I'd yell through the letter-box, "I'm off into town, do you need anything?" or "It's stopped raining, how about a stroll in the park?"but though I'd hear movement and sometimes see his curtains give a little twitch, the fellow, he never came to the door. Oh Grandad! His flat smelt of medicine and wee, and once a week a nurse would turn up in a green plastic apron and a big bag of tubes. Was it you old friend? But no, you've forsaken this hole for sunnier climes, warm white-washed stone and little shady squares, and in the meantime I live in a world of widows, where the ashen-grey foliage sways noiselessly in the wind, where grey silhouettes of people glide along the grey ground, where... but, hm, what's the use in complaining? Even if these are no more than phantoms, at least the pictures are still moving! And of course, the thatch on my head just keeps on growing, from the bristles in my ears to the stalks up my nose, like a waterfall, a mighty deluge of hair, or rather an ancient parchment, a great long scroll just like the page I'm writing now, with loose threads and scraggly bits and kinks and curls which go round and round and drive the widows crazy....

Once I was walking down the road when the heavens suddenly opened and in the twinkling of an eye I was soaked, like a wet dog I was, my hair and beard hanging down so I couldn't see at all, and I heard people joking and laughing because they all had umbrellas and my only umbrella was the thatch that was hanging down to my chest, all limp and lank. And the heavier my head got, the more my body seemed to disappear, till I was just this hair piece, an ill-sized wig above two dainty little shoes, and when I went into a cafe I drank my tea from a saucer like a little doggie, a westie, but even there the waitress was kind, and she wrung out my beard and said, "Tch, old timer, such whiskers," and my fleece, it was even whiter than her apron, than her note-book. Of course, the downside is that I get hairs everywhere — wrapped around my soap, bobbing in my soup, long strands curled round everything I touch. I tell you, Memling, you could stuff a cushion with my wool! And yet more and more hair keeps on sprouting. I don't know, maybe I should let Mrs McTavish at me with her scissors and her bowl, but I just don't trust those shaky hands, like twigs on a windy day they are...

Not that my own handwriting is much better. See what large letters I use as I write to you with my own hand; the letters get bigger as my eye-sight gets poorer, and even my corn-flower peepers are losing colour, turning grey like everything else, like my underwear or my shirts or the very air in the sky. Sometimes it feels like I'm at the bottom of the sea and all I can see are the shadows of great fish floating somewhere above me, blobs, marks, shapes. What a world this is; grainy as an old film and grey as fog, scratched and stained. But I'm sure your world is very different, old pal. Yes, somewhere you're sitting by an azure sea with your pretty wife and pretty house, and the white stones and the white-washed houses are so bright, it's enough to make your eyes water, enough to knock you off your feet. Ah, such things! Often I think that my life is just a pale version of yours, even if yours is no more than a kind of haze or daydream. The sun, the waves, the stones; tell me Memling, do you spend your days gazing out at the infinite blue of the horizon, or does the pasta pot and your jolly round wife draw you away? Can you see some kind of sign out there on the horizon? Is there a spot where the blue of the sky meets the blue of the sea, some kind of mark or break, like that betwixt life and death? Or is everything blue, luminous, as clear and bright as glass, like in a little kiddie's painting of the sky? What is this colour, this light — is it a view or a mirage? And why does this vision seem so much more substantial than my own digs, the wee charcoal sketch which makes up this life? Discoloured, toneless, feint; tell me, old friend, how did things come to this? And everyday I get thinner, like a shadow made from cardboard — Oh Memling, these are not the things of life but the things of death! Little wonder then, the picture is so grainy, the monochrome images as silent as the grave...

Ach, Memling, sometimes I think I've lived two lives, yours and mine, one *in colour and one in black and white. And yours is the more real, old buddy, even if it's no more solid than the heat-haze on the horizon, no more than the distant blue light of what might have been...*

What's that, old friend, the truth? It seems to me that I have lived my life in a kind of fog or a cloud, a cloud that has grown and grown, until it swallowed everything. Oh, my friend! I remember when I was wee, and my dad looking and looking for me in our little grey yard, but I'd climbed into this big wet sheet just above him, a great white cloud smelling of soap and bath-time and sleep and when he yelled my name I just lay there in my make-shift hammock, above the yard, above the adults, above the life that lay in wait. And some days it seems that I never did come down, that my two dainty feet have never really made contact with the world and its weight. Tch, what do you think, old friend? The jobs I've done, the girls I've dreamed about — was it just laziness, Memling? Lethargy, lassitude, indolence, the listlessness of man? Or was it that I could somehow make out something else, something that made me shun this world: a form or a shape, some kind of feeling in the night?

Ah, Memling, Memling, Memling! When did I last see you, old friend? I remember a rakish cravat, an artist's beret and a rather jaunty moustache, but was that you or me? But I know there was some kind of art school and a great black building and a long, narrow class-room which looked out onto a steep park of black trees and ashen skies, where the grass was grey and the blossom too... And in my head, Memling, I remember life-classes and models and a girl shaped like a guitar, or a guitar shaped like a girl, I forget which, and this tall white room full of sculptures made up of holes, gaps, missing parts, and the girl who made them, she told me to think of these spaces as windows, intimations of the numinous, like port-holes or eyes, and this girl, she wore glasses which were like windows too, mysterious apertures... And in another room there were paintings of long, Slavic-looking faces, all with necks like storks and slim, tragic lips... And in the hall off that there were plaster casts and mannequins and bits of wood and row after row of empty bottles, all ready to be broken up into shapes, patterns, things. Do you remember any of this stuff, old buddy? Some kind of jazz song with very sad words but played very fast... Smoky cafés full of earnest young things talking about abstraction and action painting and absolute graphics, pyramids of cigarettes piled up in the ashtrays... That girl who went to classes spattered with paint and one day turned up all yellow, though of course she was just showing off 'cause if you wanted colour in this drab city you had to daub it on yourself... But Memling, where were you in all of this? Is that you with the painted moustache and oily rag, the one whose arms barely reach to the easel? Ach, Memling, that canvas you're working on, what's that supposed to be? That's not a window but a closed door, or maybe the inside of an eye, all squiggles and specks, like the dust on a light bulb before it's turned on. No, you should listen to that girl standing next to you: the shape of things are but windows on the ineffable, encumbered by curtains and drapes and other material things....

Hey, who was that girl you used to pal around with, Memling? You know, the one with the bobbed hair and the bright red lipstick, the one whose little red mouth used to run down the corridor in front of you... What happened to her, old buddy? I remember going to this show she put on, and all the pictures were of strange black lakes or streams and in the middle of each was a little boat or a sofa or maybe a pair of lips, and this shape, whatever it was, it seemed to bob there in the gloom like a life-buoy or an island, a solid blob of paint sticking up. Ah, Memling, do you remember? That girl, the one who looked like Clara Bow. She had a little round face, like it had been drawn by a compass, and this little round face was balanced on her body, like a moon, like some kind of funny satellite. And she was crazy about you, Memling! When she saw you she'd light up like a spotlight and she was always showing off for you, messing around, taking off her clothes....

Mm, she was great! Dark hair, dark eyes, and two little eyebrows like black fish, fish that swam round that round face of hers as if it were a fish-bowl or a diving helmet, a cartoon face, d'you remember? Oh, Memling, that girl of yours, she was something else, like a speech-balloon with an exclamation mark after everything she did! And then one time she turned up at your place in the middle of the night with an enormous suitcase and a whole bunch of bags, hopping about from leg to leg as if in desperate need of the lavvy.

Do you remember that night, old man? The girl with the suitcase, the gal with a bruise on her cheek and ants in her pants? That girl, the real girl, the one who makes all the others seem like mere sketches. Ah, old timer, you must remember! The girl you've been following all these years, trailing after her in your old man's pyjamas and your grey washed-out underwear — the girl with the dark eyes and mouth like a little red boat.

And there she was in your pokey wee flat in the middle of the night, hopping from foot to foot and batting her eyelashes at you coquettishly.

"Okay," Clara said. "Who wants to take me to the station?"

Ach, Memling, what did you say? "Ah, Missy, I don't have a car," you mumbled, but by then the girl was already in and splayed out on your sofa.

"You're great," she said. "A real pal."

Yup, the girl was quite something, her pretty round head balanced on her shoulders like a medicine ball, black bob, big, dark eyes. The girl who looked like Clara Bow! What happened that night, Memling? The night she turned up at your flat with her suitcase and all her bags...

"Um, I don't have a car," you repeated, pulling up your pyjamas.

"Mm, that's okay," she said, "I don't mind, you can call me a cab. Have you got much money?"

Ho, Memling, such a thing! But what about the state you were in — horrible grey trews, pale unshaven mug, hair sticking up all over the place. Honestly Memling, you looked a right state, don't try and deny it...

"D'you know what time it is?"

"I forgot my watch. Have you got anything to eat?"

The girl, pretty, coquettish. She rubbed her tum and batted her eyelashes suggestively. But Memling, Memling, what could you do? So you made her a sandwich and got her a cup of tea and after that you said you'd walk her to the station, it wasn't that far.

"Are you sure? Mm, you're really great," she said, spitting crumbs all over your sofa.

"Just give me a sec to get dressed and..."

"Dressed? Hey, just put a coat on, it'll be okay, let's go," and she hoyed the remains of the sandwich in the bin and you were out of the door, Clara hanging over you as you headed down the stairs with her bags, your slippers flapping as you went.

"What if we bump into someone?"

"Ah, c'mon, you look great. You know, you're a real pal, helping me out..."

And the girl plonked herself on you like a coat, and those big eyes of hers, they were like wells, or like dark caves, with a little pool of light at each centre. Mm, who could resist her, even though that clumsy great case she'd been lugging around with her, it weighed a ton...

You must remember that night, Memling, and how things turned out, I mean, between the two of you. Look, there you are coming out of the stairwell, *you in your pyjamas, Clara a pretty round face on a stick.*

"What have you got in here anyway, a body?"

"Hey, don't scuff it, I only borrowed it, you know..."

The whole city felt strange, the volume switched off and everywhere deserted.

"Are you sure there's a train at this time of night?"

"Sure. Why wouldn't there be?" *She walked past the streetlights and she was a streetlight too.* "Say, you're quite strong aren't you? You know, for a little fella..."

"Mm, thanks. These handles are killing my hands, you know."

"My hero!"

"What have you got in here anyway?"

"Just my stuff — I'm moving out and moving on!" *The girl pulled a funny face.* "Out of my way daddy-o, it's the open road for me!"

"You're crazy. What about your classes? Or your flat? It's the middle of the night..."

"Just look at your muscly wee arms — like little bags of nuts. Hey, don't drag the case on its bottom..."

The night was silent, soft, strangely insubstantial, though the girlie's bags weighed a ton. Clara paused to look at herself in a shop window.

"Does my hair look alright? I had to get ready in a terrible hurry. And then I had to pack all my stuff and the bags started ripping and it was hard carrying all my things. Um, are you okay?"

"Mm."

"I mean, I chucked away all I could, you know. I threw everything on the floor, and everything in the left went in the case and everything on the right out the window. I don't know what I was doing — I've brought no tights at all! But who cares, I'm getting out of here, blowing this hot dog stand..."

"Um."

"Listen, I've got it all planned out, where to go, what to do. I'm sick of this place... the weather, the cold, the people..."

The girl's case really was heavy; who would have thought one piece of luggage could weigh so much?

"There must be more to life than this! Something else, you know, some kind of opening or door-way..."

When Clara walked past a shop-window, you could see a whopping great bruise on one cheek.

"I'm kicking the dust off my heels and if you don't like it then, well, out of my way fella, I'm coming through!" Then Clara stopped and looked at him. "But not you, you're really great, a real sweetie... Say, are you okay? You look kinda funny."

And you thought, What am I doing here? It's the middle of the night, and while everybody else is fast asleep I'm schlepping down the road in my slippers and overcoat, humphing this great lump from pavement to pavement....

"You look tired, peaky..."

"No, no, m'okay."

"You're a pal you know, I couldn't do this without you..."

Memling, I'm writing all this down so you don't forget it. Ach, you must remember, old buddy... the night the two of you stumbled along like sleep-walkers, past the statues and the trees and the deserted benches, following the long line of bins, heading for the cutting which led down to the station. There was nobody anywhere, no traffic, no drunks, no cops.

Ah, my back, you though, what is this, a ton of feathers? My poor hump is killing me....

Clara skipped down the steps like she was in a musical.

"The night's a funny feeling, isn't it? I leapt out of bed, got my stuff together and thought that's it, I'm off, no one can stop me now..."

"Oh yeah? And what about that fella you were seeing, that guy with the motorbike? Why isn't he lugging your suit-case down these stairs?"

She shone her face in your eyes like a torch.

"Listen, I don't even think about him," Clara said, without missing a beat. "I'm free like the birds in the trees..."

"Right..."

"It's true! You're a doll for helping me, a real angel..."

But when the two of you got to the station, it was the strangest, I mean, the strangest thing. You see, whilst the rest of the city seemed mysteriously devoid of life, the station itself was unbelievably packed, though it was hard to imagine where all the folk had come from or were going. Mm, there were bodies everywhere — by the ticket-office, in the shops, the snack bar, over by the barriers, everywhere — like there'd been some kind of mass evacuation or the general resurrection of the dead.

"I... just...need... to put this down," you said.

"Woa, it's busy isn't it?" Clara said, standing on one foot. "Lucky we don't have to worry about a ticket..." And with that she pushed her way along the platform, like a swimmer heading through choppy seas or a waitress navigating a packed room.

"Hey, c'mon," she yelled, "we gotta go..."

"Go?" you called. "Go where?"

The place was completely packed, and the only way to get anywhere was by pushing. But what if somebody saw your jimmy-jams beneath your long coat? And what were you doing here in the first place? Clara's suitcase kept tripping you up and your hands were awful sore.

"Over here!" she yelled. "Hey pally, what are you waiting for?"

The train was waiting on the platform, its carriages crammed with tired-looking passengers, each compartment full-to-bursting.

"Are you sure this is it?"

"Yeah, help me with my case willya? Just shove it between those old folks, that'll be fine..."

How tired your arms were! Like you'd been lugging that thing around all night...

"I can't get the case in there, are you crazy? There isn't even room to breathe..."

"Ah, c'mon — look, there's a space over there, you could fit a double-bed in that..."

And all the time more people were piling on, and there were guards shouting things, and whistles blowing and flags being waved and the crowds on the platform were pushing forward.

"You want me to shove it in there?"

"Be a pal, huh?"

The whole carriage suddenly swayed.

"What d'you think I've got, a step-ladder?"

"Ah, c'mon, put your back into it..."

But even as you tried to push it in, the carriage swayed again.

"You're crazy, I can't reach that from here. People are staring..."

"C'mon baby, that's it..."

Then the whole train started to move.

"It's going! What are you doing? I gotta get off!"

"If you could fit my bags under that seat, that'd be great..."

"What are you talking about? I'm in my pyjamas! I haven't got a ticket!
I've got to go!"

The coach rocked from side to side and you could see the platform starting to
slip away. There was the waiting room, the news-kiosk, the cigarette machine,
and then they were gone. There were things and then there weren't. Things
vanished.

"Hey, is it my fault your arms are so short? Don't get mad with me!"
But then Clara stared at you and seemed to switch on some kind of light in
her eyes. "Shh, don't be cross. Come with me — it's okay, it'll be fun. No,
really; I mean, what have you got to lose?"

And all the time the grey canopy of the station was being slowly, soundlessly,
rolled away, replaced by an enormous expanse of dark sky.

"But…"

"Ah, c'mon. Hey fella — let's get lost!"

And, Memling, there was nothing you could do. The train lurched from
side to side and the station was fast disappearing.

"Okay, well, let's find somewhere to sit down."

"You're so great, such a pal."

Memling, Memling, what about the black sky, what did you think it
meant? But maybe you weren't thinking about that or about anything else
but the girl. You see, the carriage was really packed, with no seats anywhere.
The aisle was piled up with people's stuff, great heaps of luggage, and those
who had made it into a compartment were hemmed in from every direction.
On one side there was an empty trolley abandoned by the loo door, and on
the other side somebody had piled up several bags' worth of what looked like
dirty washing. The corridor itself was in a right old state: the heating felt like
it was on the blink and cold air whistled in from the windows.

"Maybe the next coach along," said the girl.

"I can't believe I'm still here. I must be crazy…"

"Listen, I'll make it up to you. Just you wait, you'll see."

"Mm."

"It's true! Trust me, I'll make it worth your while."

Who could tell what she was thinking? Inside her dark eyes, something
shone like stars, mysterious wee specks.

"We'll just have to wait here. Didn't you reserve a seat?"

"Reserve a seat? I didn't even buy a ticket. Hey, c'mon, don't pull that *face, we'll be fine....*"

Clara rubbed herself up against you, like a cat.

"*Where's this train going anyway?*" you asked, trying to rescue your slipper from under some oaf's foot.

"*Home, you'll see. But just for a while. We'll kick over the traces and then there'll be no stopping us. Hey, be a pal, huh? You've always been my favourite, you know...*"

The train hurtled through the darkness and the window reflected back an enormous heap of things, luggage and people, form and formlessness.

"*Mm, did you split up with that guy, then?*" you asked, feeling Clara's hot breath on your face.

"*Him? He doesn't even exist. Who cares?*" And she pulled a face.

"*I thought you'd been spending all that time with him...*"

"*He was just a... jerk. The world is full of them. It's a world of jerks.*"

"*Mm.*"

"*I can't even remember his name.*"

"*Okay.*"

The train went over some bumpy track and the lights suddenly flickered.

"*I've got to write an essay tomorrow, you know,*" you said.

She laughed. "*Oh yeah, what on?*"

"*Hans Memling's Triptych of the Weighing of Souls. You know, the one with the pictures of heaven and hell...*"

"*Hey, that's just where we're going!*" she laughed, and the little fish above her eyes swam up and down. Her eyes were as dark as ink but at the centre there was something else.

The corridor rocked from side to side and the travellers swayed restlessly — old folk, crumpled businessmen, shift-workers — all of them crushed into one enormous scrum. But at the other end of the carriage a ticket-inspector was making his way toward them, his dull blue uniform methodically traversing the crowd.

As soon as you spotted him your heart sunk.

"*We've had it,*" you cried, but Clara just shrugged. "*What do you mean? All we have to do is hide in the loos...*"

But the lavvy was occupied, and besides there was a queue of people outside, though whether they were actually waiting or just crammed into any available space, it was hard to tell.

"There's nowhere to go," you hissed as the fella in the cap got closer.

"Ach, it's fine, don't panic…"

"But we haven't got any tickets."

"Don't worry, we'll be okay."

"We haven't got enough money either."

Frantically, you pushed your way to the door and tried opening the window.

"What are you doing?" asked Clara, balancing herself by the luggage rack. "It's freezing out there."

Shoving hard at the catch, you finally got the window to open, but the girl was right; outside a gale was howling and the air was black and cold. You squinted your eyes but couldn't see anything. There was just the pale smoke of the train, bits of soot, grit.

"Listen," you hissed through clenched teeth, "if I can just get the window jamb open then we can hide outside, maybe climb on top…"

"You're funny," said Clara, her white teeth gleaming between her lips. "A crazy guy!"

You stretched out your arm, but once again it just seemed too short.

"If… I… can… just… reach the handle…."

Clara laughed and tugged on your coat.

"Get… onto… the… roof," you muttered.

Outside the wind yelled as the very darkness seemed to tear itself into rags.

Clara giggled, her dark eyes flashing.

"Look, the fella's gone off to get some change, we'll just change coaches when he's on his way back. Say, are you all right? You're shaking…"

"What? Oh, sure, sure." But when you pulled yourself back from the window your face was black with dirt, which set Clara off in peals of giggles again. "You're a loopy guy, you know?"

"Look, let's just get past the ticket-inspector, okay?"

"Okay!" and Clara laughed again, 'cause your face was as black as the coalman's balls. "We're going, we're going…"

You pushed your way along the corridors but there was no sign of the ticket-fella anyway. Eventually you found a space and used the case as a seat. It was very late. The train was hot and stuffy with an occasional blast of ice-cold air. It smelt of BO and its windows were very dirty.

"Nearly there!" whispered Clara, dangling her shoe off the end of one foot. "And then, well, just you wait…"

There may have been shapes in the gloom outside but it was awfully hard to tell. Nothing seemed to have definite shape or substance, just odd marks and squiggles. Clara nestled herself against your shoulder and slurred her speech.

"Yup, we made it. We're heading down the track, ain't ever coming back…"

"Mm."

To the left there was darkness, and to the right also. Outside the window there were no colours, lines or shapes of any kind. Blocks of grey and black passed, but indistinguishable from each other, without weight, without substance. No, nothing seemed to have any form. All was empty, insubstantial, fleeting. The night was a void.

But not for long. For after a while the train began to slow down and lights began to appear again, blurry and smeared, like dots from the girl's strange paintings. One minute you were struggling with the carriage-door and next you were humphing her case onto the platform, and finally you were shuffling past the deserted ticket barrier with all her stuff, two more little black dots in the night. Nobody got off with you. The station was very cold and draughty. In an instant the train was gone.

"Well, that's that then," she said.

"Right."

Everything seemed mottled and discoloured — the posters, the walls, the very air. It was as if everything was speckled with some kind of dust or film, made up of dots and blemishes. The windows of the ticket-office were particularly dirty.

"Hold on a minute. I know this place." you said, hauling her luggage out past the taxi rank and then over the cobblestones.

"Mm? Oh, yeah, yeah. Don't worry though, we aren't staying. Just one night, okay? Just one night then we're off…"

Memling, I'm writing this as clearly as I can, though my hand is getting cramped and the paper is running short. Can you read it, despite all the scribbles and the rewriting and the crossings-out?

Look — there are the little grey shops near the clock tower and there are the railings that mark the edge of the river, and after these, the grey tenement blocks and the shadowy silhouette of the hills, broken-backed and weary. All *this is very familiar, Memling! Like my own wee town — the cobbles, the twisty alleyways, the looming shape of the castle. Yes, there's the monument and the cannon and the steep little hill, the one with the chip-shop and the ironmongers — Memling, Memling, I can see my house from here!*

And there the two of you are, lingering outside the only hotel in this little grey town, the one with the views of the castle, with the flags and the sad-looking banner...

"Okay, let me just slip this on," Clara said, and with that she produced a little gold ring and poked it on her finger.

"What's that? What are you doing?"

"Well, you know, they won't give us a room without it."

"A room? We haven't got any money. I'm in my pyjamas. I've got an essay to write for tomorrow..."

"Don't be such a wet blanket. Don't you want to come with me?"

"Well, you're a nice girl and all..."

"C'mon, what do you want to do, stay with my mum and dad? It'll be fun. Just make up a name. We'll scarper in the morning."

"Um, I don't know, this is crazy, it's practically morning already..."

And then you were standing in the wee drab lobby, surrounded by dark wood panels, dreary watercolours, and all sorts of tartan kitsch. A squat old fella was asleep behind the desk, an amazingly ugly guy with a fat nose, like some kind of troll.

"Um, hi," you said, in a strange, strangled voice. "We're looking for a room. Um, just for the night."

The fella opened his eyes and stared unblinkingly, like a toad.

"A room?"

"Ah, if you have one."

The mannie licked his lips but still didn't blink.

"A room," he said.

"Yes, a room."

The fella still didn't move. Smiling brightly, Clara pushed herself forward and propped her elbows on the reception desk, using the light from the guy's desk light to make her cheap ring sparkle. "Mr and Mrs Memling. Hans Memling. I'm afraid we don't have a reservation because my husband is an idiot..."

"That's right," you said.

Clara perched herself by his desk and gave the wee homunculus one of her most dazzling smiles.

"Do you have any rooms? It's okay, it doesn't have to face the castle. We can look onto the old tenements, we don't mind. Have you got anything? We're awful tired…"

The gal's face shone like a sunflower. Boy, she could really turn it on when she wanted to.

"A room," said the guy.

"Yes please!"

He jerkily reached toward his rack of keys, and then slowly, reluctantly, produced a thick black book.

"Sign here."

"That's great!" said Clara. "You're really kind." And in your best handwriting you wrote 'Mr and Mrs Hans. Memling', though all the time you were thinking, What am I doing here, I ought to have my head examined….

The fella moved out from behind his desk and retrieved a bunch of keys. He seemed to be moving erratically, like something in a stop-motion film. The fella was heavy-set, smelly, covered in a thick, uneven pelt. He eyed his guests up one more time and then led them over to the stairs. Clara pinched your bum as you passed.

"This is really nice," she gushed, "What a terrific place…"

It was only when you got to the top of the stairs that you remembered your mug was black as coal from the train.

"Lovely!" you echoed.

But the guy didn't seem to care. Wordlessly, he opened the first door at the top of the corridor and led you in. He didn't help with the suitcase.

"Great, mm, look at this…"

The room was okay, actually. A big window. Heavy-set dressing table. Pot-bellied wardrobe. Two single beds.

The girl looked disappointed.

"Well, of course, it's really nice," she said, "but have you got anything else? It's just that, um, I don't really like the colour…"

Betraying no emotion, the little troll-fella nodded and showed you the next room along. But this was no good either: window too small, room too cold. He showed Clara another but this one was facing the wrong way. Did he have a room that wasn't looking out onto the castle? You staggered with her case up the stairs. The fella unlocked another door. Nope, too cramped.

"What are you doing?" you hissed as Clara slipped past. But she just sidled up to the wee gnome. "Have you got anything on the top floor?" she asked. "Facing that block of flats?"

Still without a flicker of response, the silent figure led you back up the stairs to the top. He was panting heavily by now, but that was nothing compared to the state you were in, humping that heavy case. Was she deliberately trying to tire you out?

The very last room (the rest of the hotel was empty, or so it seemed) was a cramped little attic room filled by a sagging double bed and an enormous wardrobe. A manky-looking sink and toilet were in a cubicle just outside the door.

Clara rushed in and immediately opened the curtains.

"It's perfect," she cried, "we'll take it!"

The little troll didn't say anything. He just handed you the key and silently shuffled off along the hallway, another funny shape.

"What do you think?" asked Clara, spiralling around the room. "Nice, huh?"

"Mm."

As if in a daze you walked over to the bureau and switched on the radio. Loud, fast jazz immediately started playing, but when you tried to switch it off you couldn't find the knob.

"Um…"

"No, just leave it. It's great, don't you think?"

You didn't know what to say. The music swirled and crashed like some kind of demented circus.

"Why don't you get cleaned up?" said the girl. "Freshen up."

"Okay".

The bathroom was tiny, with a titchy wee sink, a horrible looking flannel, the merest sliver of soap. What a dump! You washed your face and stared out of the little frosted window. Like the bedroom, it looked onto the block of flats opposite, but you could also make out a little grey garden, a patch of waste-ground, and alongside this, a low railing, against which someone had left a motor-bike. Above it a line of washing flapped fitfully in the breeze.

You quickly finished washing and wondered what to do next. You wanted to go to the lavvy but was afraid that the girl might hear. Should you take your *pyjamas off? They looked really manky but what if you'd got it all wrong? You undid one button and sniffed suspiciously at your pits. The music from the room was very loud. What if someone complains? you thought.*

But then your ears picked up on another sound: a window being opened, followed by a crash, then a pause, and then another bang. Pushing open the door you saw Clara leaning out of the window in her underwear, looking to see what she'd managed to hit.

When she pulled herself back in, she had a funny expression on her face.

"Oh, hi, hi... I didn't hear you," she said.

She hid something in her hand and surreptitiously put it back on the bureau. Had she been chucking stuff out of the window?

"Whatcha doing?"

"Nothing."

"What d'you mean, nothing?"

"Nothing. Hey, come here, look at this..."

All of a sudden she started to dance jerkily to the music. All the lights in the room had been switched on and the girl was just wearing her bra and pants. She was skinny but still a knockout. Singing crazily to the song she shimmied her way past the bed and jitterbugged up to you.

"Well," she said, "what do you say to that?"

Ah, Memling, what could you say? The music was loopy, raucous. The girl's head bobbed about on her skinny bod like the head of an enormous flower.

"You're beautiful," you said. "Beautiful..."

"C'mon sweetheart, let's dance," she yelled over the clamour. "That's it, there you go..."

You were quite a bit shorter than the girl, but she didn't seem to mind. Her underwear was very skimpy. She whispered something in your ear but you couldn't hear it.

"What?"

She whispered something else and smiled. The lunatic music banged and clanked.

"I can't hear," you murmured and started to pull away but Clara dragged you closer and started to undo your jim-jams. She seemed to be pulling you in the direction of the window.

"You're sweet," she yelled.

You kissed and pressed your hot clammy hands to her bra strap. But then there was another crash and when you opened your eyes she'd chucked her hairbrush out of the window.

"What was that?"

"Nothing. Kiss me again."

Once again you gave in to bliss, but the girl seemed to be trying to manoeuvre you back to the window. Why had she opened the curtains? And what was that in her other hand?

"Yes…" *you whispered, panting heavily.*

But when you tried pulling her gently toward the bed she resisted. "No, no, not yet…"

She dragged you roughly back to the window, and whilst you were kissing again, there was another bang, followed by the sound of breaking glass across the way.

When you pulled away, she'd chucked a pitcher and an alarm clock out too.

"What are you doing?"

"Who?"

A dog started barking and several lights came on in the flats opposite.

"You, what are you playing at? Look, get away from that window, people will see…"

"Who cares? Come here baby…"

"Are you crazy? What's that in your other hand? There's people out there…"

Clara looked back over her shoulder and gazed intently at the window almost directly across. Yes, the light was on and some young guy was staring back, more a silhouette than a man, the merest shape without substance or weight. But who was he? Clara squeezed out of your grasp to turn and look. He wasn't wearing anything. Was he the guy with the motorbike you'd heard she was knocking about with? But you didn't want to look and you didn't.

"Come away from the window, what are you doing?"

The girl just stood there, frozen like a sleepwalker.

"Whatchya doing? Look at all those people." *Lights were on in most of the flats, and there were people in nightshirts, pyjamas, pants, nighties…*

"They can see us," *you hissed.* "Close the curtains".

But the girl wasn't listening. All of a sudden, her mug didn't seem so animated or bright; her eyes were dull, her mouth tired and thin. The guy stared back at her impassively. He seemed barely there, more a cut-out than a man. What was he doing? He just seemed to hang there, suspended in space. He was an outline, not a person.

Clara put her hand up to the glass and made a funny kind of wave, but it seemed a terribly sad gesture, the saddest thing you'd ever seen. The guy didn't wave back. His expression was inscrutable. Was he tired, bored, upset? He looked pale and drawn. He had a bruise on one cheek also.

A shudder went through the man's body, but otherwise he still didn't move. He was terribly pale, like a shop-dummy. In fact, the more you stared at him, the harder it was to be sure that he was alive at all.

And you, Memling, what were you thinking? Were you jealous, upset, mad? Something about the girl confused you, drove you crazy... Clara waved again but then the fella turned away and closed his curtains. It's true! The space where he had stood was empty and there were people shouting, swearing. The window beneath the guy's was broken, and some fat bloke in a pair of Y-fronts was holding up an alarm clock. The fella's window remained empty.

Clara put one little hand up against the glass. She seemed to be mouthing something but the fella wasn't there to see it.

"Come on, let's go..." you said, and pulled her back from the frame. This time she didn't protest. Whilst you hastily drew the curtains and switched out all the lights the girl climbed silently into the bed. All of a sudden she seemed absent, closed-up. Not knowing what else to do, you switched off the radio and climbed in next to her.

"What are you, a maniac? Who was that guy anyway — your boyfriend?"

Her voice came from very far away, as if underwater.

"Him? He's just a jerk. I can't remember."

"What do you mean you can't remember? You're talking like a crazy person. What was that all about?"

For a long time she didn't reply; when she did it was as if her voice had travelled a long way.

"You're my pal, aren't you? You know, we have fun..."

"Fun? You ought to be locked up. What are we going to tell the guy about his alarm clock? That guy knows it was you, you know."

Clara pressed her face into her pillow and made a noise. Her body *seemed to be closing down.*

"Hey!" you squarked. "Don't fall asleep! I wouldn't be surprised if a million people are up here in a minute. What are we going to tell 'em? We haven't got the money for anything. Hey, don't you nod off, we're in big trouble..."

The girl's voice drifted up from her pillow, muffled and sad.

"Let's get away from here. What do you say, just you and me? This place is a dump, let's get out of here, jump on a bike and zoom off... d'you want to?"

You felt confused, angry, mixed-up. A million different thoughts were rushing through your head.

"Yeah, well, we gotta get out of here before the owner turns up. It won't take them long to work out which room it was..."

"No, let's really get out of here... out of here, this dump... let's just go. No more classes, no more assignments. What do you say? Where the sun shines once in a while, where it isn't always so cold..."

"Go? We'll be lucky not to go to prison. We'll be chucked out of college at any rate. And what am I going to tell my mum and dad? There's going to be so much trouble."

She rolled over to face you, but all you could see were the two little lights in the middle of her eyes. "I mean, go for good. Chuck away our stuff, jump out of the window, shinny down a drain-pipe..."

The girl's eyes were like little headlights in a tunnel, but her voice was cracked, desperate. Her mouth felt very close to yours.

"We have fun don't we? Hey, whaddyasay? Just the two of us, hitting the road, quitting this dump. It'll be great, just imagine it, they won't see us for dust..."

You shook your head.

"Look, get dressed. Maybe we can sneak out some back-way. There must be some kind of fire escape. Hey, what are you waiting for? We gotta get your case and go."

But by now Clara's voice was very soft, almost inaudible. "Don't you wanna go?"

"Hold on, I've got to get my coat." You were out of the bed and stumbling around in the darkness. "Have you seen my slippers?"

Her voice was tiny, only just there.

"Don't you like me?"

You couldn't find your slippers but didn't dare switch on the light.

"Don't we have fun?"

Outside you could hear heavy footsteps stamping up the stairs. Confused, you started to flail about but couldn't seem to find a thing; where were your tiny little slippers? There was a general banging and clattering, just outside your room.

"D'you know where my slippers are?" you whispered, but then somebody started hammering on the door.

Clara pushed her face further into the pillow.

"Shhh — let's ignore it," you hissed, but the banging was getting louder and louder. You looked out of the window but there was no way down. There was no way out to the toilet either. The only place left was the wardrobe.

"It's no good — we'll have to hide in here," you said, though the thing was full of rusty coat hangers and old shoe boxes. "Don't just lie there — we've got to get in…"

There were shouts and blows, as if somebody was trying to break the door down.

"I'm not fooling, we've got to get inside…"

But the girl wasn't moving. She was just a little lump in the bedclothes.

The troll from behind the desk was yelling obscenities and suddenly you felt a great wave of tiredness. Tch, what could you do?

"Clara?"

There was no response.

"Are you asleep?"

The girl didn't move and to be honest you felt pretty weary too.

"Open up in there," the landlord yelled, and all of a sudden you felt that you couldn't really be bothered, everything was falling away, broken.

"Okay," you said, "okay…"

How knackered you felt! It was as if you'd been hypnotized too.

"Just a minute…"

There was no sense to anything. Your limbs didn't seem to work.

"I'm coming, hang on…"

It was all a mess, a jumble, a muddle of disparate things.

When you opened the door the fella from behind the desk and the fella with the alarm clock were both facing you, the two of them as mad as hell.

There were loud accusations and threats of legal action. Curses, swear words. The two fat, ugly guys blustered and raged about malicious damage, criminal intent, personal property… You tried to protest but couldn't find the energy. Ho, why struggle? It was incredibly late and each passing second felt wearier than the one before.

"I know, I know," you said.

You tried closing the door to the bedroom, but the two guys roughly pushed you out of the way, saying all sorts of things. What were the pair of you up to in here? How old were you anyway? Mr and Mrs Memling, my arse…

Yes, everything was falling away. You felt light, ghostly, insubstantial. Nothing seemed to matter anymore. Lassitude overwhelmed you.

"Okay pally, we're coming in …"

The two guys pushed their way in, two enormous guts. Their voices were angry, threatening.

"What's going on here?"

But the girl wasn't there. The bed was completely empty and instead the window was thrown wide open, the curtains pulled back, something on the ledge. There was a shape, a blur. The two guys started to rush over.

"Hey…"

And you? What did you do? It was as if you weren't even there, as if your limbs were not your own. Fatigue gnawed at every part of your body and you had trouble keeping open your eyes.

"Clara…"

The two guys were peering down into the yard, their backsides framed by the shape of the window. Out there, there were endless lines of washing, long strings of nighties, pinnies and thermal breeks. At one end there were nappies, at the other some kind of plastic sheeting, a line of straps dangling from its cord. Apart from that there was nothing, absolutely nothing. Bits and pieces of laundry flapped erratically in the breeze. It was nearly morning and the sky was changing colour. You closed your eyes.

Sitting at his little desk, the old man closed his eyes also. His head was bowed down over the worktop and his beard spilled out over all the sheets of paper. Old man, old man, what are you doing? But the old fella wasn't listening; rather, he swung his pen about as if it were a baton, listening to some kind of music in his head. Yes, he was a tiny man — if you cut round him then you'd be left with just a speck, the tiniest hole imaginable. His eyes were blue and mysterious in the half-light, the colour of eternity and extinction. But what was it he thinking about? His lips mouthed soundlessly whilst his thoughts drifted here and there. Funny little man! It was as if he was growing smaller and smaller, rubbed out almost, removed from the page. Then he licked the top of his whiskers and once more began to write.

And then, old buddy, and then? Ah, Memling, what can I tell you? Well, a little time later I was either thrown out of art-school or else I quit, I can't remember, and I found myself working on building sites or factories, and then in a laundry or else in a pub, but my soul, it was shrivelling up, Memling, turning in on itself, and I felt myself shrinking and puckering up, I didn't write, didn't paint, I even stopped cutting my hair, and over the years my mane grew to resemble a great fall, a mighty river of hair, as you can plainly see... But I didn't lose my marbles, old friend, my hair just seemed to flow free, and in other ways I still looked after myself, I got up in the morning, put food on my table, brushed my teeth, went to bed and so on, over and over again, as if in a dream....

But all this time I was getting smaller and my beard was getting longer until one day the foreman at my factory said to me, "You'll get that fleece of yours caught in the machinery, you'll have to chop it off," so I walked out, Memling, still with my hard hat on and everything, 'cause I knew that I would forever be dissatisfied with this world and dreaming of a different one instead. It's like this wifey once said to me, "The way you walk, fella, it's like you've both feet in the air," and she was right, Memling, though she too wanted to cut my hair, just like old Mrs McTavish, but I wouldn't let either of 'em, 'cause I was afraid that when they'd finished I wouldn't even be there, there'd just be a pile of white hairs in a bowl, like frost, like ash, and some voice saying, "What are you up to now, you old fool, come back here this minute."....

And then I started to get this pain in my back, stabbing pains from my neck to my spine, and on top of that I had terrible trouble with my innards, old buddy, I was getting skinnier and skinnier, until I was as thin as a rake, not like snow but sleet. What a fate, eh Memling? Like a stick bending under a heavy load... And as the jobs got worse so did my back and even my cornflower eyes weren't as blue as they used to be, more like clouds or puddles, grey pools reflecting a grey sky, and then I realised that they didn't want to see anymore and my back was bending down to touch the ground... Ah, Memling! It was like the strings that held me up were irretrievably tangled, twisted round upon themselves, and all I had to do was wait for the strings to fray, for the last line that attached me to this sad world to snap, and I would fall, old friend, fall just like that girl, as if through an open window....

But the strange thing is, old buddy, this fall went on for years and years, and all the things falling past me, they were just shadows or holes, the space where things used to be. Such a thing... it was like riding on a train of shadows, but at the same time it wasn't really a carriage, more a platform, or a waiting room, or maybe even a little flat, where one might live for years. Do you know what I mean, old buddy? This fall, it seemed to be the end, but it turned out to be the thing itself. And when I looked out of the window, all I could see were blocks of grey and black, as fleeting as the view from a moving train, and the facilities, tch, they were dreadful, Memling, broken pipes, dodgy heating, mess and litter everywhere. I'm not kidding, old buddy — rubbish on the floor, scratches on the table, big rips gouged out of all the cushions, and as for the loo, trust me, old man, you really don't want to know. But tell me my friend and tell me now: how did I get to be so old? How did that train take me from there to here, from adolescence to senility without stopping at maturity in the middle? I know, I know, I'm exaggerating, but still... After all, what is old age, my oldest friend? A bent branch on an old dark tree, some apple-cheeked idiot astride it with a saw....

Ah, Memling, it's true! When I got out of bed yesterday it was like waking up in somebody else's life, as if I'd been born with the words 'when I got out of bed...' No, really! It was like brushing a stranger's teeth or combing some old bloke's beard, and when I looked in the fella's wardrobe all the clothes were cut very small, as if to fit a tiny man, but when I tried them on, they fitted me just fine. Ah, who can tell, eh old friend? All I know is that when I went in the bathroom and washed and scrubbed behind my ears, it felt really strange, like trying to tie a tie on someone else, and when I put my dainty wee feet in a waiting pair of shoes, they felt kinda snug but also very cold, and then I was ready to go out and had a key in my pocket, and this key, it fitted the door perfectly, so I went out.

Well, you can imagine what happened next. This town, it was quiet and peaceful, as grey as a pigeon, Memling, and it turned out I owned one of those *little kiosks up by the castle, you know, one of those places selling tartany knick-knacks, dollies and mugs, um, pencil-cases and stuff, and that's where I ended up, behind the counter... what else could I do? I opened the shutters, set out the postcard stands and the little folding maps, arranged the plates, the pictures, the little plastic models of the castle itself, and then I settled back in my chair, which had a little box poked under it so my legs wouldn't have to dangle. And after a while, visitors started to appear, gaggles of tourists in scarves and knitted hats, and one of them asked me, "Say, that castle up there, what's it like?" and I said, "Um, I'm sorry, my friend, I can't help you there," and he said, "Well, why ever not?" and I had to confess that I'd never actually been inside, and he said, "Never been?" and I nodded my head sadly and the visitors, they tutted and muttered, and said, "Well, what are you doing running this place if you're not from round here?" And I said sadly, "Ah, this grey town with its drab walls and dreich brick, that's me, that is," and they looked at me like I was a crazy thing, like I was the wild man of Borneo. But what else could I say, Memling? After they'd gone I walked up to the castle esplanade and stared up at the gate-house and the draw-bridge and the great stone walls, though I didn't go in, I never went in, Memling, not until this very night, when something lifted me out of my flat and brought me here, to this tower, to this desk...*

Why do you think that was, old friend? Fear, laziness, old age? I mean, visitors would turn up in their rain coats and macs, or later in anoraks and puffer-jackets, their hats pulled down and hoods pulled up, and they'd all troop up to the castle like clothes being pulled in on a line, rack after rack of 'em, not people but vestments, apparel, garments, and all the time I stayed where I was, my beard getting longer and longer, hanging over the counter like a scroll, a mighty screed... And when it was quiet I'd take out an enormous black ledger from under the table and do my accounts, carefully calculated figures and sums all arranged in strict perpendicular columns, but when I looked down what I'd really written was a letter to you and my handwriting was all over the place and sometimes my beard was shut in the pages, and sometimes it was stained with ink or with soup...

And when I read it back, there was Clara with her suit-case, her big black eyes and head like a light-bulb, a little yellow filament glowing inside her dome... but my pen seemed to tremble and twitch, and the more I wrote about her, the more my scribbles danced all over the place, the wee scratchy little lines scumbling up and down the pages, wandering over lines, stumbling across borders, waltzing off from time to time onto the counter instead, and there were so many crossings-out and broken sentences, the whole thing was a mess, like bits of scaffolding rather than any kind of house itself. And I'd sit there in my shop near the castle in the middle of the night, mug of tea on one side, big black ledger open on my knee, and it would seem like mine was the last light on anywhere, the last pin-prick in the universe, and even the castle wasn't there, it was just an even denser patch of darkness, like some kind of reef at the bottom of the ocean, and there I wrote and I wrote...

You see, I thought to myself that maybe I could save her somehow. After all, wasn't that what all writing was about? Rescuing time, retrieving things, whether they be people or places or feelings we'll never feel again. I don't know — maybe that barmaid had been right: though the frame was fragile, form was eternal. But it sure didn't seem that way. No, it seemed that the more I wrote about Clara — her big black eyes, her dainty wee brows, bold red lips, like a boat, like a lifebuoy, bobbing crazily out to sea — the more I was just painting round her, like leaving little sign-posts where she used to be, wee crosses like kisses, just spaces, holes. What d'you think, old buddy? Is it true that even if a thing perishes, its shape is left behind, like an outline of the possible? I don't know, Memling, I don't know... Maybe I've gone about this all wrong. Maybe instead of trying to bring the girl back to dry land, I should have carried on and followed her to the further shore, jumped out through that open window, that portal or opening...

After all, when she jumped, who's to say she fell? Maybe she dropped past the first washing line and came out in a big pair of bloomers, flew past the second and snatched a big flouncy top, plummeted past a third and collected tights and a jacket, till she came out at the bottom fully dressed, sliding out of a big white sheet like she'd just got up in the morning, like a scene from a slapstick comedy, the greatest stunt in the world! And when she looked up and waved, it wasn't like to that pale fella in the flat opposite, but crazily, happily, as if to say "Not so shabby eh? Whaddya say pally, let's go...." And then she'd hop on the fella's motorbike, her hair sticking to her head like a helmet and that big face of hers shining like a headlamp, and, ah Memling, how could you not fall for her, she was like a movie star, like Clara Bow...

And what if the two of you had gone off, eh old friend? Maybe you'd have made it out of there, kicked the dust off your shoes, blown that hot-dog stand...

And maybe you'd even have made it all the way over the page, buddy, to the open highway and thence to a distant shore...

What do you say, old buddy, did you get there? Maybe you're there right now, opening this letter in some warm, sun-kissed garden, snatching it from that gal with the frizzy perm and the heavy make-up, her big red mouth like a slice of water-melon perched on her face... And the gal is hopping around and yelling, "Hey, who's it from, let me see," and you say, "Ah, just a letter from a friend," and when you read it, you're amazed, no, more than amazed, astonished, and you think to yourself, Yes, such a life, a little grey town, long white beard, a pot of soup bubbling on an old stove... like a second life, a dream life, and suddenly your cornflower eyes grow thoughtful, grow sad. And this garden, it's flooded with light, the colours glowing, shining, from the lemon trees to the myrtle bushes to the reddish clay of the soil, and in this garden there's a little table, with a jug and two glasses, and the gal with the red lips and the wobbly face is beaming at you and saying, "Old friend eh... sure it isn't some old flame? I know you, you rascal..." and you smile and say, "Ach, just look at that handwriting, like hen's feet," and Memling, this garden, it smells of camellias and lemons, and there are low buzzy things and the stones are white, candescent, bright enough to make your eyes water...

And you turn the pages round and round on your little table-top, all the scribbles and diagrams and doddery mistakes, and think about that little grey town, maybe for the first time in years, that ashen wee place with its castle and its cobblestones and its monochrome square, and when you look out over the myrtle bushes, you can see the blue of the sea, maybe even the spot where the blue of the sky comes down to meet it, the vaguest intimation of a line or break, like the thread between life and death...

What are you thinking, Memling? Why do you look so sad? Look, that gal of yours is pouring you something from the big stone jug, and ah me, her lips are so red, it's like they've been painted on, and there's blobs of paint in her hair and on her hands too ...

Ah, if only this was true! If only I could leave you there, suspended on that invisible thread between this world and the next. White house, green garden, yellow fruit, and all the time the smell of cooking, a smell as strong as the colours themselves....

Memling, if this letter reaches you, think well of me. Though old age has fallen on me like snow, like an avalanche, at least I managed to put pen to paper, made something of myself at last. Yes, I found a line and followed it to the very end... And if this letter makes it through, somehow makes it across that great distance which divides us, then don't be sad. This little grey town is no more real than the sea before you, the merest illusion, a trick of the light. After all, who's to say that one is more real than the other? No, Memling, look at that sea which is as blue as anything you've ever seen, bluer than the bluest blue paint, even bluer than your cornflower eyes. And give that gal of yours a kiss from me!

Look after yourself young sir and goodbye,
Your affectionate friend,
Hans Memling.

VI

When he'd finished, the old man laid down his pen and stretched. Outside of the room it was as black as ever and his back was awful sore. Such a night! The room seemed fusty, foul smelling, and the fella's head felt awful heavy. Hm, what was wrong? He examined his desk, pulled on his beard, rocked on his chair; then, when he looked over at the stove, he saw that his soup had boiled over, putting out the wee flame beneath it. Ho, such a thing, he thought. He got up to switch it off, but didn't feel so steady on his pins. Hello, he thought, what now?

The old man felt queasy and light-headed but still managed to drag himself over to the stove and stumble awkwardly back, pausing to gather up the funny-shaped scraps of paper on his desk. "Nearly there, old buddy," he whispered. "Nearly done." In a drawer he found scissors, string and several sheets of stiff brown paper, and began to wrap the bundle of papers — notebooks, pads, napkins, even old bits of newspaper — in a big, untidy pile. It took a while, but eventually he had a single ill-shaped parcel, like a large dust-wrapped stump, and with this he made his way, painfully, unsteadily, toward the door. When he passed the stove he saw the contents of the pot were completely burnt-on, a thick orange crust covering the bottom. "But who can eat at this time of night?" he asked. The room still stank of gas and he had a sick feeling in the pit of his stomach. "Poison," he thought. Then he took one last look around the little pad and switched off the light, plunging the whole place into darkness.

Little Hans, little Hans! But by now it was far too late. I mean, who's to say? Maybe these weren't the fancies of a flighty old man but the last thoughts of the fella in his portakabin, the gas hissing, the wind blowing outside, the dog howling at the gate...

Listen: the gas filled everything — his pyjamas, his sheets, the pot-bellied wardrobe in the corner. And thus, without even knowing it, the mannie crossed over the border one last time, swimming blindly to the farther shore, to the country that had always claimed him...

And as he crossed the line, passing that point beyond which no one can travel with any thought of ever coming back, only one thought occupied his mind: if only he could find a post-box... yes, if he could find a post-box then his whole task would be complete. But the parcel was terribly awkward and weighed heavily on his arms. What a lump! he thought. And what am I? Just an old fool abroad in the dark.... The great hall seemed to have disappeared, and with it the banners and the tables. In fact, as he wandered around, the whole castle felt deserted. The fella was lost, disorientated. Where should he go? Confused, he found a way up to the battlements and climbed up the rough steps. There, he stumbled out onto the crumbling parapet and gazed out at the little town below, his eyes struggling to pick out familiar landmarks amongst the murk. At least the town's still here, he thought, though it was faint, indistinct, almost part of the black sky that enveloped it. And yet, and yet... there was something gentle about it tonight, its granite shapes softened somehow, almost serene. This little town, he reflected, maybe I've slandered it after all.... As the old man gazed down on the twisty alleyways and badly painted roads a strange wistfulness stole over him, and he felt light-headed, almost giddy. He wanted to use his parcel as a box and scramble up to have a better look but the battlements were too high and the arrow-holes too thin. Better not, he thought. Not here.

Struggling with his great hump, the fella then followed the line of the ramparts, and came to a kind of stunted tower on the west side of the castle. From there he could see the other side of the great kirk, but his best view was of the tumbledown graveyard which ran alongside it, an ill-kept squiggle of crosses, angels and ancient mausoleums. There, everything looked soft and scumbled, from the little chalk monuments to the lines of charcoal benches to the angelic white shapes of the statues. Oh, such forms! All the grass had gone to seed and small animals lay sleeping on the gentle mounds of earth. But why had he been brought here? The old man looked for one headstone amongst all the others, but couldn't see it. What kind of marker would she have anyway, what stone? The old man sat down on his parcel and rubbed his knees. It was all a mystery. There were things and then there weren't things. There were merely blobs, specks, marks. The old man stroked his beard and slowly blinked his eyes. Maybe she'd made it after all. And as he was thinking this he heard a woman's voice.

"Whatcha doing here, it's freezing," yelled the wifey from the ball, her ample figure swaying seductively from side to side. She was standing in the yard down below, arms crossed and nightie pulled round her, trying to keep warm.

"Oh, nothing," cried the old man. "Just thinking, really." His eyes crinkled and shone. "But, tell me my dear, why aren't you at the ball? That baldie fella too much for you?"

"I came looking for you, you dope," said the gal as she climbed the steps, still shivering from the cold. "Why? You jealous?" She sniffed the air and rubbed her arms. "Gee, it's like the Arctic up here. Or does that beard of yours keep you so warm?"

The old man smiled. "But don't you think it's peaceful up here? Gentle, restful…"

"Hm, I don't know about that." The woman stretched out one veiny leg. "Listen, why don't you come back to the dance? What have you been up to anyway?"

The fella's eyes shone.

"Well, I had this thing to write, but I'm almost done. All I need now is a post-box, somewhere to post this, and my friend, he'll…"

The gal eyed up his parcel, kinda sceptically.

"You still scribbling away?" she sighed. "Even at this late hour? C'mon, fella — the night's nearly over and you don't want to miss it…"

But the old man shook his head and pulled on his beard.

"The ball? No, no, I fear it's far too late for that. Just help me find a box and then somehow I'll get this great lump in and…"

"Ah, let your friend go jump! Come on, I'm in the mood for dancing…"

"Oh Madam, I…"

"Hey, no more excuses. What are you waiting for? It's gonna be morning soon and then before you know it, it'll be Monday, the working week…"

But the old fella, he knew the working week wasn't for him. He felt terribly old. His knees throbbed and his back ached.

"Oh, my dear…"

"Ah, c'mon. You know, you should be asking me anyway."

The woman's face was shiny and round, like a bowl. So clean and bright, he thought! When he looked into it was as if the old man was looking at the reflection of his younger self.

"What d'you say?"

Mm, what could he say? The fella nodded uncertainly. "Well, maybe I could accompany you back to the hall. I mean, it's kinda dark out here and awful hard to keep your bearings. How about that? Do you know the way?"

"Sure. The castle's not so big, you know..."

The woman grinned and the fella bent down to collect his bundle.

"Hold on... just let me... get... this..."

"That old thing? What d'you need that for?"

"Um... just... a... minute..."

"Why don't you just leave it? All you need are your two left feet..."

But the old man persevered and struggled with his bundle. Ah, why did it feel so weighty? He hauled it to his side and the two of them made their way slowly, doggedly, back past the cannons, the guard-house, a statue of some fella on a horse. Ahead of him, the woman's red lips floated mysteriously in the darkness.

"You're not so past it, old timer. C'mon, come with me..."

As they passed what looked like some kind of rose garden, the faint strains of a jazz tune could be heard, comic, mocking, happy.

"It's funny, you know," said the old fella. "It feels like I've heard that music once before..."

The woman's mouth was like a little boat, bobbing in the blackness. "Mm. Do you think we can still get drinks?"

"Ah, who could deny you anything?" said the old fella, his blue eyes flashing.

"See, I said you were a charmer," replied the gal. "An old rogue..."

The old man smiled but was finding it awfully hard to keep up. "Can you see a post-box?" he asked, panting.

"Look — there's the courtyard and there's the hall. C'mon, we're just in time..."

"Hold on... got to get a.... better grip...."

Why was the parcel so heavy? It seemed to weigh as much as another man.

"It's okay, we're in luck. See? There's still couples dancing…"

The woman's lips led the way, like a torch, like a beacon. But the fella's papers were very awkward and his knees felt awful sore.

"My dear…"

And then he realised where he was. Yes, there was the tower, and before it the scaffolding, the bags of straw; and there in the alcove, the recumbent legs of the skinny young guy, obviously still fast asleep.

As quickly as he could, the old man stole over to him.

"Kid, kid, wake up!"

He shook the lad awake and looked deep into his eyes.

"Look kid, can you do me a favour? Can you take this parcel and post it? I mean, drop it in the first box you find. Ho, my lad, what do you say? Can you do that?"

The young fella blinked his eyes and looked about himself, mighty sleepily.

"Mm?"

The jazz tune played crazily, jauntily.

"Take this letter and find a post-box, as quickly as you can, this very night! All you need do is drop it off, there's no call for postage. Hey, will you do it? I'm sorry kid, but I've got to go…"

The lad looked at the sheaf of papers suspiciously.

"Post it?"

"That's right! Can you do that for me, can you? The first box you come to…"

The kid stared bleary-eyed at the little figure and tried hard to focus.

"I was asleep…"

"That's it, kid. Take the parcel. Yeah, you're a pal…"

The kid still didn't know where he was but he reached out his hands and took the parcel, a great sheaf of ill-shaped papers…

Sounds from the ball filtered into the alcove: horn, accordion, double bass. The music was crazy, raucous, played at double-speed…

"Okay… okay…"

The old fella smiled.

"You're a pal, you know? A real pal…"

"Mm…"

"You're a pal…"

And with that the fella was gone. His cornflower eyes seemed to disappear in the gloom, only to reappear by a pair of ruby-red lips in front of the main hall.

"C'mon," yelled the woman. "What's keeping you?"

The huge double-doors opened up and there was the ball again, dancing figures, the band, line after line of flapping clothes.

Pyjamas swirled, nighties swung, pants and night-things flew everywhere. But where was the old man? One minute he was there and then he wasn't. There were things and then there weren't things. A door, a shape, a window opening…

Then the door to the ballroom swung shut and the kid groaned and stretched. Ach, what had he agreed to anyway? There was a scribbled address on the front but he couldn't really read it. Ah well, he thought; that was somebody else's problem. He picked himself up and staggered out of the alcove. What time was it anyway? It seemed as if he'd been asleep for a hundred years.

The music banged and clattered and Hans wandered back down the slope, picking his way through the discarded glasses and paper cups. His head was throbbing, and he felt kinda cold in just his pants. What was he doing up here anyway? He had essays to write, things to do. This thing, he thought. This weight…. All around him things were changing, the shadows replaced by a more general grey, lines becoming straighter, shapes more distinct. Was it nearly dawn? Hans rubbed his knees and wondered how he was going to get home. The distance seemed vast, impossible. He looked down at the package and it seemed the only proof that this night had really happened, that he was actually here and not tucked up in his bed. The new day was squat, grey, mundane. The gravel felt sharp and painful, the stones uneven and old. How did I even get here? he thought to himself. To save his feet he cut down across the grey lawn and there he came upon a little bundle fast asleep in the gloomy grass, a girl turned in on herself, a wee slip of a thing, breathing hard through her nose. There were grass stains all down the waitress's apron and her tray lay upended in a bush.

"Um, Miss?" he said. "Miss, are you okay?"

The girl sighed and gave a little twitch.

"Mmm."

She sniffed and scrunched up her eyes.

"You all right?" he asked.

Clara gave a long languid stretch and rolled over.

"Mm."

There were funny marks all down one side of her face, from where she'd been sleeping.

"Ah, I was having the strangest dream," she said. Then the girl opened her sleepy eyes and smiled. "Nice pants! Hey, give a gal a hand willya?"

He helped her up and watched as she picked bits of moss and leaves from her hair.

"Where is everybody?" she asked, straightening her skirt and tights.

"Um, I don't..."

"Has it finished?"

Hans shrugged.

"Ah well, there goes another job. My boss will have my guts for garters! Still, what can you do? Another shift over! But will you look at my uniform? Those stains'll never come out. Still, if I'm not going back and all..."

The girl's make-up gave her big panda eyes and her hair was stuck up in a funny sort of tail. But for all that, Hans thought to himself, she was kinda pretty.

"Say, have you got a car?" she asked.

"Me? No, no..."

"You haven't got a motorbike have you?"

"'Fraid not."

"Walk me home then?"

The faintest trace of the music could just be heard, mingling with bird sounds.

"Um, okay..."

"Great, let's go!"

Their backs were to the castle now, and they could no longer see its shape. As they walked, the road took on a more definite form and substance. A cold wind blew and the girl snuggled up closer.

"So, did you have a good time?" she asked, hanging on his arm.

"A good time?"

"At the ball."

"There was a ball?"

"Sure! At least, I think so…"

The pair of them wandered out through the gates, past the little knick-knack shops, filled with tartan tat; what a place, Hans muttered to himself. Nobody else was around, though the odd car could be heard on the road which ran along the bottom.

The girl beamed at him.

"You're awful kind."

"'S'okay…"

"Are your feet okay?"

"What? Oh right, um, don't worry…"

They wandered down past the cannons, and took the wee steps from Castle Hill. At the bottom was a little park, trees. Some fella was taking his dog for a trot.

"So what d'you do?" Clara asked, tugging on his sleeve.

"Me? I'm a student. A photography student."

"Really? Wanna take a picture of me?"

Hans laughed.

"Who wouldn't?"

She stuck to him like a burr. Close-up, her little round face looked caked in stage make-up, but that didn't stop her from being very pretty.

"What's that you're carrying? A present?"

"This?" Suddenly Hans looked strangely perplexed. "Um, I don't really know…"

"Oh yeah." Clara's eyes darkened. "It's not for some girl is it?"

"No, no … I mean, I can't remember."

"Hm."

Hans' head felt heavy as if he'd been drugged somehow, or gassed.

"Do you remember tonight?" he asked. "What happened…"

"Mm, sure. Double shift and no tips."

"No, I mean, this thing, the castle…"

But she was no longer interested. Her little lips puckered up and her panda-eyes looked elsewhere.

"So don't you like being a waitress?"

"It's rubbish. But I need money to buy a bike…"

"A bike?"

"Yeah." She yawned and leaned in, closer. "I'll tell you later…"

As they walked down the hill, the first few pedestrians were starting to drift by — tired, grumpy, sick from lack of sleep. Ach, thought the kid. What must we look like? But what could he do? The girl looked like some exotic beauty from the Twenties and he was happy just to be with her.

"That's a great uniform, you know," he said. "The black and the white. It makes you look very glamorous…"

The girl laughed.

"No, it does. Like a movie-star in some old fashioned film…"

"Mm."

A bus passed, full of bored looking commuters. One bloke flicked through a *Daily Record* while another nibbled at a greasy pasty, the folds of his chops lined with ink.

"Are you cold?" she asked.

"Freezing."

"Mm. Come here."

"What are you doing? Oh."

Some old dear cycled past on a bicycle and the traffic at the bottom of the hill was starting to build up — delivery trucks, skip lorries, vans. Yup, it was the working week but the girl didn't seem to care; she plonked herself on her fella like a hat, and Hans could feel her skin, her lips, the taste of last night's wine…

"Mm."

Clara wrapped herself around him and Hans felt strange, somehow heavy and light at the same time.

"Um…"

But even as they embraced he could sense something over her shoulder: a box, a shape. Yes, there was something he still had to do, some last task to perform. What else could Hans do? Even as they kissed he felt the pull of the letter in his hand.

"Um," he said, "I've got to…"

Clara felt him pull away and scowled.

"Hey…"

"Wait here, I'll just be a sec…"

He dashed across the road and made for the post-box, but when he got there, he felt oddly unsure, as if the box were somehow the wrong shape, its slot all dark and mysterious. This hole, this endless space, thought the kid, where does it take us and why? He heard a strange hissing in his ears and the letter trembled and shook. But why did he feel such a sense of panic? It was only a slot, a hole, and yet his brain reeled and his limbs trembled. What a fate! It was as if he was no longer in charge of his own body, his eyes unable to see, his ears deafened. Hans shuddered and the gas hissed.

This space, this hole…

But even as Hans trembled on the brink, standing over the box with his hands shaking and his ears roaring, the letter suddenly dropped into the slot and immediately the whole thing was over. Yes, the letter was gone! And whatever the old man had written, it was gone too, passing mysteriously from this place to the next, changing, transforming, disappearing. Hans could no longer even imagine it. He stepped back from the box, his heart pounding in his chest, the pump beating away ten to the dozen. Old man, he thought, old man. The space howled and there was a strong smell of gas. But on the other side of the road the waitress hopped from foot to foot as if she had ants in her pants, her face beaming and her uniform flapping comically in the wind.

"Hey," she mouthed. "Hey!"

The picture flickered and jumped. There were blobs and daubs and flashes of light. Hans ran over to take Clara's hand, and all of a sudden the two figures were just shapes, shadows, a trick of the light. The young guy sighed; all he wanted to do was run away with her, run as far and as fast as he could. After all, why not? His knees didn't hurt him yet, and the girl was still so young. He could hear traffic, birds singing, the barking of a dog. No, he thought, it's all real, not a dream at all.

"Hiya," Clara said to him as he reached her, her dark eyes flashing. "Miss me?"

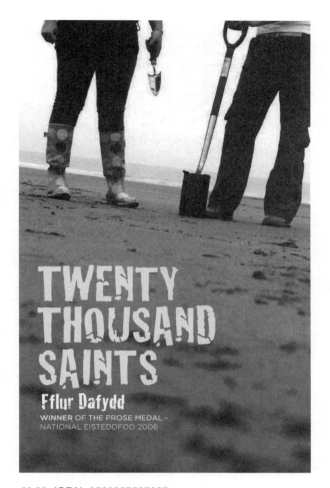

TWENTY THOUSAND SAINTS

Fflur Dafydd

WINNER OF THE PROSE MEDAL –
NATIONAL EISTEDDFOD 2006

£9.99 ISBN: 9780955527227

The most compelling novel I've read in years; a love story, a thriller, and a profound meditation on language and identity. **Peter Florence, Guardian Hay Festival Director**

A wild, exhilarating read.
Catherine Taylor, **The Guardian**

2008 Pick of the Year. *Compelling.*
Prospect Magazine

Dark, comedic thriller that explores intense bonds between people and their loved ones... a gripping read.
The Spokesman Journal

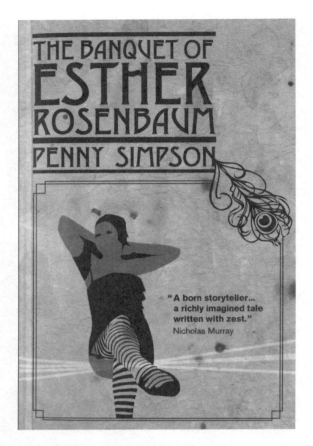

THE BANQUET OF
ESTHER
ROSENBAUM
PENNY SIMPSON

> " A born storyteller...
> a richly imagined tale
> written with zest."
> Nicholas Murray

£9.99, ISBN: 9780955527234

[An] extravaganza where the real and the imagined take turn and turn about... sumptuously detailed and fantastical... [this novel is] at once full of disturbing delicacy, and at the same time [forceful]... [marked by its] humour, verve and hallucinatory strangeness. **Clare Morgan, Times Literary Supplement**

Magic realism at its political best, echoing the sense of unreality that reigned as Hitler and the Nazis gradually gained power in a country still reeling in the aftermath of the Great War. True to the genre, Simpson uses plain language and an understated narrative voice to speak of extraordinary things. When I turned the last page, I found myself wanting to start the book all over again. **www.gwales.com**

A feast of language... akin to those depicted in the Biblical Book of Esther... *served on a platter of metaphors so strong that their aromas permeate the text.* ***Jewish Book World*** *(USA)*